Twelve Mile School

Also by Judy McGonagill

The Widow Jane Parker

The River Rider

The Twelve Mile School

Honor Versus Lies

Twelve Mile School

HEARTS OF TEXAS
BOOK THREE

JUDY MCGONAGILL

PHYLLIS ROSALEZ

Book design by eBook Prep
www.ebookprep.com

Released June 2023
Paperback ISBN: 978-1-64457-610-6
Hardcover ISBN: 978-1-64457-611-3

ePublishing Works!
644 Shrewsbury Commons Ave
Ste 249
Shrewsbury PA 17361
United States of America

www.epublishingworks.com
Phone: 866-846-5123

This book is dedicated to my sister-in-law, Betty DeLoach McGonagill, for sharing the story of her maternal grandmother, which gave me the idea for writing this fictional story based on scant facts. Betty's grandmother taught in a one-room school, supported by several ranching families, near Del Rio, Texas. A young woman, miles from any help, practiced Pancho Villa drills with her students in the event the Villistas or outlaws posed a threat.
This book is also dedicated to all teachers, past, present, and future.

Prologue

Mexican Revolutionary General José Doroteo Arango Arámbula, also known as Pancho Villa, was a prominent figure in northern Mexico from 1910 to 1920. He and his followers, known as Villistas, often robbed haciendas and trains. They shared the spoils with the poor and his faithful soldiers.

It is well documented in history that Pancho Villa and his troops are believed to have directly attacked several places along the United States' southern border.

Perhaps the most famous attack occurred in Columbus, New Mexico on March 16, 1916. Pancho Villa became enraged when President Woodrow Wilson withdrew U.S. support and gave it to Venustiano Carranza, who became President of Mexico after overthrowing dictator Huerta in the summer of 1914. President Wilson hoped Carranza could establish a stable government in Mexico.

In retaliation, Villa and his forces attacked the U. S. 13th Cavalry Regiment Garrison at Camp Furlong and Columbus, New Mexico. Some of Villa's men told him it was a small garrison of about thirty men. In a predawn attack, they were surprised to find the garrison contained 330 soldiers, well equipped with machine guns and Springfield rifles. Villa's troops seized one hundred horses and mules and set fire to part of the town of Columbus. Eighteen Americans and eighty Mexicans were killed in the melee.

This incident led to General John J. Pershing and ten thousand soldiers entering Mexico, where they unsuccessfully pursued Pancho Villa for nine months. Pershing was recalled when the United States entered World War I.

In May, June, and July of 1916, there were three more attacks along the Texas border, taking several lives and wounding a number of soldiers, customs inspectors, and one civilian. It was believed these were further retaliations of Villa and his forces but was never proven.

It is reasonable to believe citizens living along the U.S. and Mexico border were intimidated by reports of Villa's aggressive acts and on constant guard of being attacked by his forces as well.

The southern boundary of Val Verde County is also the boundary between the United States and Mexico. That part of the Rio Grande River marking the county line and international boundary stretches for approximately one hundred miles from northwest of Langtry to twelve miles southeast of Del Rio. The county covers 3,232 square miles making it about one and a half times the size of the state of Delaware.

While visiting with one of my sisters-in-law, Betty DeLoach McGonagill, she related that her maternal grandmother Catherine Lewis (later married name Tagert), as a young woman, had taught in a one-room schoolhouse for several ranching families during this time period. The school was located on Mud Creek, which meanders along part of southeastern Val Verde County, Texas.

Betty laughed and said, "I remember Grandmother saying they had Pancho Villa drills in the event of an attack." A woman teacher with a schoolroom full of children isolated from help needed to know how to protect them in case such a terrifying incident should occur.

This was the catalyst for the story told in *Twelve Mile School*, which is fiction based on a limited bit of factual information about a young teacher and the infamous Pancho Villa.

Chapter One

Eleven-year-old Slim Fitzpatrick threw the hard ball with all his might to his best friend, twelve-year-old Willie Hoffman, who let out a yell of disgust when he missed it. Willie scurried across the schoolyard, chasing after the fast-rolling ball, uttering a few swear words under his breath. While waiting for Willie to retrieve the ball, Slim noticed an unusually large column of dust rising over the hill to the south. Slim intensely watched the curious scene, realizing it wasn't just a dirt devil skipping across the hilltop. The cloud of dust was much too large for that. Then he caught a glimpse of the possible reason for the ominous plume of dirt. He did not hesitate but took off at a full run toward the schoolhouse.

Ester Hammon sat at her large teacher's desk, observing a few scratches marring the top and several ink stains that wouldn't come off no matter how hard she scrubbed. The old desk was the focal point in the large one-room schoolhouse. She looked with pride at the neat stack of freshly graded papers. For the most part, the students were progressing very well in their studies.

Ester breathed in the fresh scent of autumn's first cool air. It was a welcome change in the normally stuffy classroom. She dreaded the thought of winter's approach when the doors and windows would have to be closed against the cold. The stench of unwashed bodies and clothes would be extremely unpleasant.

She sat waiting for morning recess to be over, waiting to see if the Pancho Villa drills they had practiced were really necessary. The Villistas had been causing a great deal of unrest along the borderlands. Ester seemed to be waiting and waiting for something significant to happen in her life.

Although she had only been teaching at Twelve Mile School for about two months, Ester could already identify all of her twenty-one students' voices and laughter as she listened to their cheerful play during morning recess. She knew the four school-age Cremwelgy children well since she lived with their family three miles from the school. There were three more children at home. The remainder of the children belonged to the other three ranchers that built and funded the school. There were seven Fitzpatrick children, three Hoffman children, and seven Miller children. One more rancher was involved in the school in a remote way. Ester was told that during Christmas break, from the middle of December until the middle of January, and in the summer, she would go live at the McKie Ranch eight miles farther up the Devils River. Mr. McKie was a widower with a six-year-old daughter. Eight miles was too far to send a six-year-old alone to attend school, so this arrangement had been made in exchange for his financial support for the school.

"Miss Hammon, Miss Hammon! Riders are comin'," Slim yelled as he came running into the classroom. He was breathing hard and his eyes were huge with anticipation as he pointed toward the south.

"It might be hi—hi—him!" he stuttered in animated expectancy, thinking about who might be riding toward the school.

Ester quickly rose and hurried to the window to look at the approaching riders. She strained her eyes to see how many riders were coming toward the school. She could make out a dozen or more riders moving fast, she speculated, as she squinted her eyes again in an attempt to see more details. She couldn't see any particulars of their dress at this distance, but so many riders looked very suspicious. Ester blinked her hazel eyes to clear her vision. The cloud of dirt their horses were kicking up drifted toward the clear morning sky.

Ester was a tall woman, five foot eight inches in her stocking feet. She wore her straight dark blonde hair pulled back and tied at the nape of her neck. Her features were rather plain, with thin eyebrows, a straight nose, and small hazel eyes. Her one point of beauty was her full lips that turned up at the corners, making her look as though she were constantly about to smile. Ester normally possessed a pleasant demeanor, but she could be firm or even defiant if necessary!

An uneasy feeling of foreboding filled Ester as she keenly watched the oncoming riders.

"Go ring the bell and give the signal," she told Slim in as calm a voice as she could muster. She didn't want him to become more alarmed and scare the other children.

Ester could feel her entire insides begin to quiver, and her palms began to sweat. She started closing the windows and securing shutters. Ester had to remind herself again to remain calm so the children would not panic.

Slim did not hesitate as he grabbed the bell rope and gave it a fierce yank to set the bell in motion. He shouted at the top of his voice, "PANCHO VILLA COMIN', PANCHO VILLA COMIN'!"

The girls dropped their jump ropes, and marbles were left on the ground as the children came running at full speed into the safety of the school. As they arrived, the older students helped Ester close the remaining windows and shutters.

Six-year-old Susie Hoffman began to cry, her chin quivering as tears streaked her dusty cheeks.

"Don't cry, Susie," Ester soothed, as she pulled the child into her arms. "Here, crawl under this desk next to Lilly and hold her hand.

Don't come out until I tell you it's safe," Ester said, still managing to maintain her calm manner.

Ester felt her stomach begin to knot as she watched the frantic activity around her. She quickly counted the number of students and found one missing. She counted again as she knew everyone was present. Then she realized who was missing.

"Where is Walter?" she shouted above the clamor.

"In the outhouse," several answered in unison.

"Oh, dear me," Ester mumbled as she ran to the back window. She yanked back the shutters and raised the window.

"Walter!" she yelled. "Stay in the outhouse; riders are almost here; don't come out now, just stay there. Do you hear me, Walter?"

"Yes-um, I hear you," came Walter's muffled response.

Ester slammed the window shut and secured the shutters.

Someday, when she knew Walter better, she needed to ask him why he spent so much time in the privy, Ester contemplated, worried he might have some stomach disorder.

She hurried to the door and lifted the loaded Winchester from the rack. Twelve-year-old Willie Hoffman and eleven-year-old Slim Fitzpatrick lifted two other guns and positioned themselves on either side of the front windows near the gun portholes. The third porthole, where Ester stood, was to the left of the huge front door. They were small side-to-side rectangular openings with hinged doors that could be opened from the inside. This gave Ester and the two boys a fairly good view of the road in front of the school. There were several more portholes around the other walls in the event someone tried riding around the building.

Although Daniel Cremwelgy was twelve, he seemed to have an aversion to guns, so he did not offer to take one of the Winchesters. She had noticed two of his younger brothers carried guns around the ranch. She had asked Vincent why such young boys already knew how to shoot a gun. Vincent had told her he started teaching the boys to shoot on their eighth birthday. It was a necessity living on a ranch where dangerous animals still roamed the area along with poisonous snakes, and outlaws frequently holed up in one of the caves along the Devils River. Ester realized the ranch boys were far more mature than the boys she had taught in Dallas.

Ester had thought Vincent Cremwelgy was joking when he told her she had to know how to shoot a gun and be willing to shoot anything, whether it crawled on its belly or was a snake wearing boots, if it was a threat to the students or to her. He had patiently taught her how to shoot a pistol and the Winchester. At first, Ester had asked herself many times if she could take the life of another human, but finally, the answer came to her. Yes, if that human presented a dangerous threat, she could. Ester had heard stories about rotten men abducting girls, even young girls, and ruining them for life. Oh yes, she could shoot such a varmint without hesitation, she finally decided. But now her hands shook, and she could feel the sweat running down her neck from beneath her hair. She could feel the rivulets of sweat between her breasts as she stood beside the door, waiting for the riders to pass. As she waited, she could feel the tension build and run through her body. Hopefully, they would just ride on by and not cause any trouble, she wished, as she listened for every sound that came through the barred door.

Ester could hear the pounding hooves slowing as the riders approached. Then several men yelled, "VIVA MEH-HEE-CO! VIVA PANCHO VILLA!"

She could tell the riders were slowing to a stop in the schoolyard. She felt her heart lurch, and now the sweat was running down her forehead into her eyes. She swiped her face with the long sleeve of her crisp, white blouse to clear the sweat from her eyes. How could she shoot if she couldn't see?

Ester listened to Lilly's sweet voice trying to console not only Susie but Ruth Fitzpatrick as well.

"Aleyne, go help Lilly with the girls," Ester told the older girl, in hopes of keeping the younger girls from bursting into full-blown hysteria. Ester had no doubts that Aleyne could calm the two girls as well as she could.

Although Aleyne Cremwelgy was only eleven, she shouldered great responsibilities at home. She was a pretty girl, with long auburn hair kept in braids and sparkling blue eyes, and her body was already developing. Ester shuttered to think Aleyne could be a prime target for some unscrupulous man's pleasure.

There was near silence inside the schoolhouse and silence outside. Ester gingerly moved the cover from over the gun porthole and took a cautious look. A dozen or more riders dressed in white shirts with fringed vests, black pants, high-top boots, and straw sombreros were lined up single file, facing the school. Ester noticed they were all armed with pistols and rifles, but all arms were in their holsters. Most of the men wore a single bandolier filled with bullets across their chests. At least they were no immediate threat, she decided, as she observed the group. What did they want or expect them to do, she wondered, as she continued to peek through the porthole? How long would they just sit and stare at the closed schoolhouse? As she observed the men, she tried to figure out which one might be Pancho Villa. They all looked much the same. Of course, every man had dark hair and eyes, very brown skin, and most had some type of mustache. She had never seen a picture of Pancho Villa and wasn't at all sure she could pick him out of this group even if she had seen his picture.

Slowly one of the riders nudged his horse forward a few feet. He removed his sombrero as though he were entering someone's home and wanted to make a gesture of politeness. Maybe that is he, she thought, as she studied his features and watched every movement.

Ester waited. The minutes seemed to be dragging by, and she worried the students would become restless after a while.

Finally, he spoke in a strong voice for her to hear but not overly loud or aggressive. "I am Juan Antonio Perez Talamontez," he announced, as though he were introducing himself to a crowd of spectators. "We mean you and the children no harm. You have nothing to fear from us," he paused. "We come only to buy horses from the ranchers and nothing more." His English was articulate.

Ester did not know if she was expected to respond to his speech or just listen politely. She said nothing but waited to see if he said more, or would ride on. She wondered if he spoke the truth about his name, or did he just say that so they wouldn't be as frightened and maybe let down their guard?

The silence seemed to stretch on for several minutes.

"We will depart now. Do not be afraid," he said, as he turned his horse and rode to the head of the line. The other riders turned their horses in unison and followed their leader on past the school.

Ester stood for several minutes without moving or speaking, just listening to the receding sound of the departing riders. After taking several deep breaths, she placed the Winchester back on the rack and motioned for the boys to do the same. When the students saw them replace the guns, there seemed to be a huge sigh of relief.

Ester turned to Slim. "Go tell Walter he can come to class now."

The children crawled from underneath the desks and took their places in a subdued manner.

"Should we open the windows and door?" Willie asked, showing no fear about what had happened.

Ester considered the possibility of the riders' return.

"Yes, open both, but you and Slim keep a close watch."

Ruth Fitzpatrick looked nervously toward the open door. Then she asked, with a quiver in her soft voice, "Do you think they'll come back today?"

Ester cleared her throat and spoke with as much confidence as she could muster. "I hope not, but we will keep a close watch. Now, third graders, open your readers to page 32," she continued on as though everything was normal again. She couldn't let the children see her unease, her fear of what might have happened.

Ester felt edgy the rest of the day and could sense the unease among the students.

As Ester and the Cremwelgy children walked home that afternoon, she reflected on the circumstances that had brought her to Twelve Mile School. She had taken this teaching position to escape her well-intended family's constant attempts at matchmaking with every eligible bachelor in Dallas. At age twenty-two, her family was horrified to think they might be stuck with an old maid schoolmarm. She had dated a number of eligible men, but none had held her interest past the third date. Ester had decided she'd rather be single than stuck in a loveless, unfulfilling marriage.

When Ester had read an advertisement in the Dallas Morning News newspaper for a teacher for Twelve Mile School in Val Verde County, Texas, she immediately wrote to Mr. Vincent Cremwelgy, applying for the position. Much to her surprise, she received a prompt reply saying she was hired and would start immediately after Labor Day.

Twelve Mile School had seemed an unusual name when she first read it. Vincent explained that while the ranchers were building the school, a surveying team from Fort Clark happened by, and one of the surveyors commented that if you followed the Devils River as it meandered southwest, it was twelve miles to where it emptied into the Rio Grande River, and if you followed the wagon road twelve miles southeast you would reach the dusty little town of Del Rio. Thus, the name stuck.

The large one-room schoolhouse sat on the high bank overlooking the Devils River. It faced east to take advantage of the best breeze with the river running behind it and the wagon road in front. The building had been constructed on the high bluff in order to avoid floods. A few scrubby mesquite trees provided sparse shade near the building. The surrounding area was covered with bushy ceniza plants, prickly pear cacti, a variety of weeds, and sparse grass.

At first, Ester had found the changes from living in a large city to living on a remote ranch and sharing a room with three young girls, who were also her students, a daunting adjustment. After a few weeks, she had found her niche in the Cremwelgy household. With some ingenuity, she had even managed to find a little privacy in the crowded living quarters.

Vincent and Olga were a warm, friendly pair and tried to make Ester feel a part of their family. Ester appreciated their efforts in making her feel so welcome. In return Ester gladly helped Olga in the kitchen in the evenings when they returned home from school. Nor did she mind helping with the cleaning, laundry, and ironing that took up most of every Saturday. Thankfully, they were a religious family and believed in resting as much as possible on the Sabbath.

Church services were also held at the school. The first family to arrive on Sunday morning would move the desks to the sides of the room and retrieve benches from a lean-to behind the building and fill the center for Sunday services. It was an efficient plan. The same families that supported the school also attended church along with some of their married ranch hands and a few of the single cowboys. After church, they all shared lunch together, referred to as "dinner on the ground." Ester thought most of the single men came as much for the good home-cooked food to nourish their bodies as for the scriptures to nourish their souls.

When Ester and the Cremwelgy children got home that afternoon, the children could hardly wait to tell all about the riders.

Vincent idly rubbed his day's growth of whiskers as he listened to the children and Ester talk about the Mexican riders. Olga shook her head in disbelief and looked at her husband with fear showing in her eyes, as though she thought he knew the answer as to what should be done.

"I sure don't like to hear about those Meskins crossin' the river to buy horses or goodness knows what else," he told the group with a worried look on his normally pleasant face. "I'm glad this is Friday. We'll have to have a meetin' after Sunday services to discuss what needs to be done before somebody gets hurt. I better send one of the cowboys up to McKie's place to let him know what's goin' on."

Eight-year-old Owen piped up. "Papa, I could ride to Mr. McKie's tomorrow. I ain't afraid of no dirty, stinkin' Meskins," he said, with scorn.

"Don't be too big for your britches, young man, and be careful how you speak of those different from yourself. Remember, God made us all in His image," Vincent lectured as he pointed his finger at Owen. "Where did you hear such talk?" Vincent asked Owen, with a look of displeasure on his face.

Owen looked a bit deflated. "Sorry, sir, that's what Sonny and Willie Hoffman call 'em," he answered as he ducked his head in shame. A lock of brown hair fell forward covering most of his face. "I could still ride up to Mr. McKie's place," he answered, in a more subdued voice.

"Well, young man, we don't talk like that around here. I think it best one of the men go this time," Vincent said, and Owen knew better than to argue further with his father. "Besides, from the looks of that hair I believe we need to do haircuts tomorrow," Vincent stated.

"Ah, I like my hair like it is," Owen complained.

"I don't, and there will be no more said about it," Vincent declared.

Owen knew the conversation was over.

Chapter Two

As each family arrived for Sunday services, the talk was all about the incident of the riders on Friday. There was a strong underlying current of dread, and maybe fear, as to what might lie ahead for the ranchers.

John Fitzpatrick, a stocky man with thinning red hair, turned his attention to Vincent, Wilber Miller, and Delmar Hoffman. "Did them riders come to your place?"

The men shook their heads.

"Nobody at my place saw 'em," Vincent answered.

"Nobody came to my place either," Delmar confirmed, with a shake of his head. Delmar was a tall man, but his shoulders were already beginning to slump forward, preventing him from extending to his normal height of well over six feet.

"I wonder where they were goin' to buy horses?" Vincent pondered.

"Do you think they went all the way to McKie's place? He has the best horses in Val Verde County. I don't think he'd cotton much to sellin' them to some of Pancho Villa's henchmen," Delmar ventured.

The other men shook their heads and chuckled in agreement.

"I heard just last month, two times the women and children in Del Rio were sent to the courthouse while the men stood guard 'cause Pancho Villa and his Villistas were fighting across the river in Villa Acuña," Delmar told the group of men.

"You just never know where he'll show up next," John added, with an uneasy look.

"There comes McKie now," Vincent said, as he pointed toward the approaching wagon.

"It takes a real calamity to get McKie to Sunday services," John put in, with a slight laugh.

Ester noticed the approaching wagon pulled by a pair of fine-looking horses. She had not met the McKie family yet as they did not normally attend Sunday services. As the wagon pulled to a stop, a man who stood well over six feet tall climbed down first. He wore a straw hat that made it difficult to see the color of his hair, but she caught a glimpse of blond hair touching the collar of his white shirt as he turned to help the woman that sat next to him down from the wagon. Ester knew that must be his mother, Corabell. She was a woman of medium build and height. She also had blonde hair, pulled up in a bun with a few strands of gray running through it. Corabell had a pleasant smile as she greeted those nearest her. Mr. McKie then helped the other woman down from the wagon. She was hardly five feet tall and rather plump. She too had blonde hair, pulled back and tied at the nape of her neck. It was obvious when you looked into her eyes and saw the vacant stare that she was mentally afflicted. Olga had told Ester that Molly McKie was slow thinking, kind of like a small child. "Her mind is about like a four- or five-year-old child, and she doesn't speak but a few words," Olga had said, with concern. Last to be helped out of the wagon was an adorable little girl with long golden curls, bright blue eyes, and a face like a cherub. She let her father help her to the ground.

This must be her prospective student, Christine, Ester knew, as she watched the child run toward the other children as soon as her feet touched the ground.

The poor child must have few opportunities to play with other children, Ester reflected, as she watched the excited child.

Mr. McKie tipped his hat toward the ladies and shook hands with each of the men that stood near his wagon.

Vincent Cremwelgy motioned Ester to come nearer. Ester complied with his request.

"Grant, I would like you to meet our new teacher, Miss Ester Hammon, from Dallas," he said, gesturing toward Ester.

"Ester, this is Grant McKie," Vincent finished the introductions.

Grant removed his hat and extended his hand to Ester. "My pleasure, Ma'am," he said. His large work-hardened hand surrounded hers as he gave Ester a brief handshake.

"It is nice to meet you, Mr. McKie. I've been told I will be going to your ranch to teach your daughter," Ester said, with a responsive smile.

McKie simply nodded. "Christine is looking forward to having you come to be her teacher," he said, and then turned to converse with the men.

Ester felt the sting of his dismissal as she turned to join the other women. She was quickly introduced to Corabell and Molly McKie before services started. Ester did not care for Grant McKie's indifferent attitude and hoped the rest of the family would be more accepting of her presence at their ranch. After all, it wasn't her idea to go there; she had just as soon stay at the Cremwelgys' during the Christmas break. It was going to be difficult to not be with her family during Christmas, but to be in a place where she was not particularly wanted would make it even worse.

The McKie family sat two rows in front of Ester, so she had time to observe them during the service. She noticed again how tall Grant was when they stood to sing. He was several inches taller than the other men. He was a bit on the slender side, with broad shoulders, and she noticed how the material of his shirt stretched across the muscles of his upper arms. Ester had to admit he was a nice-looking man as she caught an occasional glimpse of his profile when he turned his head to look at Christina when she became restless. What a shame he isn't very friendly like his mother, she thought. Well, she wasn't going to the ranch to socialize with him but simply to teach his daughter, Ester reflected, as she turned her attention back to Mr. Fitzpatrick reading the morning Bible lesson.

Two Sundays in a month, a preacher from Del Rio would come to conduct the Sunday services, and on the remaining Sundays, John Fitz-patrick conducted services. In Ester's opinion, John was about as good a preacher as the visiting minister.

After Sunday service everyone shared lunch. Two tables were set up on the south side of the building to break the north wind in cooler weather and take advantage of the southeast breeze in the warmer months. One table was filled with food. There were always several platters of fried chicken and roast beef or ham. There were plenty of vegetables, deviled eggs, yeast rolls, and a variety of desserts. The other table was where the adults sat to enjoy their meal and visit. This was about the only social contact the ranchers experienced. The women very rarely went to town with their husbands when they went in for supplies, so Sunday service was about their only social outing. When the children filled their plates, they sat in small groups under the trees.

Ester was one of the last to serve her plate and found the only empty place at the table was directly across from Grant McKie. She wished there had been another place to sit, but, much to her chagrin, there were no other places left. She hoped he would concentrate on eating and not bother with polite conversation, especially after the brush-off he had given her earlier. For a few minutes, it seemed her wish was being granted.

Grant lifted his head, making eye contact with Ester. "I understand you came here from Dallas."

"Yes, I did."

"I'm curious to know what possessed a city lady to accept a teaching position in such a remote part of the state."

Ester was taken aback by his question and did not care to reveal the circumstances of her family badgering her to get married. "I wanted to experience teaching in a different environment," she hedged.

"I see, and what do you think of this environment thus far?" Grant asked as he made a sweeping gesture with one hand as he continued to gaze at Ester as though he would know if she were not being truthful.

Ester paused before answering, "I have found it interesting and challenging at times."

"I suppose having to deal with the riders from Mexico was a bit of a challenge for a city girl," he said, as though he had doubts about her abilities.

Ester narrowed her eyes slightly and stared at him. "Mr. McKie, I know how to shoot a pistol and the Winchester and would not hesitate to do so if I felt the students or myself were being threatened!"

Grant was a bit surprised by her vehement answer but was glad to see she had spunk. "What would you do if they shot at you? It's one thing to think you have the upper hand in shooting, but that isn't always the case. These men are trained soldiers, and some are outlaws as well. They would not hesitate to shoot right back at you. Could you stand your ground if that happens?" he challenged, in a tone that indicated he had doubts about Ester's courage and stamina in such a situation.

Grant saw he had wrangled Ester with his statement and questions. He noticed she narrowed her eyes again causing a small crease in her forehead, and her mouth hung slightly open in disbelief. He had certainly seen prettier women, but she did have a certain attractiveness, he supposed. Then he wondered why he would even be concerned with her looks. His only interest in Ester Hammon was her qualities as a teacher.

Ester realized her mouth had dropped open and quickly closed it. "I guess we will find out if that situation ever arises," she stated, in a tone that she hoped would let him know she did not appreciate his line of questioning.

Grant did not answer but turned his attention to Molly, who was sitting beside him. "Molly, stop playing with your food," he scolded, much like a parent would do but in a low tone so most others would not have heard what he said.

Ester found she had little appetite after their exchange but was not about to let Grant McKie know he had upset her, so she forced herself to continue to eat.

Elanor Fitzpatrick, who was seated beside Ester, turned to ask about how her children were doing in school. Ester was glad for the opportunity to talk with someone besides Grant. Thankfully, Elanor continued their conversation for most of the remainder of the meal.

Ester was about to rise to go get dessert when Grant addressed her again.

"Will you bring the books and other materials you will need to teach Christine, or do I need to buy some supplies?" he asked.

"Yes, I will bring everything we need for her lessons." Hoping to ease the tension she sensed between them, she added, "I'm sure I will enjoy having Christine for a student. Does she know the alphabet, and can she count to ten?"

"She knows some of the letters in the alphabet, and she does count to ten. She scribbles a lot, so I know she's anxious to learn to write," he answered, with a softer expression than she had previously seen.

"Does your mother work with her on any of those tasks?"

Grant rubbed his hand over his lower jaw and looked as though he were searching for the right words. Ester noticed how dark his eyes were. She had thought they were brown, but in fact, they were a deep blue that reminded her of a darkening sky. He had small lines around his eyes indicating he spent many hours out of doors in the sun. That would also account for his deep golden tan. He leaned toward Ester and spoke in a low rumbling voice, "Mother has no formal education, so she can't help Christine, and, unfortunately, I'm away all day and have little time to spend helping her with school subjects."

Ester felt a twinge of sympathy for the man. She was sure he wanted his daughter to have an education, and she would certainly do all she could to help Christine while she was at the ranch.

While the women were putting the food away, Ester noticed the men had moved to one end of the table. She overheard John Fitzpatrick ask Grant what he thought they could do about the Mexicans coming across the border to buy their stock or maybe even steal them.

Ester walked over to the group of men and politely said, "Excuse me, I think the other women and I should be in on this conversation. I have already had to deal with these men, and your wives may be at home alone when they come to your house. What should they do?" she questioned, as she looked at each man in turn.

All of the men looked at her in stunned silence. The women had stopped clearing away the food and stared at her as well. No one spoke.

Grant cleared his throat and finally spoke. "I think Miss Hammon has a good point," McKie told the group. "We do need to decide what your women folks should do if you aren't home and these men come," he pointed out, as he turned to look at the other men.

They all quickly agreed and began to make room for the women to join them again.

As Betsy Hoffman walked past Ester she whispered, "Good for you speakin' up for us women."

Betsy seeming to be such a meek little woman, it surprised Ester to hear her comment. Ester had noticed she often sat with her head down as though she were afraid to join in the conversations with the other women. Any opinion Betsy expressed was prefaced with "Delmar says" or "Delmar thinks" as though only his opinion counted. Ester suspected that at the Hoffman house his opinion was the only one that counted.

As the discussion moved forward, it became obvious to Ester the other ranchers seemed to hold Grant McKie's opinions in high esteem. She decided it must be because he was the largest landowner and apparently raised fine horses as well as cattle, along with some sheep and goats, while the others raised mostly cattle and sheep.

McKie revealed the Mexican riders had come to him wanting fifty horses. Grant told them he could only spare thirty-five horses and would need several days to get them gathered up and ready for the Mexicans.

Grant looked directly at Ester and said, "I suggested they come for the horses next Saturday, so there should be no problem at school; that is if they do as I asked, but with these people, you never know what they may do. I suggest you be on guard just in case they come early," he warned, as he turned his attention back to the others.

"It's a darn shame these Mexicans are permitted to run back and forth across the border at will," Vincent commented.

"It sure is," John agreed. "Just look at what happened last March. They attacked Columbus, New Mexico, killin' a bunch on our side and stealin' horses and burnin' the town!" he concluded, with a shake of his head.

"Yeah," Delmar joined in. "What kind of a chance would we have against them thievin' killers?" he asked, with obvious loathing.

"They've been across at Glenn Springs and several other places, killin' and robbin' folks just like us," Wilber Miller grumbled.

"It looks to me like President Wilson sold us down the river by backin' Carranza, and here we sit on the banks of the Rio Grande with no protection. Pershing and his troops are runnin' all over Mexico tryin' to catch Pancho Villa with no luck. Old Pancho is a slick one. If I had what Pershing has, I bet I could catch them thievin' bandits," Delmar stated, getting even angrier.

Delmar Hoffman struck Ester as a disgruntled man. He complained about everything, it seemed. Just last week he was complaining about the rain washing out several fences. She had heard the other ranchers say how glad they had been to have the rain.

Grant had remained silent throughout their discussion. He knew what they said was true. They were sitting in a potentially volatile position. The nearest soldiers were forty-five miles away at Fort Clark Cavalry Post, and the local law couldn't cover this entire county of over three thousand square miles with much success. They were each one pretty much left to protect their own family and property. Grant had more men than the other ranchers, but they were spread over thousands of acres except for the few stationed at the homestead. They were not trained fighters. Yes, they all carried a pistol and could shoot a snake or wild animal, but he wasn't sure how well they could stand up against trained soldiers and outlaws.

Grant looked around the group when the conversation lagged. "Everything you say is true, but to my way of thinking the best thing to do is to try to remain calm and cooperate as much as possible with the Mexicans. We may not like it, but what choice do we have? None of us have the men to stand against them."

Delmar spoke up, "I sure don't like it! The soldiers should be over here campin' on our doorsteps to keep them varmints away!" he spat with disgust as he gestured in the general direction of Fort Clark.

Grant didn't directly comment on Delmar's view but turned to John instead. "John, could you ride to Del Rio tomorrow and have the sheriff contact Fort Clark about what's going on? Maybe they can send some troops to parole the area for a while."

John nodded his consent.

Chapter Three

Each day during the next week seemed to drag by as Ester and the older boys kept watch for suspicious riders. By the time Friday afternoon came, everyone was happy to have the weekend away from his or her unnerving vigil.

As Ester and the four Cremwelgy children walked home, she noticed a slight change in the countryside. The leaves on what few trees there were along the river and in the pastures were beginning to turn a pale orange and brown. There wasn't much fall color here like in east Texas where there were many varieties of trees whose leaves turned vivid colors of gold, orange, yellow, and brown in the fall. This harsh land had a quaint beauty, though. The rugged limestone cliffs along the river with their layers of white rocks made Ester think of her mother's layered cakes. The ceniza plants were stunning a few days after a good rain when they turned from their pale green to brilliant hues of pink, although the locals called them purple sage. Ester even found a certain beauty in the lacy leaves of the craggy mesquite trees.

The Devils River was wider than most rivers in Texas but shallow for the most part. It could be treacherous in places, though. Ester had seen the older children and Vincent wading in knee-deep water, unexpectedly step off into a channel, and all of a sudden be in water up to their waist or over their head. Vincent said the rocky bottom was like a honeycomb, full of holes with sharp edges that would cut your feet if you were barefoot. Ester knew the children looked forward to swimming in the cool river during the long hot months that usually stretched to mid-October. The Cremwelgys often packed a picnic supper on Sunday afternoon and went to the river for relaxation, away from the seemingly endless chores at the ranch. Now, the weather was turning cooler, so they would miss their Sunday outings.

About halfway home, they climbed the highest hill, and at the crest there was a stunning view of the surrounding countryside. Ester admired the view looking north along the weathered cliffs of the river that finally faded into shades of blue and purple marking the distant hills. Looking south along the meandering river toward Mexico, you could see the purple outline of the Sleeping Lady Mountains. The children had pointed it out to Ester the first day as they walked home from school. There was a long flat mesa that dipped slightly to indicate the lady's waistline, then rose to the gentle swell of her breasts; it sloped down to indicate the valley at the base of her neck and rose almost straight up to form the chin and face. Then her silhouette faded into the other mountains. Ester wished she had her own house sitting on the top of this hill, so she could enjoy the splendid view.

When they arrived home, Olga was in a state of panic.

"What's the matter?" Ester asked with concern when she saw Olga's normally jovial expression changed to one of worry.

"Sarah's been in labor all night and all day. Hank's gone to Del Rio for a doctor, but I don't know if the poor dear can hang on until he gets back or not," Olga said, with a worried look. "I've been over there most of the day but came home to start supper."

"Who's with her now?"

"Vincent went and got Elanor Fitzpatrick about an hour ago. She's helped deliver lots of young'uns but even she's worried about this one not comin' yet."

"Should I go sit with Elanor?"

Olga paused and looked at Ester. Then she shook her head. "No, I don't think it would be proper for a maiden lady to be there for the birthin'," she told Ester.

"Oh, Olga, I may be a maiden lady, but I know about where babies come from," Ester said, with a slight laugh. Yes, she knew about where babies came from and how they were conceived, but she certainly had never been present for their birth. Her family had protected her from that too when her sisters delivered their babies. Ester wasn't afraid to go sit with poor Sarah and as for the rest—

"I know, but I just don't know," Olga hesitated.

"Well, either let me fix supper or go sit with Sarah and Elanor," Ester said, a bit exasperated.

"Well," Olga hesitated again. "This old stove is kind of cranky, so I guess you could go sit a spell, but if things get too rough, you just come right out of there," Olga instructed, as though Ester were her child instead of a grown woman.

Olga watched Ester cross the yard toward the Days' small house. It struck her how different her life had been from Ester's. She and Vincent had married when she was fifteen and he had just turned nineteen. Aleyne was born eleven months later. By the time she was twenty-two, she had three children and had miscarried one more. The farthest she had traveled was from her family ranch near Uvalde, about ninety miles, to this ranch she and Vincent had bought shortly after they had married. She had never traveled on a train, never checked a book out of a library, never eaten in an elegant restaurant, or never heard a symphony orchestra play. There seemed to be a vast difference between her life and Ester's, yet they had formed a close friendship and spent hours talking together as they worked.

Hank Day had been the ranch foreman several years before he and Sarah married. Sarah had already had two miscarriages in early pregnancies. The couple was so looking forward to finally having a baby.

When Ester entered the small house, she saw the woman looking like one of six-year-old Lilly's limp rag dolls. Sarah lay in a tangle of sweat-soaked sheets. Her pale skin was covered with a sheen of sweat, although the day was cool. Her face was almost the color of the white sheet that covered her from the waist down. She looked utterly exhausted. Ester heard the low, pain-racked moan escape from deep in her throat that sounded as though she may never utter another sound.

Ester gave Elanor a questioning look, then whispered, "What can I do to help?"

Elanor shook her head and pursed her lips, "Ain't much you or anyone can do. Just pray to God Hank gets back here soon with the doctor."

Ester looked at the woman as she heard another painful moan escape her pale lips but then she was quiet.

"I've delivered and helped deliver lots of babies but I ain't never seen one like this. This one is bad," Elanor whispered, with a shake of her head and an anxious look.

Ester saw a washcloth lying beside a pan of water on the table beside the bed. She dipped the cloth in the cool water, wrung it out, and gently bathed Sarah's face and arms in an attempt to soothe her.

Sarah looked at her with tired sunken eyes. "Ester," she whispered her name. "When is Hank comin'?" she asked, hardly loud enough for Ester to understand what she was saying.

"Soon, very soon, I'm sure," Ester told her, although she had no idea how much longer it would be before he might return. She instantly felt guilty about the lie but thought it was better than saying she didn't know.

"Is there anything you need? Perhaps a little something to eat to build your strength," Ester offered, in hopes something would give the poor woman some strength.

Sarah shook her head slightly and murmured, "No, nothing."

Ester gently sat on the bed beside her and wiped her face and arms again with the damp cloth. She listened to the intermittent excruciating moans and prayed Hank and the doctor would come soon.

She glanced at the old oak mantle clock that sat on a shelf near the door, and the hands seemed to be in the same position as the last time she had looked. She saw they had moved only slightly. Another hour passed. Eventually, Ester heard the rumbling of a wagon nearing the house and prayed again it was Hank bringing the doctor.

The door flew open and Hank came rushing toward the bed as he gave each woman a questioning look.

"Still no baby," Elanor answered his unspoken question.

Before anyone else could speak the door opened again and a tall, dark-headed man carrying a black bag entered the house. Ester breathed a deep sigh of relief. This must be the doctor, she thought.

The man walked forward and introduced himself. "I'm Doctor Will Hudson," he said, and gave Ester and Elanor a slight smile. Ester noticed his golden-brown alert eyes and truly striking face.

He stood looking at Sarah for several seconds and then sat his bag beside the rumpled bed. "I hear she's been in labor for over twenty hours," he said to no one in particular.

"Nearer to twenty-four," Elanor answered. "I've delivered many a baby but ain't never seen one take this long afore. Somethin' just ain't right," Elanor said, with another shake of her head as though to emphasize her point.

"I'll need to examine her," the doctor said, as he looked at Hank. Seeing the man's pale face Will suggested, "Hank, you better go wait outside. I won't have time to tend to you if you keel over," Will said, with a chuckle.

"Doctor, Ester here is a maiden lady, so maybe she best wait outside too," Elanor suggested.

Will looked at Ester and asked, "Do you think you might faint at the sight of blood?"

Ester had seen blood in plenty of other circumstances and even witnessed a woman being thrown from a carriage in downtown Dallas. Her face and exposed parts of her body were covered in bright crimson blood. She died almost instantly. While these things were certainly unpleasant, Ester felt certain she would not faint.

"No, I won't faint. I've seen blood in other situations, and it didn't bother me," she answered ardently, which wasn't exactly the truth either. She was normally a stickler for the truth, but sometimes the conditions didn't warrant a long explanation to get to the absolute truth.

"Being an unmarried woman, will assisting in the birth be offensive to you?" he asked, without looking up as he prepared to do the examination.

Ester did not hesitate. "No, I won't be offended by helping with the birth."

Doctor Hudson glanced up and gave her an encouraging smile. "Good, because I will most likely need both of you to help," he said, as he glanced from one woman to the other.

Ester watched him painstakingly examine Sarah. She lightly bathed Sarah's face when she let loose with another one of her gut-wrenching moans during his examination.

"Umm, just as I thought, I am going to try to turn this baby to the right position," he told the women.

"Sarah, this will be unpleasant, but I have to try to get your baby in the right position to be born. Take deep breaths and scream if you feel like it," Will told Sarah, as he started the procedure.

Minutes later he straightened and asked Elanor to wipe his brow. Elanor scurried to the cabinet where the washbowl sat and brought back several rags.

"Ester, get on the bed and, when I tell you, sit Sarah up at about a forty-five-degree angle. You may want to get behind her to brace her with your body as she is going to be pushing back. Elanor, get on the other side, and when Ester sits her up, you take both hands and rub in a downward motion starting under her breasts all the way down," he demonstrated with his hands in the air. The two women took their positions and followed his directions.

Ester was amazed at the strength still left in the nearly exhausted woman as she pushed back against her with each new contraction. Soon Ester was damp with sweat from the energy it took to hold Sarah in the upright position.

Ester noticed how the lamplight flickered and highlighted the waves on the doctor's rich, dark brown hair. When he would look up to give instructions, she was drawn to his golden-brown eyes enhanced with long thick eyelashes that any woman would be jealous of. A small dimple played in his left cheek when he smiled. He was truly the most handsome man Ester had ever seen, even more handsome than any of the actors she had seen at the theater in Dallas.

After several hard contractions, Will said in an excited manner, "Okay, here it comes. Push, Sarah, push!"

The scenario was repeated several times. Sarah heaved with her entire being and within seconds the baby slipped from her body. Will held the child up by the feet and gave it a sound swat on the buttocks. A wail of protest was heard throughout the house and reached Hank who was still lingering nearby outside.

Will looked at Ester and gave her an alluring smile that made her catch her breath. "If I hadn't known better, I would have thought you had done this before. Don't you agree, Ms. Elanor?"

Before Elanor could answer the door was flung open, and Hank came gingerly to Sarah's bedside. His eyes were wide in disbelief, and his face showed his relief that the ordeal was finally over.

"Congratulations, you have a fine son," Will said with a grin, as he held the baby toward Hank.

Hank stepped back a few steps.

"I uh, I uh, better not take him, I might drop him right on his little head," he said, a bit flustered.

Will smiled and turned to Elanor. "Here, Elanor, will you clean him up and give him to his mother?"

Before Elanor could answer, Will glanced down when he heard Sarah give another heart-wrenching moan, and his eyes widened in astonishment. "Take him," he said, as he almost shoved the child into Elanor's arms. "We have another one coming!"

Everyone in the room gasped except poor Sarah, who let out that final scream full of gut-wrenching pain.

Will repeated the procedure he had performed minutes earlier. Then he announced with a broad grin on his face, "Congratulations again, you have a beautiful daughter."

Hank beamed at his fatigued wife. "Sarah, we have two babies," he almost cooed. "Just what we always wanted, a boy and a girl," he said, in awe and almost disbelief.

Sarah gave her husband a wan smile. "We are blessed," she said, as a tear slipped down her pale cheek. She knew these two children were likely all they would ever have. Her body was too weak. After the miscarriages, it just didn't seem likely more children would come, she contemplated as she cradled her newborn babies in her arms.

The Cremwelgys had invited Will to come to the house for supper and to spend the night. It would be too dangerous to try to return to Del Rio late at night, Vincent had told him.

Will had graciously accepted their invitation. Vincent and Olga had excused themselves to retire as the hour was getting late, and life on the ranch began early.

Ester was glad for the chance to visit with Will in the quiet of the kitchen as they ate. At last, she had found someone to discuss the symphony with, talk about interesting books each one had read, and some they had both read. Ester was eager to talk about something besides her humdrum daily existence living on a ranch and teaching in a small one-room school. What a refreshing conversation. By the end of the meal, Ester felt so invigorated that she doubted she would sleep for hours and wished they could continue their conversation. However, Will looked near exhaustion.

"Oh, please forgive me for prattling on and on, but it seems an eternity since I've had anyone to discuss these things with," Ester said, as she looked a bit embarrassed.

Will smiled, showing the dimple that had captured Ester's attention earlier. "I have thoroughly enjoyed sharing this meal with you and conversing on interesting topics too," he said, with a chuckle. "Most of the men I attend talk of livestock and Pancho Villa coming to steal their stock, and the women talk of all their children and each ailment every one of them has ever had," he told her with a smile.

Ester was reluctant to end their delightful conversation but realized it was getting late as she stood and quickly cleared away their dishes.

"Let me show you to your bed. It's in the room with the two younger boys. The older ones are sleeping on the front porch before the weather turns too cool at night and runs them inside," Ester explained.

"Ah, I remember summers long ago when my cousin Charles and I begged to set up our tent in the backyard. Living in town was not as conducive to camping out as living in the country. Our parents let us do it quite a lot in the summer. Of course, we had considerably shorter summers than you folks have down here," he concluded, with a faraway look of pleasant memories reflected in his expression.

"Where are you from?"

"I grew up in upper New York state, in a town of about twenty thousand."

"What did your father do there?" Ester asked, wanting to learn as much about him as their short time allowed.

"He was a doctor too."

"You mean you didn't return home to take over his practice after medical school?"

"No, he had already retired, and they had moved to live near Mother's sister in Pennsylvania by then, and I didn't know anyone there, so I decided to head south away from the long, dreary winters," Will said, as he picked up his bag to follow Ester.

She carried a lamp to light their way into the otherwise dark house and pointed out the bed Will was to take for the night.

"If I don't get up early, please wake me. I haven't had much sleep the past couple of nights," Will said, as Ester started out of the room.

Ester nodded her head to indicate she had heard his request.

The life of a doctor must be exhausting, she thought, as she turned down the cover on her own bed. She had felt tired by the time Sarah had delivered her babies and they had finished with her care. Now her eyes seemed wide awake. Ester thought about the handsome doctor sleeping in the next room. She had learned he was single with no apparent love interest. There was far more she would like to know about the fine-looking Doctor Will Hudson, but she doubted she would be seeing much of him in the future. The fifteen miles into Del Rio was like a visit to another town and one she seldom made. Probably Will would not come to the Cremwelgys' again unless there was some serious mishap. Country people didn't ordinarily seek the services of a doctor. They relied on old home remedies and took care of one another.

Ester remembered watching Vincent remove an embedded fishhook from Homer's leg last month while they were fishing. Flossie had thrown her line, but, instead of landing in the water, her hook landed in Homer's leg. It was buried halfway up to where the line was tied onto the hook. Homer was brave while his father worked the embedded hook out of his leg with a small pair of side cutters. Homer screwed up his face and squeezed his eyes shut in an attempt to ward off the pain but hardly made a sound during the ordeal. When they got home, Olga had put iodine on the wound and that was that.

If that had happened in Dallas, they would have immediately gone to the doctor to take the hook out and care for the wound to avoid infection. Yes, things were certainly done differently here in the country, Ester mused as sleep finally claimed her.

Will lay in the lumpy bed staring up at the dark ceiling. He was thinking about the rather attractive young woman sleeping just a few feet and one wall away in her own bed. Ester was certainly the most interesting young woman he had met since coming to Del Rio five months ago. She was rather pretty, he reflected, and had a regal quality about her. He wished it weren't so far out to the Cremwelgys' so he could visit more often, but the distance and long hours he put in daily tending the sick would probably prevent any such pleasure trips. Will was curious as to why Ester had chosen to come to such a rural place to teach when she had obviously enjoyed all of the amenities Dallas had to offer. As his thoughts wandered, he finally gave in to the long-awaited sleep his body so desperately needed.

Chapter Four

The following Saturday, in the early afternoon, Ester and Olga saw the Mexicans along with Grant McKie and several of his men headed toward the Rio Grande. They supposed Grant was accompanying them in case they encountered the military patrol to vouch for the horses being sold and not stolen. It could have also been to keep them from plundering any additional stock on their way back to Mexico. Hopefully, the Mexicans had what they wanted and wouldn't return any time soon.

At Sunday services, little was said about the Mexicans coming to buy the horses from McKie. The subject had turned to the war raging in Europe. Many expressed their concern that President Wilson would let the U. S. be dragged into the faraway conflict. The Millers were the only ones with boys near the age to go to the army, and one could see their worried looks as the war was discussed. Prayers were offered for the allied forces fiercely fighting the dreadful Germans.

The war seemed so far away, Ester thought, as she looked around the room while the minister read the morning Bible verses. It seemed they had their own war of sorts here on the border. The constant fear of invasion from Pancho Villa and outlaws seemed to run rampant through the rugged country filled with arroyos and caves, where they could hide until they could slip across the border to Mexico where they knew they would be safe from the law. Ester could understand the ranchers' fears. How awful to have the things you worked so hard for be stolen, and if you protested you would likely be killed. It was depressing to think that there was some kind of war going on in most parts of the world.

On Monday morning, a troop of soldiers from Fort Clark stopped at the school to inform Ester they would be patrolling in Val Verde County during the next couple of weeks. Lieutenant Noble Young, a strikingly handsome young man with light brown hair and alert hazel eyes, was very cordial. He gave an extensive explanation of their mission to Ester while the children were at morning recess. When she called the students back in for class, the lieutenant and troop went on their way to visit the ranchers to make their presence known.

Ester felt safer already, knowing the soldiers were in the vicinity. Then she remembered the vast number of miles they would have to cover in the county, and the feeling of security quickly waned.

The weather turned colder, and the north wind reminded them of winter's approach. Ester had begun to dread the three-mile walk to school in the frosty morning air, and the afternoon walk was just as unpleasant when they had to walk home facing the biting north wind. She had bought a new winter coat before leaving Dallas, but its weight only added to her discomfort by the end of the walk.

Ester had saved all of her wages and wondered if she had enough to buy a horse and buggy. She would talk to Vincent about it and see if he would be willing to care for the horse when she went to McKie Ranch for a month in the winter and three months in the summer. Of course, she would pay him for the horse's upkeep.

She wished she had money for an automobile, but the road from the five-mile turnoff was so rough it would be hard driving. The main road went on west across a low water crossing of the Devils River toward Comstock. The sharp pointed rocks on their ranch road would likely ruin the tires and then, keeping fuel would present another problem. Maybe she just wasn't cut out to live in the country, she supposed, as they trudged along toward home on Friday afternoon.

She really needed to go back to school tomorrow to give everything a good cleaning since most of the children had runny noses and colds. Maybe the weather would improve by then, she hoped, and the trip wouldn't be so disagreeable.

Ester had worked steadily all morning washing each desk thoroughly with soapy water and then rinsing each one. She had cleaned the windows and swept and mopped the wood floor. She sat at her desk admiring her clean classroom when she heard voices coming from the front steps. She walked to the door to open it and realized the man spoke with a strong Spanish accent. She hesitated, listened intently, and heard a man speaking English answer him. Ester was curious as to why the two men were sitting on the school steps on a Saturday morning, visiting.

She pressed her ear to the door and could just make out part of their conversation.

"No need in you payin' the boss big prices for them horses when I can get them for you at half his price," the English speaker said, in a low rumbling voice.

"Si señor, he is a fine man, but I must buy for the better price," the Mexican answered in broken English.

"Yeah, he's a decent sort. I've known him for about fifteen years," the English speaker agreed rather begrudgingly. "When you send someone to the ranch be sure they ask to speak to the foreman of the east range and speak to no one else. If someone asks what he wanted I will just say he was looking for work, and they won't question that," he cautioned.

What ranch was he talking about? she wondered. Could he be the foreman on McKie's ranch or some other ranch? She pressed her ear harder against the thick door in hopes to catch more of their conversation.

"I will send someone in about ten days. He will let you know then how many horses and cattle we need."

"I'll keep an eye out for him. I'm sure we can do much business together that will benefit you and me," the English speaker said, with a low laugh.

"I am sure we can, amigo," the Mexican answered.

"We better get movin' before somebody happens by and sees us together. That sure wouldn't do," the English speaker told the other man.

Ester could tell they were walking away from the school as their voices faded. She dared not peek out the window in case they caught sight of her.

Who could the foreman be? If only she knew who to warn they had a dishonest employee, she pondered, as she waited for the men to ride away. The only foreman she knew was Hank Day and that was not his voice she heard through the door. Should she tell Vincent what she had heard, or should she wait until she went to the McKie ranch in a few weeks and tell Grant? After all, he was the one who had dealt with the Mexicans. He might have a better idea about what rancher had a dishonest foreman.

As she walked home, she had an uneasy feeling. Had she known about the danger posed by the Mexicans coming across the border at will, and the outlaws that roamed this area, she would never have taken this teaching position. She looked at a distant cave in the side of a cliff across the river and wondered if some outlaw might be hiding inside watching her as she walked home. A shiver went down her spine at the thought, and she quickened her steps toward the Cremwelgys' ranch.

Maybe, she pondered, she was just getting homesick since it was only a few days until Thanksgiving and then Christmas wasn't far away, as she buttoned her coat against the north wind that was becoming increasingly stronger. She watched the heavy gray clouds to the west and wondered if rain was headed their way. She disliked winter under the best of circumstances and living out in the country was not the best by any means. The house was drafty and at night she piled so many quilts on her bed it was hard to turn over. Walking to and from school in the winter was not appealing in the least. Perhaps she should resign at Christmas break and go back to Dallas, she rationalized, feeling a bit downhearted.

Then she remembered Christine McKie and how excited the child had seemed to have a teacher coming to the ranch. What a shame the child couldn't attend school with the other children! It must be a lonely life for the little girl. She had lost her mother at such an early age. She was loved and cared for by Grant, his mother, and even his sister; she had no one to play with and would only be taught for such short periods of time. No, she couldn't disappoint Christine, and where would they find a teacher in the middle of the school year for the other children? Ester chastised herself; she had made this commitment and she would keep it through this school year no matter how miserable the circumstances.

Ester reached the top of the hill and stopped to savor the view. There was a harsh beauty about this country. The formation of the rocks and craggy hills and the meandering river blended in to make a pleasant scene, even in winter, when the grass was brown, and the trees were bare of their leaves. It was a strange land but one that drew you in and did not want to let you go. Maybe that was why the ranchers came and endured the hardships year after year. They all seemed to have a kinship with the land.

Thanksgiving morning was full of constant activity in the Cremwelgy kitchen. Olga stuffed the large turkey Vincent had killed the evening before and put it in the huge oven to bake until lunchtime. She directed Ester and Aleyne in cooking sweet potatoes, preparing the yeast rolls that would bake as soon as the turkey came out of the oven, and making two pecan pies. Olga had baked a delicious-smelling fruitcake the previous day.

Ester had no doubt that Olga was queen of the kitchen. She longed for the time when she could be the one in charge of a kitchen. She considered herself to be a decent cook. How else was she to improve her skills unless she had more practice? Yet, with a hint of jealousy, she reminded herself this was not her house and she must respect Olga's supremacy while staying here.

Sarah, Hank, and the twins also joined them for the feast. Sarah brought green beans, fruit salad, and two pumpkin pies.

By one o'clock, the kitchen was filled with wonderful aromas, and the counter was laden with delicious-looking dishes. Three of the ranch hands also joined in the celebration. Everyone seemed to enjoy the festive occasion. Ester had dreaded the day thinking she would be even more lonesome for her own family. She had been so busy helping that she had not even thought about her family being together at home, except for her. When she did finally think about her family, she had to admit she really didn't feel she had missed out on anything.

When the guests had departed, Olga called all of the children into the parlor. "Aleyne, get the paper and a pencil from my top bureau drawer. Flossie, go get the new Sears Roebuck Catalog from under my sewing machine," she instructed the two oldest girls.

They soon returned with the items, and the children began to smile and clap their hands with excited anticipation.

Ester watched the proceedings and wondered what the excitement was all about but did not ask.

"If you go to school you can pick your own shoes, with my final approval," Olga added.

Olga laid a piece of paper on the floor.

"Aleyne, hold Jason still so I can trace his feet," Olga told her daughter.

Aleyne picked up the squirming child and placed his feet on the paper. He began to kick and fuss, wanting to be free from her restraint. Flossie quickly came to help by holding his feet still while Olga traced around each foot and then wrote his name on the paper.

"Can I pick out shoes for Jason?" Flossie asked.

"Yes, pick out some high tops," Olga told her. Then she called Maggie and each of the remaining children in turn. There was much discussion about the shoes and Owen was sent back to search the catalog three times before Olga approved his choice.

At last, Ester had to ask, "Is there a Sears Roebuck store in Del Rio?"

"Oh, heavens no," Olga replied, with a laugh. "We mail these drawings in and Sears matches them to the right size shoes and mails them back. It only takes a couple of weeks to get the new shoes."

Ester sat listening with her mouth slightly open. She had never heard of such a way to buy shoes.

"We always get new shoes for Christmas," Flossy told her.

When Olga saw Ester's expression, she gave a hardy laugh. "I expect you're used to going to the store to buy shoes, but we don't have much choice in the local stores, so we just mail order."

Ester was still amazed at the way they determined the sizes, but apparently, it worked. She must remember to tell her family about how country people bought shoes. They would truly be amazed, she mused.

Chapter Five

The first Friday in December, the Cremwelgy household was in a state of near pandemonium. The entire family and Ester were going to Del Rio to shop for Christmas. Ester was almost as excited as the children. This was her first trip to town since she arrived in September. Ester found it hard to believe she had been here for three months and not gone on a single shopping trip. Oh, how her sisters would laugh if they knew what a bleak life she was leading. No trips to the department stores to see the latest fashions, no trips to the theater to see the latest play, no trips to the symphony performances, no trips to the library, which she dearly loved, and no dates with prospective beaus. Oh, how they would marvel at her meager existence and would likely demand her immediate return to Dallas.

The bone-jarring ride in the farm wagon seemed to last forever, but at last, they could see the little town in the distance. It was indeed small, but it was populated and must have some decent stores, Ester hoped. When they finally arrived on the main street, Ester was surprised to see the businesses span for several blocks. Once they had secured their rooms at a nearby boarding house, Ester could hardly wait to start shopping, although it was near closing time for the stores. At least she could see what stores there were and plan her shopping for Saturday. They would spend two nights in town and return to the ranch on Sunday.

Oh, it felt wonderful to be among people and buildings, with things to do, she mused, as she strolled along the main street gazing at the display windows of each store.

She was equally surprised to see a number of automobiles parked along the main street. They must be city dwellers, she decided, because, if all rural roads were like the one they lived on, they certainly wouldn't be driving automobiles. She was pleased to see signs for several department stores, two five-and-dime stores, four barber shops, two beauty shops, one bakery, three apothecaries, one opera house, and three cafés. Being late on Friday, the streets were almost void of people, but she was sure by tomorrow the town would be bustling with shoppers.

It was strange to see the buildings lit with electric lights. Of course, they had electric lights in all buildings and their homes in Dallas. Here none of the ranches had electric lights. At times she felt as though she had stepped back in time about twenty-five years. Yes, it was certainly different living in the country.

As she retraced her steps back to the boarding house, suddenly a door from one of the barbershops was flung open, almost hitting her. She staggered in an attempt to avoid being thrown to the sidewalk by the flying door. A strong arm grasped her around the waist to prevent her from falling.

"Beg your pardon, Ma'am," a familiar voice said, near her ear.

"Ester! What in the world are you doing here?" that same voice asked in amazement.

Ester regained her balance and looked up into the familiar face of Doctor Will Hudson. She was glad to see he looked far more rested than the last time she had seen him. His fresh haircut and shave enhanced his good looks, and his eyes twinkled with recognition. Ester breathed in the pleasant spicy smell of his aftershave.

"I've, well we, the Cremwelgys and I, have come to Christmas shop. We just arrived a short time ago, and I wanted to see what stores were here so I could plan my shopping for tomorrow," Ester explained, a bit breathless from the near mishap and perhaps from her nearness to Will. She felt her cheeks growing warmer and was afraid she might be blushing like a schoolgirl.

Will released her and stepped back now that she was stable on her feet.

"Where are you staying?"

"At the boarding house just around the corner," she gestured.

"Ah, one of my favorite places to dine," he said, with a hint of satisfaction in his voice. "May I join you and the Cremwelgys this evening for dinner?" he asked, with a charming smile.

Ester could feel her heart beating a bit faster. It must be due to the near collision, she tried to reason with herself. "I would, I mean, we would be delighted to have you dine with us. I am sure the Cremwelgys will be happy to see you again."

He took her elbow as they walked toward the boarding house chatting as though they were old friends who normally walked together enjoying one another's company.

When they entered the dining room the Cremwelgys were already seated with only one empty chair left at their table. The proprietor quickly ushered Ester and Will to a nearby table set for two. This arrangement was satisfactory to all, especially Ester, who wanted a chance to enjoy Will's private company again. They continued their conversation through dinner and lingered through three cups of coffee. The dining room was empty except for them, but the owner assured them they could stay as long as they liked.

"Ester, would you like to have dinner with me again tomorrow night and then go to the Opera House for the show?" Will asked as he started to rise from the table.

"That sounds delightful," she responded, filled with excitement at the thought of seeing him again and spending an entire evening together.

"Great, I'll meet you here at six o'clock. The show starts at seven. In case I get called out I will send someone with a note to let you know I won't be able to keep our date," he said, with a warm smile but with an attitude of regret in his voice.

Will wanted to meet her for dinner and escort her to the Opera House, Ester was thinking with a thrill. It had been over three months since she had been out with a man. "Oh, I hope you don't get called out, but if you do, I certainly understand. It is just that you are the only person I have met to discuss books, theater, and so many other things with that it seems like I am starving for good conversation. Oh, don't misunderstand, the Cremwelgys are wonderful people and make me feel so welcome, but they just don't talk about the things we talk about," she hastened to explain.

Will smiled, "Yes, I know. I don't get to enjoy much conversation of quality either, except occasionally with Doc Williams."

He reached for her hand and gave it a gentle squeeze. "I'll see you tomorrow at six," he said, and gave a conspiratorial wink.

To her delight, she found a large selection of materials in one of the nicer department stores and selected fabrics for a new Sunday dress. She had three skirts and three blouses for teaching and two Sunday dresses. One dress was beginning to look faded, so she could wear it as a housedress on the weekends. Ester spied some navy blue material, and next to it was a bolt of navy blue with white polka dots. Oh, that would make a smart frock, she surmised, as she glanced toward the Simplicity pattern book. She soon found an appropriate pattern. It was a double-skirted dress, with long puffy sleeves, and a large collar. The mid-calf underskirt would be the solid color, and the overdress would be made from the polka dot material. Then she chose some white material and lace to trim the collar and cuffs. She could easily imagine what a pretty frock it was going to make. Ester felt certain she would have enough fabric left to make Lilly and Maggie new rag dolls for Christmas.

At lunch, she returned to the boarding house to deposit her bundle of purchases. After a light lunch, she returned to the stores to complete her shopping. She bought new spinning tops for the boys, pretty ribbons to make two hair bows each for Aleyne and Flossie Cremwelgy, and two for Christine McKie. She bought a pair of ready-made pillowslips for Olga and Vincent. She would embroider their names on each one. Since she scarcely knew the McKies it was hard to buy gifts for Corabell, Molly, and especially some token for Grant. Ester finally made what she felt would be appropriate selections.

As she returned to the boarding house with her arms loaded with packages, she met Vincent also walking in that direction. He relieved her of most of her packages.

"When you put your packages away would you like to go look at a buggy I found for sale at the livery stable that might suit you?" he asked.

"Oh yes, what about a horse too?"

"No need to buy a horse, I have enough to spare one for you to use," Vincent assured her.

"How will I get it home?"

"Daniel will trade the horse he rode to town for another and it can pull the buggy home. He will teach you how to manage the horse and buggy."

"Daniel likes to work the horses, doesn't he?" Ester stated more than asked.

"Ah yeah, he seems to have a knack for horse trainin' 'n' tradin'. He trades up with every horse and usually has some pocket money to boot," Vincent said, with a chuckle.

"Trade up?" Ester asked, as she was not familiar with the term.

"That means he has a horse, say worth two dollars, but he

convinces some fellow that his horse is really more valuable and will trade his two-dollar horse for a three-dollar-and-fifty-cent horse," Vincent explained, with a fond smile. "Daniel takes every horse and works with it until he has improved the horse, so he is in a better position to get a better price. Yeah, he is becomin' quite a horse trader," Vincent mused, with a note of pride in his voice.

The sleek, black buggy had two seats that could easily accommodate Ester and the five Cremwelgy children. Well, Daniel usually rode his horse, but there would be plenty of room if he chose to ride with them. Suddenly the winter trips to and from school didn't look so bleak.

At a quarter to six, a boy arrived at the boarding house with a note for Ester from Will.

Dear Ester,

I have to make a house call but will join you at the Opera House as soon as possible. Sit by the aisle and save me a seat.

Will

Ester naturally felt disappointed that she would not have the pleasure of his company for dinner but was glad he could meet her later. At least she hoped it worked out as he planned. How patient would she be with a husband who could never be certain of keeping their plans? Would she be content to attend functions alone?

Ester laughed at her absurd thoughts. Why was she even thinking of such things? Especially since they had just met. This might be her only opportunity to go out with the attractive and equally charming doctor.

The performance had just begun when Will slipped into the seat beside her. She could feel the cold from the damp night air on his clothing. He coughed slightly several times. Ester looked at him with concern and then whispered, "Are you coming down with a cold?"

He coughed several more times and was finally able to answer. "No, the cold, damp air doesn't agree with me. It has started to rain, and I just got a slight chill, but I'll be fine once I warm up."

Within a short time, his coughing subsided, and they sat shoulder-to-shoulder enjoying a variety of entertainment. The performers did melodrama skits and sang funny songs that brought uproarious laughter from the audience. Several of the songs were played with a beat that enticed the audience into clapping or tapping their feet to the beat of the music. After a while, Will reached for Ester's hand and held it in his. When she glanced at him, he gave her his special smile that made his dimple seem to wink at her. Toward the end of the show, a couple sang a medley of romantic songs as though they were wooing one another. Will gently caressed her hand, and during a tender love song, he raised her hand to his lips and gently kissed her fingers. Ester felt her pulse race and completely lost her concentration on the songs being sung. No man had ever kissed her fingers, and the sensation was amazingly enchanting.

They emerged from the warm theater into the cold rainy night air. Will held his umbrella over their heads to shield them from the gentle rain. He slipped his other arm around Ester's waist and pulled her snugly against his side. They walked back to the boarding house discussing how much they had enjoyed the evening's entertainment. When they reached the steps leading up to the front porch, Will gently kissed Ester on the cheek. She could feel his warm breath against her skin and inhaled the fresh scent of his spicy shaving lotion. She longed to feel his lips on hers, but he did not fulfill her wish.

That night she lay in her warm bed reliving his tender kiss on her fingers and then his parting kiss on her cheek. Oh, how she wished the miles did not separate them for such long periods of time. The time they spent together was like a refreshing breeze on a warm day. Will filled the need she had for male companionship and meaningful conversation. He was so handsome and such an interesting man. She felt sure every eligible woman in town would pursue him relentlessly. What chance would she have in winning his affection when their meetings were strictly by chance?

As Will walked back to his cold and almost empty two-room apartment at the back of Doctor Williams' house, he thought about the last two evenings he had spent with Ester. He longed to spend more time with her but also knew it could lead to the danger of his eventually having to reveal his secret. Will knew he must guard his mounting feelings for Ester and should never let her fall for him as it would only break her heart in the end. The hacking cough shook his body as he entered his apartment. He quickly disrobed and covered himself with a mound of blankets to warm his shaking body in hopes the coughing would soon stop.

Chapter Six

The days between Thanksgiving and Christmas break seemed to pass in a whirlwind of activity.

Ester spent every free minute sewing her new dress to be worn for the first time on Christmas Day. She was pleased with her handiwork as she inspected the dress. Ester gazed at her reflection in the big round mirror on Olga's dresser. It looked far more stylish than what the other women wore. She hoped they wouldn't think she was putting on airs.

She made rag dolls for Lilly and Maggie Cremwelgy and still had enough material left to make one for Christine McKie. At night she would work by the dim lamp light in her partitioned-off corner of the bedroom behind the old quilts Olga had hung to give her a bit of privacy. She patiently stitched Olga's and Vincent's names on the pillowcases for Christmas. Ester joyfully wrapped all of her gifts in gaily colored paper and ribbons. She left them in Olga's care to put under their tree on Christmas Eve.

Ester wished over and over that she could stay at the Cremwelgys' for Christmas but knew the time was quickly approaching when she must go to the McKie Ranch for a month. While she was anxious to begin teaching Christine, she dreaded the day-to-day living in another strange household. It seemed she had just adjusted to the workings of the Cremwelgy household, and she had an underlying feeling she might not feel as welcome at the McKies' as she had been at the Cremwelgys'.

Grant arrived just after noon on Saturday. He quickly loaded her bag and box of gifts into the wagon, and they were on their way to his ranch.

In several places, the road was almost impassable because the recent rains had washed trenches in the dirt and numerous rocks had slid onto the roadway. Ester had never been on such a treacherous road. It was much worse than from the Cremwelgys' to the school. They bounced along for quite a while and finally topped a hill that gave a spectacular view of the main ranch compound nestled on the slope of a hill across a wide valley. The late evening shadows cast the surrounding hills in shades of deep blue and purple. A slow-moving stream meandered through the valley where sheep and goats grazed. It was a tranquil scene.

In the distance, Ester could see a large ranch house. There were two huge barns, several pens, and two large arenas for training the horses. Several other buildings were scattered around the headquarters. As they drew nearer to the house, she could make out a number of rough cedar posts supporting the roof over the porch that extended across the entire front of the house. A porch swing at one end with several chairs nearby made it look like an inviting place to sit on nice days. The house and surroundings had a pleasant, hospitable look, and Ester hoped that impression would prove true.

She and Grant had talked pleasantly enough on their trip back to his ranch. Ester had learned his wife had died in childbirth when Christine was three. His father had settled this land in 1883 at age twenty and worked himself into an early grave at forty-five making the ranch successful. His heart seemed to give out, Grant had said with a note of respect for what his father had achieved. Grant had stepped into his role as owner at age seventeen.

A number of folks thought he was far too young to manage such a large ranch, but he had proven them wrong. Grant had managed the original ranch and more than doubled its size to over a hundred and forty thousand acres, and he employed about forty men. Some were married with families, but most were single cowboys. He ran cattle along with some sheep and goats. Grant McKie had built a reputation for raising some of the finest horses in this part of the state. Grant and most of the ranchers were leaning more toward raising sheep and goats as the cattle had about grazed the early range grass down. Ester found she admired Grant's ability and stamina to oversee such an operation.

Grant certainly was not a boastful man but answered her questions in brief statements. She suspected he didn't think she would understand too much about the details of ranching, and he was probably right.

Ester had wanted to tell him about overhearing the conversation between the two men at the school a few weeks previous, but she had not been sure how to approach the subject. She found Grant a bit difficult to talk to. He had what she called a *standoffish* manner. Ester supposed it might be that their interests were so different. She knew next to nothing about livestock, and he certainly wouldn't be interested in discussing the books she read. Ester doubted he had ever been to a symphony or theatrical production. Hopefully, she would soon find the right opportunity to tell him about the two men and prevent some hard-working rancher from being cheated out of fair prices for his livestock.

Perhaps she would meet his foreman soon and would be able to tell if it was his voice she had heard outside the school.

When they reached the ranch house Christine bounded out the front door and ran toward the wagon before it came to a full stop.

"Christine! How many times have I told you to wait on the porch until the wagon's stopped before you come running out? You could easily get hurt or spook the horses with that behavior," Grant scolded his daughter in a stern voice.

Christine gazed at her father with large blue eyes that looked as though tears might overflow at any minute. "Sorry, Daddy, I forgot again," she answered, in a subdued manner.

Ester felt sorry for the child who probably had little company, so a visitor was something to become excited about.

"Hello, Christine, I am so glad you are happy for me to come to your house," Ester said, trying to smooth over the incident. She hastened to add, "Your father is right though, you must be careful around the animals. You wouldn't want to get hurt or have one of them get hurt either, would you?"

"Oh, no," Christine assured her with a shake of her head, setting her long blonde curls into a swinging motion about her head.

Then she brightened with a smile and a twinkle returned to her eyes. "Did you bring lots of books for me to learn?"

"Yes indeed, I brought lots of books for you to study. I know you are going to be a good student," Ester returned, as she started to climb down from the wagon. Before she could reach the ground, strong hands encircled her waist and gently set her feet on the solid earth. She made a startled sound in her throat, as she had not realized Grant was so near.

He instantly released her and reached for her bags and box.

"Christine, why don't you show Miss Hammon to her room?" Grant suggested in a milder tone than he had previously used.

Ester followed Christine as she skipped up the steps and opened the large front door leading into an enormous room filled with a variety of sturdy furniture that looked to be handcrafted. Large rust-colored pillows were placed on the seats and backs of the two sofas and several large chairs to add to their comfort. The room was filled with a warm glow from several oil lamps placed on tables. Two lamps sat on the rustic wood mantle over the enormous rock fireplace that ran along the back wall.

Ester could smell the aroma of yeast bread blended with other delicious odors that made her realize how long it had been since lunch.

"Come this way," Christine instructed. She led Ester down a hall to the right off the large room. They passed two doors on the left, and at the second door on the right, Christine paused to open it. They entered a large bedroom with a full four-poster bed. A white ruffled bedspread covered a fluffy mattress that looked most comfortable. The dressing table and library table sat near a bookshelf void of books. A large chair with the same rust-colored pillows sat beside the table holding a lamp. Double windows looked out onto the large front porch. It was a cozy room and Ester wondered if she would share it with Christine, but her question was promptly answered.

"Christine has the room across the hall, Mother has the first room on the left, and Molly is on the right," Grant told her as he sat her belongings on the bed.

"Thank you. This is a lovely room, and I'm sure I will be very comfortable." She remembered there were several more doors down the hall and a door at the end. Ester wondered which room Grant occupied and what the other rooms were used for.

Corabell served a plentiful supper and coconut meringue pie for dessert. Just as the meal began, their foreman, Charlie Stroud, arrived and joined them for the meal. He was a jovial man with thinning red hair and a round body. He carried on a lively conversation throughout what might have otherwise been a dull meal. Christine giggled and laughed when Charlie teased her. When Molly noticed Christine laughing, she would join in. Ester noticed that Grant would remind Molly to finish eating. She wondered why it was Grant instead of Corabell, her mother.

Ester was relieved to know it was not Charlie's voice she had heard outside the school. She wondered if she should even mention the incident to Grant. How would he know who the man might be? Yet, it bothered her to think some rancher was going to be cheated out of fair prices for his livestock. Ester finally decided she would bide her time and see if an opportunity arose to bring up the subject.

After assisting Corabell in cleaning the kitchen Ester retired to her room to read before bedtime, a luxury she was seldom able to enjoy in the Cremwelgys' crowded household. The house was soon quiet. Thinking everyone was already sleeping Ester took her lamp and quietly left her room. She made her way to the kitchen for a glass of water before retiring. As she stood at the sink drinking, she suddenly felt she was not alone. She turned to see Grant standing in the doorway watching her. They just stared at one another for several seconds before he spoke.

"I heard something and thought it was Christine sneaking in here to swipe a cookie," he explained, with a pleasant grin.

"No, I just needed some water," Ester answered. "I'm sorry I disturbed you." She felt a bit ill at ease in her gown and wrapper, as Grant never took his eyes from her. She had always been fully clothed in front of men, even her own father. She had made it a point to dress before she left her bedroom while at the Cremwelgys'.

Ester could not help but notice Grant's good looks in the lamplight as it shimmered over the masculine features of his face and muscular frame. Its flickering light made his blond hair seem to take on a soft glow.

"Well, good night," he finally said in a husky voice as he turned to leave.

Grant sat at his desk for a long time trying to concentrate on the ranch books, but he could not get the pleasing picture of Ester from his mind. She looked so feminine and appealing standing in his kitchen late at night clad only in her nightclothes. He had to admit he was tempted to cross the room, take her in his arms, and steal a goodnight kiss. Grant shook his head to clear that image from his mind as he finished off half of a glass of whiskey. Such behavior could only lead to trouble, he was quite certain. Then he forced his attention back to the ranch accounts.

Ester was thankful she did not see Grant except at the evening meal, and fortunately, Charlie always kept the conversation on a lighter note. He delighted in telling stories about the antics some of the cowhands pulled on each other and some of the idiotic things they did all on their own. He loved to laugh, even if it was at some of his own doings.

Christine proved to be an eager student, and the days passed quickly. Ester was pleased with her progress. From time to time, Molly would come and sit for a while watching what Ester and Christine were doing. Ester tried to engage Molly in some simple activities, but she seemed more content to just watch. When Ester wasn't busy teaching, she would help Corabell around the house. Corabell was not as talkative as Olga but was pleasant enough and they got on well.

One of the Mexican ranch hands' young wives, Sonya, did all of the household laundry, including Ester's. Sonya spoke little English, so their conversations were quite limited. Ester decided to learn some Spanish words from Sonya, and that seemed to please and, at times, amuse the quiet, young woman.

The first Sunday after arriving, there was finally a break in the normal routine. Ester slept until eight o'clock, which was a real luxury. Then she spent a quiet time reading her Bible and meditating since they would not be attending Sunday services at the school. The eight-mile drive in the wagon took an unusually long time over the treacherous, bone-jarring road. Ester wondered if the isolation became easier with years spent in such a remote place. Corabell didn't have any close friends, nor did Christine. Grant had plenty of men for company. Ester wondered if he ever considered remarrying. She also couldn't help but wonder where he would find a wife living so far away from town or even his closest neighbors.

When Sunday lunch was served, it was a large meal with apple pie for dessert. Corabell was a wonderful cook. Charlie did not join them, and the meal was largely spent in silence. Toward the end of the meal, Grant announced they would be having the Christmas party on Friday, the 23rd of December. Most folks spent the night and returned to their own homes on Christmas Eve, he told Ester.

Ester was full of questions about the party. "Who all comes?" she wanted to know.

"Most of the ranch hands and their families, if they have one, and a number of the surrounding neighbors," Grant explained.

"Where does everyone sleep?" Ester questioned. The house was rather large, but she doubted it would be large enough for all of those people.

"We put the married couples in the bedrooms and make down pallets for the older and younger kids. The ranch hands make extra room for bedrolls in the bunkhouse. We hang the rest from nails, so that's what you might call wall-to-wall people," Grant added with a chuckle. "The ones that live near enough to the ranch go on home for the night."

Ester listened to every word, thoroughly amazed, and she could feel her excitement building in anticipation of the approaching event. At last, a social gathering, Ester mused. At home, there would be a number of parties to attend during the holiday season, but it seemed a rarity here.

"There'll be lots of food to cook, although all the ladies bring food too. When folks get to dancin' and nippin' the eggnog or somethin' stronger it seems to boost up their appetite," Corabell added with a good-natured chortle.

"Just let me know any way I can help. I'll be glad to cook, clean, or do anything else to help get everything ready. I love to decorate for the holidays and am sure Christine would be lots of help too," Ester volunteered.

"Well, thank you, Ester. I'm sure there will be plenty to keep all of us busy. Molly takes care of the dusting. That's her favorite chore, and she does a good job too," Corabell added, as she gave Molly a hug and smile.

Molly smiled in return and nodded her head. "Me dust," she said with a big grin as she continued to nod her head several times. Then she returned to her meal, seemingly ignoring all else.

"I want to help Ester decorate," Christine put in.

"I'm sure there will be plenty you can do to help," Ester reassured her. "Will the Cremwelgys be coming?" Ester asked, in hopes the answer would be yes.

"Oh yes, they are usually the first to arrive and last to leave," Corabell grinned. "They love a good party."

Ester was so excited she could hardly contain herself. She would be counting the days until the big event. A real country Christmas, she thought with pleasure.

Once again, she had dreaded the holidays as she was afraid homesickness would set in, but it looked as though there would be plenty to keep her mind occupied.

Christine leaned one elbow on the table and propped her hand under her chin as she continued to eat.

"Christine," was all Grant said in a stern voice. Christine straightened up and removed her elbow from the table. The silence continued.

"Daddy, is Ester old enough to get married?" Christine asked, out of the blue.

Grant looked a bit surprised by her question but cleared his throat and answered, "Yes, I expect she is old enough to get married if she chose to do so."

Christine brightened, "If you married her then I would have a teacher and mommy all at the same time," she suggested, with a brilliant smile.

You could have heard a pin drop! Everyone sat in silence not quite looking at one another.

Ester was so shocked by Christine's suggestion that for once she was literally left speechless. She finally looked at Grant and found he was looking at her. She supposed he was hoping she would answer Christine's question, but she was certainly waiting to hear his answer.

He cleared his throat again and began, "Two people usually get married because they love one another," he paused, "not just to give someone a teacher and mommy."

Christine looked thoughtful. "You could kiss Ester, and she could kiss you. I'd like that! Then you could get married and have lots of babies like the Cremwelgys," she continued, with a bright smile.

Grant gave Christine one of his stern looks that made the skin on his forehead between his eyes became a bit wrinkled. "Christine, that is quite enough on the subject. Now finish your lunch!"

Christine stuck her bottom lip out in a full pout. "I'm not hungry!" she fumed, with a trace of temper in her voice.

"Finish your lunch anyway!" Grant insisted.

"I don't know why you don't want me to have a mommy like the other kids do!" she almost yelled and ran from the room shrieking shrill, piercing sobs that could be heard all the way to her bedroom.

The three adults and Molly sat in silence just looking at one another.

Grant rose from the table, wiped his mouth with his napkin, laid it beside his plate, and simply said, "Excuse me." He left the room, and the women remained silent as they continued to pick at their food.

Before long, they could no longer hear Christine's sobs.

Grant returned in a few minutes and resumed his seat.

"I apologize for Christine's atrocious behavior," Grant said, as he looked at Ester.

Ester looked at him and she knew he had read her thoughts as though she had spoken them aloud.

A slight grin touched the corners of his mouth as he said, "What's the matter, Teacher, don't you think the rancher knows some educated words?"

Ester felt the color rush to her face as she blushed like a schoolgirl and stammered, "I, I was, --- just a bit surprised by your statement, that's all." She felt much like a child who had been caught with her hand in the cookie jar. She also felt guilty for misjudging him. She didn't know how much formal education Grant had, and it shouldn't matter. He had just caught her off guard, that was all.

Then he had the audacity to laugh at her lame denial when he saw the expression on her face.

Ester truly wished she had the authority to send him to his room for his misbehavior.

The next few days went by in a frenzy of activity. When Ester finished teaching Christine for the day, they threw themselves into making all kinds of decorations for the tree. It would arrive on December 22, Grant had told them. Ester would draw patterns of angels, bells, holly wreaths, and so on, and Christine spent many happy hours coloring them. Then Ester would cut them out. Ester showed Christine how to fold the paper and cut different patterns to make snowflakes. After a while, they had enough snowflakes to make it look like a blizzard had hit the ranch.

Corabell was in full swing with her baking and preparing her famous fruitcake. At first, Ester hadn't realized Corabell had baked the fruitcake several weeks ago and each day added a bit of brandy to the cake. She kept it in the pantry where it was always cool.

After several days, when Ester smelled the cake, she estimated one thin slice would have enough brandy to do you in.

Charlie asked about the progress of the fruitcake almost daily and had dibs on the first big slice. "I swear it's the gall-darndest best fruit-cake I have ever tasted," Charlie bragged. His praise pleased Corabell beyond measure. She would smile when she heard him bragging about her *absolutely delicious fruitcake* and even giggled a couple of times.

Each evening after dinner, Christine would almost drag Grant into the large dining room, which was hardly used, to see their latest creations for the tree, decorations for the windows, and even some to hang from the large rafters. "Daddy, we need some mistletoe to hang from the rafters," she said in a serious manner.

Grant looked at his six-year-old daughter in surprise. "Can you tell me just why we need to hang mistletoe from the rafters?"

Christine nodded her head with enthusiasm. "Yes, Granny and Ester said if a guy catches a girl standing under the mistletoe, he can steal a kiss and not get into trouble. It is an old t-t-di-tion," she finished her explanation with evident pride.

Grant looked at her with one raised eyebrow. "Yes, I believe I have heard about that tradition. Let me ask you this, how old does a girl have to be to get kissed under the mistletoe?"

Christine thought for a minute. Then she shrugged her shoulders. "I think lots bigger than me," she answered seriously.

Grant reached out and lovingly pulled one of her golden curls. "You are right, so I better not catch you letting any boys be kissing you under the mistletoe," he told her, with a playful smile.

Christine looked up at him and giggled. "What about you, Daddy? Do you get to kiss some of the ladies if you catch them under the mistletoe?"

"You bet I do," he said, as he swung her up into his muscular arms. "But you are my favorite girl to kiss under the mistletoe or any time," he teased, as he gave her several loud smooches on her face.

Ester smiled as she listened to Grant and Christine in the next room.

On the 22nd, when Grant and one of the workers brought the huge tree into the living room and set it up beside the fireplace, they all admired its height and fullness. The women got into the full swing of decorating it from top to bottom. It did look lovely with all of the colorful homemade decorations. They had strung popcorn and cranberries for the garland. Numerous colorful angels, bells, Santas, holly wreaths, and ample snowflakes adorned the huge tree. Ester even wrapped a few empty boxes in brightly colored Christmas paper, put big red bows on them, and set them under the tree. They made bouquets of red paper flowers for the tables and small garlands to go around the base of the many oil lamps that lit the huge room. Grant and Charlie brought a ladder and hung the sprigs of mistletoe tied with red ribbons from the rafters.

They all stood and surveyed their work and found it a pleasing and cheerful sight.

"Oh, it's so beautiful, Ester," Christine cooed as she hugged Ester around her waist. "We've never, ever had a tree this pretty," she added in awe.

Ester looked down at Christine's shining eyes and smiled. She was so pleased she could help make Christmas special for Christine.

Grant caught a glimpse of Ester out of the corner of his eye as she stood looking up at the tree and wondered what it would be like to catch her under the mistletoe and give her a real kiss, not just a little peck. He didn't want to think about her too much as he knew she was smitten with the young, good-looking doctor. Grant was certain they shared far more interests than she could ever share with him. His life was ranching, and she was definitely a city gal. He suspected she and the doctor would marry within the year and probably move to a more civilized place. Even if they didn't marry, she would probably return to Dallas to enjoy the nicer things in life she was accustomed to. He didn't blame her. After all, this was a lonely and often hard life for most women, stuck miles from their nearest neighbor and soon having a passel of kids to care for as well as all the other chores that went along with ranching.

Christine's mother had had it a bit easier. She hadn't had to tend to any livestock and there had been a hired hand to help with the gardening. She and Corabell had maintained the house together. Yet, he had sensed her loneliness for the companionship of women her own age. No, it wasn't an easy life for women. He might as well get the attractive schoolteacher right out of his mind. She wasn't cut out for the life he could offer. That was for darn sure!

He had heard Elanor Fitzpatrick's unmarried sister, who must be about twenty-five by now, was visiting them for a while. She had grown up on a ranch so maybe she would be someone to get to know better at the party. He had met her some years back but honestly couldn't remember much about her. Maybe she would impress him more this time, he reflected.

Suddenly Ester could feel Grant's eyes on her, and for some unknown reason she started to blush. Surely, he couldn't read her thoughts to know she was wishing Will could be at the party. She longed for him to catch her under the mistletoe and give her a real kiss on her lips instead of just the light brush of his lips on her cheek. She couldn't help but suppress a smile just thinking about Will. They had so much in common and such fun together, what little chance they had to be together. She wished he would whisk her off her feet and marry her right away. She might not mind staying in Del Rio if they were together.

Ester turned away from the lovely tree as she heard the others leaving the room. Oh, the things dreams are made of, she contemplated, as she walked slowly toward the kitchen to help with the evening meal.

On the morning of the 23rd the sky was bright and sunny with a few low-lying dark clouds caressing the tops of the hills to the north.

Ester hoped the weather would stay clear so all of the folks could come to the party, even if a cold north wind was already starting to blow.

After lunch, Ester went to her room with a warm basin of water to freshen up and decided to wear her new polka-dot dress to the party. She dressed carefully to make sure the dress looked just right. She brushed her hair until it shone, pulled it back, and tied it with a matching polka-dot bow at the nape of her neck. Ester applied a small amount of rouge to her cheeks and put on pale pink lipstick. She checked her appearance in the mirror and then walked into the living room where Corabell and Molly sat resting before the first guest arrived.

Corabell looked up at Ester and gasped.

Ester thought it was a gasp of approval, so she twirled around so Corabell could get a better look at her new dress.

"Oh my, Ester! What in the world possessed you to make such a lovely dress out of polka-dot material?" she asked, in shocked dismay.

"I thought it made a pretty combination," Ester replied, a bit perplexed.

"Mercy me, don't you know what that will cause the men to do?" Corabell asked, with an intake of her breath to express her shock.

"No, what will it cause them to do?" Ester wanted to know, still puzzled by Corabell's reaction.

"It will make them want to poke at you," Corabell stated, with a nod of her head as though to emphasize what she was saying.

"Poke at me?" Ester asked, in disbelief.

Corabell nodded her head again with the most serious expression and almost whispered, although they were alone except for Molly. "Yes, poke at you in places they shouldn't be pokin'!"

Ester stood with her mouth half open in disbelief at what she was hearing. Then she started to giggle at the absurdity of such a notion. Soon the giggles turned to laughter, and she almost lost her breath.

"Oh, Corabell, I can't believe you really think that. It must be one of those old wives' tales people think is true."

"You just wait and see. Mark my words, you're gonna have to go change into something else before this evenin' is over," she insisted, with another shake of her head. "It just won't do. No-siree!"

The Cremwelgys arrived about mid-afternoon. Ester was elated to see them. They all seemed to be talking at once. Christine finally took two of the girls to her room to play. The women moved to the kitchen to start arranging the food. Corabell had one of the hired hands bring two more tables into the dining room to accommodate all of the food that would arrive with the other guests.

There was a steady stream of neighbors arriving along with some of the ranch hands from the homestead and the other ranches. The house and yard were filled with folks laughing and talking. The men were sharing a few sips from whiskey bottles and telling jokes among themselves. Children were playing a variety of games outside before it became dark. Soon the temperature would drop, and everyone would need to move inside.

Ester was thoroughly enjoying visiting with the other women. Once again, she realized how starved she had become for companionship with other women her age as well as the fulfillment she found in Will's company. She marveled at these strong women who just accepted their hard way of life, as the way it was supposed to be, and didn't complain.

The party continued when the evening meal was served. Several tables were laden with numerous varieties of vegetables, relishes, salads, and homemade bread, as well as the smoked turkeys, along with several kinds of dressing. The men had also dug a pit and roasted a pig overnight. All of the luscious smells made Ester's stomach start to rumble with hunger. The house was filled with appetizing aromas that pulled the guests toward the tables filled to capacity with food. One large table was filled with pumpkin, mincemeat, pecan, and several other kinds of pies, cakes, cookies, and cupcakes, and the center attraction was Corabell's brandied fruitcake.

People were seated wherever they could find a space to sit, and the children sat in groups on the floor.

Charlie amused everyone by starting his meal with a generous slice of Corabell's renowned fruitcake.

Sometimes the chatting and laughter was so loud it was hard to hear the person sitting in the next chair.

Immediately after the meal was finished, all of the furniture was scooted back against the walls. Two men brought out their fiddles, one had a guitar, and another brought his banjo. The two fiddle players were brothers, Timothy and Gerald Hines. Their families had ranched up the west side of the Devils River for twenty years or more. Although they were not twins, they looked amazingly alike. Timothy was about two inches taller than Gerald. They both had thinning light brown hair, golden brown twinkling eyes, and well-groomed mustaches. The two even wore matching red and green plaid shirts. Their movements as they played their fiddles looked like mirror images of the other.

Ian O'Toole, the banjo player, was a tall man with a head full of thick auburn curls, with long sideburns, but he was clean-shaven. His bonnie blue Irish eyes danced with the music, and his left foot never missed a beat. When he announced the next song to be played, his strong Irish accent was still very evident. Ian had worked for Grant for about five years.

Angus Matthews, an older man with snow-white hair and a full beard, sat on a straight-back chair and leaned slightly forward as he strummed his guitar. Ester thought he looked like a perfect Santa Claus as he also had a well-rounded belly and pink cheeks. He smiled and often laughed as they played the festive music. All of his family had died in a flu epidemic years ago. He had never remarried. Angus had come to terms with his loss and was a jolly sort of fellow. Some folks said he'd rather play music than eat or drink.

The room was filled with music. They started by playing and singing the traditional Christmas carols like *Joy To The World, Oh Little*

Town Of Bethlehem, and Silent Night, Holy Night. Everyone sang with gusto and his or her smiles reflected the joy of the season. After a while, the musicians took a short break.

Grant stepped to the middle of the room and asked for everyone's attention. "I have some good news that will make most of you really have a reason to celebrate and the rest of you in due time. I have been negotiating with the road authority out of Del Rio, and they will begin work on our road the first of January." An almost deafening applause and shouts filled the room. Grant held up his hand to regain their attention. "They say if the weather cooperates the road to this ranch should be finished in a couple of months." The room was filled with more shouts and loud applause.

The musicians returned to their places, and the music switched to lively dance tunes. After several dances with a number of different cowboys, Ester decided it was time for a short respite. She got a glass of eggnog and sat on the fireplace hearth watching the dancers and enjoying the festivities.

She noticed Grant dancing with a woman she assumed was Elanor Fitzpatrick's sister, as they favored considerably. She was about five feet, five inches tall, slender build, with long brown hair that hung in strands down her back. She was so much shorter than Grant that she seemed to be craning her neck to see Grant's face. He appeared to be listening intently to whatever she was saying at the moment. Ester noticed he had danced with her several times. Maybe he was beginning to think about looking for another wife and a mother for Christine.

The door opened, bringing a blast of cold night air and another group of people she did not know but supposed were also neighboring ranchers. Just as the door was about to slam shut, to keep the frigid air outside, the last person to enter was Doctor Will Hudson.

Ester's heart seemed to race with excitement, and she could feel the smile that lit her face. It was so unexpected to see Will here and quite a superb surprise.

Will caught sight of Ester seated by the hearth and immediately began to weave his way among the dancers in her direction.

Before Will reached her, Ester could see his body jerk and hear the cough she hated. She knew it was caused by the cold night air. She caught her breath when she saw Will watching her as he approached. Once their eyes met, they never wavered from one another. He gave her a charming smile between his coughing spells.

"Come sit by the fire and warm yourself," Ester suggested. "Would you like a cup of warm apple cider?"

Will nodded in agreement as he could not speak for the constant coughing. He watched Ester hurry through the crowded room and soon return with the warm cider. His coughing was beginning to subside as he warmed by the fire. As he sipped the cider Ester exclaimed, "I had no idea you would be at the party tonight. How did you happen to find out about it?"

By then his coughing had calmed, and his voice had returned. "I was called out to the Wiggins Ranch. It seems the flu is starting to go around. Several of their cowboys are restricted to bed, but everyone that came tonight isn't showing any signs of getting sick yet."

"Oh my, will they be all right?"

"Yes, probably, I left instructions with a couple of the able-bodied men there about what to do, so hopefully, they will recover. The best thing is to stay away from the others as much as possible until it has passed," Will answered.

"So, the Wigginses brought you along with them to the party. I don't recall meeting them before. Where is their ranch?"

"It's actually behind the Hoffman and part of the Cremwelgy ranches. Their children are grown and not interested in taking over the ranch. It won't be too many years until they'll have to sell out as Mr. Wiggins' health is beginning to fail. A real shame as they love ranching."

"Mr. Wiggins insisted it was too late for me to start back to town, and he said I hadn't ever celebrated Christmas until I had been to a party at the McKie Ranch," Will said, with a smile. "And from the looks of things, I think he might be right." He took her hand and lifted it to his lips for a tender kiss. "Besides, I knew you'd be here and couldn't pass up such a splendid opportunity to see you," he said, with an affectionate gaze.

Will's display of affection made her feel a bit giddy and not exactly sure how to react.

"Oh, indeed, it is a grand party. Are you hungry? There are several tables full of the best food you will ever taste," Ester responded, still elated at his sudden appearance and warm gesture.

"Maybe I'll eat something in a while, but first I'd like a dance with the prettiest woman here," he said with a wink, as he guided Ester to the dance floor. "I must say your dress is lovely and most becoming. Did you make it for the party?"

"Thank you, Will. It's for the party and for church." She wanted to tell him about Corabell's reaction but was afraid that might sound too forward. Ester found it hard not to laugh just thinking about what Corabell had told her. Well, at least so far no one had tried to poke her.

They danced to a number of tunes. Once in a while, some cowboy would cut in for a dance. Several of the McKie hands even told her how pretty she looked. Ester smiled to herself thinking not a one of them had tried to poke her. It wouldn't be long until Will would return to her side and swing her around the room. As he held her close during a slow waltz he whispered, "Oh, Ester, you bring me such delight. I just wish," he hesitated, "so many things that just aren't possible."

Ester looked into his troubled eyes. "What do you mean, not possible?" she asked.

"It's too hard to explain here," he answered and gave her a wan smile. Then he brightened, "Besides, it's Christmas, so let's celebrate all of the good things we have and share." The music became livelier and he swung her around the dance floor again.

At last, Ester persuaded Will he needed to eat, so they both got plates and he filled his plate with the turkey, dressing, a variety of vegetables, and salads. Ester had small pieces of several of the tempting desserts. Ester finished and was waiting for Will to finish his meal when Grant came and asked her to dance.

Ester felt a bit surprised, as he had ignored her all evening. Maybe he had been too busy working up to courting Elanor's sister.

"I see you were dancing with Elanor's sister quite often," she remarked.

"Trying to be a good host," was all he had to say in return.

"She seems to be mixing in well and getting acquainted with everyone," Ester commented, trying to think of something to say.

"Yeah, she's friendly enough," Grant agreed.

They danced in silence for a few minutes, and then Ester heard the banjo player call out, "Happy Christmas Eve. Now give the lady you're dancing with a big kiss!"

Before Ester could fully grasp what was happening, Grant lowered his head and kissed her full on the lips. She gasped in total surprise. Before she could move or say anything, he lowered his head and kissed her again in a more intimate manner. She felt his tongue brush the inside of her mouth as though he were kissing his sweetheart. She tasted the faint tang of whiskey and inhaled the masculine odor of his cologne. Suddenly she felt butterflies in her stomach. When Grant lifted his head, he gave her a big smile as his eyes twinkled. In a low tone, he whispered, "Merry Christmas Eve, Ester."

She just stared at him, dumbfounded. Then she pulled her wits together and managed to murmur, "Merry Christmas Eve to you too."

He danced her over to where Will sat at the table finishing his dessert and pulled out a chair for her. He nodded his head to Will and, being the host of the party, politely said, "Glad you could join us tonight." Then he walked away.

Ester felt certain her face was red but did not know what to say, if anything, about what had just happened. She knew Will must have seen Grant kissing her, and she didn't want him to get the wrong impression about their relationship. She wished it had been Will kissing her that way instead of Grant. Something about the kiss made her stomach still flutter. She didn't care for Grant, so why did his unexpected kiss affect her this way?

Why didn't Will show his affection in a stronger way? Ester knew he cared for her from the way he looked at her, the grand time they had together, and his gentle touches. Why was he so hesitant to carry his affection further? What had he meant when he said he wished for things that weren't possible? She pondered the things he said and his actions but came to no reasonable conclusion.

Will smiled. "That is the finest meal I have had since coming to Del Rio. I feel like I could dance the rest of the night away, how about you?" he asked, as he smiled and held out his hand to her.

They did almost dance the night away. Much to her relief, Grant never returned to ask for another dance. Unfortunately, there was no place for her and Will to be alone even for a minute.

Finally, everyone bedded down and soon the house was quiet. Ester slept on one of the big sofas in the living room. She wasn't sure where Will wound up for the night. In the midst of getting everyone settled, he had slipped away.

Just before she drifted off to sleep, she realized someone was leaning over her. She opened her eyes and from the soft glow of the fireplace saw it was Grant. She saw what she believed to be a gleam of desire in his dark eyes.

"Would you like a goodnight kiss since your gentleman friend seems a bit shy in that department?" he asked, with a wicked grin.

"Not from you!" she answered tersely, hoping he would get the message without further discussion.

He gave a low seductive laugh and walked down the hall toward his own room.

Some of the folks rose early and after consuming a huge breakfast, began to depart. The last to leave were the Cremwelgys, and not far behind, Ester saw Will riding toward town. He hadn't even found her to say goodbye. That puzzled her since last night they had danced and laughed, and he had at least given her a hug, and another tender brush of his lips on her cheek before everyone was parting for bed.

Will felt like a real heel. He rode slowly away from the McKie place and couldn't remember when he had ever felt worse for the way he was treating Ester. He owed her an explanation for his behavior. He pulled his horse to a stop at the top of the hill and sat for quite a while arguing with himself about how to best handle this situation. He had been a fool in the first place for letting his feelings for Ester develop and for letting her feelings for him grow stronger. He had no doubt that she had fallen in love with him, and he knew he was truly in love with her. He should have never put her through what loving him would entail. Will knew he was about to break her heart if he told her the truth, and he would also break her heart if he just rode away like a coward.

Perhaps he could think of a gentle way to let her down. Maybe he could talk to Doc Williams about the situation. Doc had become a trusted friend and almost a father figure. Will felt certain he could give him some sage advice on how to handle this matter. Yes, that would probably be the thing to do, he convinced himself as he turned his horse and continued on his way back to Del Rio.

Chapter Seven

Christmas Eve and Christmas Day seemed rather quiet after the big party on the 23rd. In a way, it was a welcome respite to Ester.

Three times a year Corabell set what she termed a fine table. She used her white linen tablecloth with matching napkins. She had brought her grandmother's china to her marriage and used it on Easter, Thanksgiving, and Christmas. Through the years, a few pieces had been broken, but Corabell didn't grieve over their loss for long. She enjoyed the beauty of the delicate pink roses that adorned each piece and admired the thin ring of silver that rimmed the edges.

Corabell and Ester prepared a huge Christmas lunch. There was a large, plump turkey roasted to a golden brown surrounded by Corabell's special dressing. She also cooked a ham garnished with molasses and cloves. Sweet potatoes were seasoned with butter and cinnamon, canned green beans from the spring garden that tasted as fresh as the day they were picked, and homemade yeast rolls. The blends of luscious aromas made Ester's mouth start watering by mid-morning. Choices for dessert included pumpkin pie, pecan pie, and more of

Corabell's special fruitcake she had wisely put aside. Each dessert was topped with sweet, thick whipped cream.

Charlie and several of the cowboys joined them for the festive meal. Each man ate until Ester thought they might pop at any moment. She felt certain this was a welcome change from the bunkhouse cook's usual fare. Not long after the meal was over, Charlie and the cowboys drifted back to the bunkhouse, probably for a game of cards or even a nap, which was a luxury.

Christine was playing contentedly in her room with her new toys. Molly was taking a nap. Grant, Corabell, and Ester sat in the living room in mostly companionable silence. Grant was reading some ranching magazine, Corabell was trying to finish knitting a new sweater for Molly, and Ester sat near the fireplace reading a novel she seemed to have started ages ago. The crackling fire lent coziness to the room. The mood it created gave Ester a feeling of placid contentment.

At times she wondered what her family was doing, but she could picture their Christmases very well as they were all pretty much the same. Their tree was not decorated until the morning of Christmas Eve. In the late evening, the family gathered to sing carols, sip on Aunt Rosie's special eggnog, and exchange extravagantly wrapped gifts. She often thought the wrapping was more expensive and exquisite than the item it contained. It was fun, she had to admit, but, as she had thought earlier, very predictable. Occasionally, she felt a bit melancholy about being away from her family but life here was so busy she rarely had time to dwell on other things.

Grant didn't like the idea that he was having such a hard time concentrating on the magazine article he was trying to read. For some reason even he couldn't explain or perhaps didn't want to fully admit, his eyes kept straying in Ester's direction. She made a pretty picture sitting near the fireplace reading. The contentment of the scene was disturbing to him. The idea of a lovely woman in his home providing companionship and --- love was definitely appealing. Perhaps it really was time to start looking for another wife, but not Miss Hammon. She would never make it for the long haul as a rancher's wife unless the ranch was next door to some big city.

Suddenly Ester felt someone watching her. She glanced up and saw Grant's eyes fixed on her as though he was studying her. He quickly resumed his reading when she caught him gazing in her direction. Why would he even be looking at her? she questioned. There was no reason to believe he was really interested in her, except to taunt her about Will Hudson. She had to admit Grant was a handsome man and one that could be charming when he chose, or he could be a bit cantankerous and devilish at times, she had learned.

"Boss, Boss!" they heard Charlie calling from the back door. "Better get out here quick, there's about to be trouble. Pete and Rowdy are making bets on which one can ride Smoky the longest," he yelled.

Grant slapped the magazine down on the sofa and rose in a swift motion. He was taking long strides toward the back door. Ester heard him say, half under his breath, "What in tarnation are those two damn fools thinking?" There was more muttering as he slammed the back door, and then she could hear him yelling at the two men but couldn't quite make out just what he was saying. It was probably just as well as most likely the words were laced with expletives that shouldn't be heard by ladies.

Pete, a tall, slim fellow, with dark hair and piercing black eyes, was chasing Smoky, a stallion that only let Grant ride him, around the arena. Occasionally the horse tolerated Charlie on his back. Pete would throw a loop and miss the horse by a mile. Rowdy, medium height and build, with shaggy sandy-colored hair, hazel eyes, and a constant grin, was trying to intercept the horse. Neither man was making much headway in catching the high-spirited horse, which was most likely to their advantage. Watching the two half-drunk cowboys in their feeble attempts to rope the spirited animal was becoming comical.

"Neither one could probably rope a fence post in their condition, much less a moving horse," Charlie murmured, half amused.

"How much have those two had to drink?" Grant asked Charlie, as they walked briskly toward the arena.

"They was hittin' the bottle some before lunch and pretty steady since then," Charlie answered, with a shake of his head. "Them two shouldn't be let loose together. They can think up more darned nonsense than all the rest of the men put together."

Grant and Charlie reached the corral and continued to watch the two stumbling drunks trying to rope Smoky.

Grant gave a low chuckle. "That horse is probably smarter than the two of them put together," he mused.

"Damned right," Charlie agreed.

"That's enough," Grant yelled, but it was an instant too late.

Just as the horse flew past them, Pete finally roped Smoky, but in the process stumbled and fell. The horse continued his pace around the arena as though nothing had happened, pulling Pete behind him.

"Let go of the damn rope, Pete!" Grant yelled, as they came past him and Charlie.

"Damn-o-mighty, I think his hand's caught in the rope!" Charlie shouted.

Just then Grant noticed Pete holding on to the rope with his other hand in an attempt to keep the horse from pulling his arm out of its socket. Grant sprang into action. He almost vaulted over the fence and yelled at Rowdy to bring him his rope. Rowdy looked a bit dazed as he watched his friend being dragged by the horse. Finally, he focused on Grant enough to understand what Grant was yelling at him.

Rowdy ran toward Grant with the rope outstretched for Grant to grab. Just as the horse made another round, Grant swung the lariat and caught the galloping horse on his first try. Grant dug in his heels and started shouting, "Whoa, Boy, Whoa, Boy!" to the horse. He managed to grab Smoky's head and pull it downward to make him stop.

Charlie reached them quickly. He cut the rope near Pete's wrist that had bound him to the galloping horse. Grant let go of the horse. Smoky trotted back toward the barn with the loose end of the rope leaving a trail in the dust as he went.

Grant knelt beside Charlie to examine Pete. They could see the red welts across his hand and wrist. His wrist appeared to be broken.

"Rowdy, bring the medicine kit!" Grant thundered in rage at the other drunken culprit.

Rowdy returned promptly with the medicine box and stood around watching Charlie and Grant work on patching Pete up.

He had apparently begun to sober up a bit and started trying to half apologize for what had happened.

"I guess that weren't the smartest bet we ever made," he said, with a slight chuckle. "But I sure didn't mean for nothin' like this to happen to my buddy, Pete. It could of been me just the same as Pete," he rambled on, still slurring most of his words.

Finally, Grant stopped what he was doing, turned, and gave Rowdy a look that would chill most men to the bone.

"If you don't shut up, I'm going to tie you to Smoky and let him drag you around this arena!"

Rowdy opened his mouth but promptly clamped it shut and just nodded his head to let Grant know he understood.

"Now get away from here before I fire your sorry ass!" Grant threatened.

In about an hour, Ester heard the backdoor slam. Grant returned to the house in a foul mood.

"What happened?" Corabell asked, hoping it wasn't anything too serious.

"I think I'm going to have to separate those two nitwits before they accidentally kill one another. Pete got his arm caught in the rope when he finally managed to rope Smoky and was drug around the arena a couple of times before I could get him free. He has a broken wrist and is scraped and bruised all to hell," he grumbled in disgust.

Corabell quickly glanced from Grant to Ester and back at Grant.

"Oh, for Heaven's sakes, surely Ester has heard the word hell before!" Grant half shouted, still in an ill temper.

A brief moment of silence filled the room.

"Will a doctor be coming to set Pete's wrist?" Ester asked, as calmly as she could manage, trying to ease some of the tension.

Grant gave an insensitive laugh. "No, your doctor friend won't be coming just to set a broken wrist. Charlie's probably set more broken wrists than Doctor Hudson ever thought about!" Grant almost snarled. He walked briskly down the hall to his office and slammed the door.

Corabell and Ester sat together looking at Grant's ramrod straight back as he walked away from them and listened to the clunk of his boots on the wood floor.

"I'm mighty sorry for---," Corabell started, but Ester held up her hand in a gesture to stop whatever Corabell had meant to say.

"You don't have to apologize to me for Grant's behavior. I know he carries a heavy load on his shoulders. He never seems to get even a few minutes of peace unless it's late at night when he's in his office. I suppose he's up late working on ranch matters," Ester said, with a note of empathy.

Corabell continued her knitting and Ester tried to concentrate on the book she had been reading, but too many thoughts interrupted her concentration. When she had come to the McKie Ranch she hadn't wanted to like Grant, thinking he was arrogant and cold. Now she had come to respect him on many levels and at times even found him likable. She could easily see how much he loved Christine. Most evenings, although he still had work to do in his office, he took time to listen to Christine read or just play with her for a while.

Yet, he was so different from Will. She couldn't imagine Will losing his temper and cursing in front of her as Grant had done. Will worked under lots of pressure too. His skills could save or end a life. Well, in a way Grant's skills could do the same thing. If he hadn't been able to catch the wild horse, she shuddered to think of the consequences. Why was she comparing the two men? she suddenly wondered.

After another hour, Corabell laid aside her knitting. "I think I'll just put out some cold turkey, ham, and bread for supper. After that big lunch, I doubt anyone will be very hungry."

"I'll come help you," Ester offered.

They heard Charlie calling Grant's name as he came through the back door. The clomping of boots on the wood floor announced more than one person coming into the house.

When the two men reached the living room Charlie paused briefly to ask, "Where's Grant?"

"He's in his office," Corabell answered.

Charlie and the other man continued down the hall. As the second man passed, he tipped his faded black hat slightly but only said, "Corabell, Ma'am," as he followed in Charlie's wake.

Travis was a tall, big-framed man, but not fat. He wore a coat that had certainly seen better days, chaps over his pants, worn boots, and spurs that jangled as he walked. Ester noticed he had a slight limp. He must have just ridden in to have not removed his spurs before coming indoors. What she could see of his face appeared to be tan from hours in the sun. He sported a long handlebar mustache and full beard.

Ester thought he looked quite unkempt but supposed he was single and didn't have a wife to make him look more presentable.

Corabell stood still waiting for them to enter Grant's office.

"Oh, dear Lord, there must be more trouble for Travis to show up here, especially on Christmas Day," she sounded worried.

"Who is Travis, and why would he bring more trouble?"

"He's the foreman on the east side of the Devils River. He don't usually come here unless something is terrible wrong," Corabell said, with an anxious look.

"Why does he never come otherwise?" Ester inquired, her curiosity aroused.

Corabell seemed to give Ester's question considerable thought before she answered. "Travis is a loner. He don't want people bothering him or giving him advice on how to run his part of the ranch, not even Grant."

"But Grant is his boss."

"Yes, but he wants Grant to respect him by showing he trusts whatever Travis does. For the most part that is how they work together. Travis thinks Charlie is too dependent on Grant and don't really pull his weight on the west Devils River section, but that ain't so. Charlie came here just before Grant's papa died. If it hadn't been for Charlie's steadying hand the ranch or Grant likely would never have made it. You see, Charlie is really the one who taught Grant how to run the ranch successfully and advised him when it was the right time to expand. Grant went pretty wild, for a while, after his papa passed. He started drinking, running around, and getting into arguments with some of the other ranchers. Charlie stayed with him, and finally, between him and Zora Mae, was able to get him to grow up and take his responsibility. When he met Zora Mae, Christine's mama, she laid down the law about his wayward ways. She told him if he really wanted her to marry him, he would straighten up, and he did!" Corabell paused as though remembering that difficult time not only Grant had gone through, but she must have been very worried for Molly and herself.

"Charlie thinks Grant needs to be more involved in all of the ranch operation and don't much like the way he lets Travis do as he pleases most of the time. I've heard them argue over it more than once, but Grant says Travis is doing a good job and it's best to leave well enough alone. I tend to agree more with Charlie that Grant should keep a tighter rein on Travis, but I don't interfere in how Grant runs the ranch," Corabell concluded with a slight frown.

"Well, he seems to be one of the most successful ranchers around so I guess he must be doing something right," Ester observed, as she and Corabell continued preparing the evening meal.

Ester sliced one loaf of bread while Corabell carved the leftover turkey and ham. The aroma of the smoked meat filled the kitchen. Although she wasn't hungry, Ester couldn't resist the temptation to nibble on a piece of the turkey. Ester always admired Corabell's ability to carve such even slices of meat while her attempts turned out to look like Christine may have been the one doing the carving. Corabell had many more years of experience at carving and cooking for that matter. She was a good cook, and it didn't seem to matter if she was cooking for six or sixteen; it always turned out good.

"How long has Travis worked on the ranch?"

"Oh, I'd say about fifteen or sixteen years. Allen hired him several years before he died when he bought the old Thornton place that expanded the ranch to the east. That was too much for Charlie to oversee. The other ranch needed some work to bring it up to Allen's standards. The Thornton brothers were two old bachelors that finally got too old to ranch proper and kind of let things run down before they decided to sell out. Grant has expanded it some more, mostly to the east, so Travis has a little more land and livestock than Charlie to oversee."

"So, may I ask, exactly how big is this ranch?"

"Let's see, I believe Grant told me it's about twenty-eight sections or about eighteen thousand acres give or take a few," Corabell answered casually, as she set a platter of cold meats on the table.

Ester paused with the knife in mid-air she was using to slice bread. She could hardly fathom anyone owning that much land. She had known the Cremwelgy Ranch was about nine thousand acres and thought that was an enormous amount of land for one person to own. Somehow, she had figured out the McKie Ranch was somewhat bigger, but she had no idea it was eighteen thousand acres. Let's see, she thought, twenty-eight sections would mean it was also twenty-eight square miles! Ester marveled.

Corabell glanced at Ester in her statue-like pose with the lifted knife and asked, "Is something the matter?"

Ester regained her poise and shook her head. "No, nothing's wrong, I just didn't realize how big this ranch really is."

They heard several loud knocks at the back door.

"Come on in," Corabell called out.

A rather short Mexican man appeared in the doorway. He held his sombrero in his dark brown hands. His hair was mostly silver with a few dark strands running through it, and his face was as dark as his hands with the weathered look of old leather.

"Excuse me, Señora McKie, I must speak to Señor Grant," he addressed Corabell politely.

"Hello, Pablo, go on through to his office. He's in there with Charlie and Travis."

"Thank you, Señora," he said. The man wiped his worn boots on the porch but did not remove his spurs either before entering the main house.

"I sure hope you ain't bringing more bad news," Corabell said, as the man passed through the kitchen.

"I must speak with Señor McKie and Señor Charlie," was all he said. He walked briskly on through the dining room and through the living room as he headed toward Grant's office with the clinking of his spurs fading in the distance.

Corabell shook her head as she continued her work "Lordy, Lordy, I hope there ain't more trouble brewin'!"

"As I was saying," Corabell continued with a chuckle, "Yeah, when Grant's father, Allen, bought the original ranch it was about ten thousand acres, and we thought we owned half of Texas."

Ester glanced at Corabell as she talked and saw the distant look of pleasure that played across her features. Apparently, she had loved her husband very much, and the mention of his name seemingly brought back warm memories.

"We worked like dogs getting the ranch running, but those were happy times. We'd be dead tired at the end of the day, but just sitting on the porch looking at what we had done gave us the courage to go on and on," she said, with a satisfied sigh. "Allen was 'bout beside himself with pride when Grant was born. You know all men want a son to leave their land to. He was just about as excited when Molly come along until we found out somethin' was terrible wrong with her. Then he just looked sad every time he looked at her. He was bitter that she turned out the way she did, but nothing could be done about it. I tried to teach her to do things for herself, and she can do some things, as you know. If I'd been educated like you, things might have turned out better," Corabell conceded. Her face revealed a hint of sadness as she wiped at the corners of her eyes with her apron. "But I never let myself get bitter over it or blame God or nothing like that."

They heard the approach of footsteps from the thumping of four sets of boots and the rhythmic jangle and clanking of spurs as the men neared the kitchen.

"Ma," Grant called out before he even entered the room.

Both women looked around just as he came through the door ahead of the others.

"Get some food ready for the men. We're being hit on both sides by the Mexican bandits stealing the cattle," he said. His tone indicated his displeasure over the developing circumstances.

Ester noticed the now familiar frown lines between his eyes that appeared when he was distressed. She also saw the set of his jaw and heard the tight restraint in his voice. All of these signs told her the situation was serious.

The other three men passed on through to the outside, but Grant stayed. "I don't know how long we'll be gone as they have a couple of hours' head start on us, but we should be back sometime tomorrow. Just in case we aren't, the bill of sale for the forty horses the Army is supposed to pick up day after tomorrow is on my desk."

Corabell was nodding her head as he talked but had already started making stacks of meat and bread.

"Ester, would you get some paper from the storeroom and start wrapping the food?" Corabell asked, as she continued to work.

Ester stepped into the storeroom to get the paper but could still hear what Grant was saying.

"I'm leaving Johnny, Sam, and Pete here to keep an eye on things and take care of the chores. I know Pete can't do much with a broken wrist, but there are some things he can help with. Charlie is taking three men with him and they will pick up three more on their way. Travis and I are taking five men and picking up two more on our way," Grant said, with a deep sigh.

"How many bandits have the cattle?" Corabell asked, as she took the paper and started wrapping the stacks of food.

Ester followed her lead and quickly added in her head how many packages of food they would need. "We need food for two more," she told Corabell as she continued wrapping.

"Travis said Cotton counted at least ten rustlers, and there may have been more. Pablo said he counted nine riders, and his son, Rubio, is watching them and trailing from a distance."

"Rubio, he's just a kid!" Corabell stated, as though she couldn't believe Pablo would leave a boy in such a dangerous position.

"I think he's about twelve now. Pablo wants to take him with us, says he's a crack shot."

Corabell didn't comment, but Ester could tell by the set of her mouth and her subtle frown that she didn't much like the idea of a twelve-year-old going with them chasing dangerous cattle rustlers.

"They've cut fences on both sides of the ranch. If they decide to take the Comstock Road on the west side, they'll likely beat us to the border. Travis' side is going to be a bit slower as it is farther to the border, and there are several fences they'll have to cut to get through the other ranches."

Ester remembered the day the Mexicans stopped at the school, and her defenders were boys about the same age as Rubio. Country children seemed to grow up faster in many ways, just by the circumstances of where they lived and all of the hard work they were expected to do. Knowing this, it surprised her a bit when she realized Corabell's disapproval of Rubio going with the men.

When Corabell finished wrapping the last package, she gestured toward Ester. "Go ahead and take these packages out to Shorty so he can start packing the saddle bags."

Ester gathered an armful of packages and went out to find Shorty. As she walked toward the two packhorses, she heard several of the men talking, and among them was Travis. Suddenly it hit her! It was Travis she had heard outside the school talking to the Mexican about getting livestock much cheaper than he could buy them from his boss. She listened closely to the deep tone of his voice. He gave a short laugh, and then she knew beyond a shadow of a doubt it had to be Travis.

Ester knew she had to let Grant know Travis was going to doublecross him, but how could she do it in the middle of all these people? To make matters worse, Travis stood right in the midst of the men.

Ester wanted to fling the packages at Shorty and hurry back to the house to talk to Grant, but Shorty seemed to be taking his time packing the saddlebags.

She kept glancing over her shoulder to see if Grant had come out yet. If he got out of the house, she wouldn't have a chance to say anything. If she didn't get to tell him about Travis, he and the other men could be in grave danger when they met up with the rustlers. No telling what Travis might do to protect his interest in this scheme, she worried. Eventually, Shorty took the last of the packages. Ester almost sprinted back to the house. Just as she reached the back porch, Grant opened the door and came out. He turned and walked toward the closet that held his riding gear.

"Grant," she spoke his name softly. Apparently, he hadn't heard her. He leaned over and buckled on his spurs, straightened and slipped into his heavy coat.

Ester walked the length of the porch and stood behind him as he reached for his hat.

"Grant," she said, loud enough for him to hear her this time.

He turned, a bit startled to see Ester standing so near.

Two of the men rode near the porch to ask Grant a question. He answered, but they remained near the porch talking to one another.

Grant turned his attention back to Ester with a questioning look.

"Grant," Ester whispered, "Pretend we are sweet on one another and you are saying goodbye. I have something important to tell you, and I don't want anyone to hear," she continued in a low voice. She nodded slightly toward the two men that still sat nearby on their horses.

Grant put his arms around her, drawing her to him. He lowered his head slightly so she could whisper in his ear as he gently nuzzled her neck like a man would do with his sweetheart.

His nearness and the touch of his cheek, with its slight stubble, and his warm breath against her neck certainly distracted Ester's train of thought, but she needed to speak quickly.

"Grant, it's Travis; I believe he's in on this," she said with urgency.

"What do you mean, it's Travis?" he asked, as he continued his affectionate pose.

"He's the one I heard outside the school when I was there one Saturday cleaning. He was scheming with a Mexican to sell him cattle or something cheaper than he could buy them from his boss. I recognized his low pitch voice when I brought the food out, and when he laughed, I knew for sure it was him," she said as fast as she could get the words out. Grant was now planting little featherlike kisses on her cheek, which was making it hard to concentrate and sending fluttering waves throughout her body.

Although it was only a ruse so she could warn him, his masculine appeal was distracting all the same.

Grant drew back a bit and looked into Ester's eyes. He had always admired their light hazel color, but this was the first time he had seen them so close in the daylight. They were beautiful, he thought, as he tried to concentrate on what she had just told him about Travis.

Somehow, he could not imagine Travis pulling a double-cross on him. Travis had worked for his father and then him for fifteen years. He had been a damn good foreman. She had to be mistaken. Often people misidentified people that were accused of some crime. She hadn't seen him. She had only heard a low-tone voice that she now believed to be Travis. Grant didn't want to insult her by saying she was totally wrong.

"Ester, I have no doubt you heard what you said you did at the school, but I think you are sorely mistaken about it being Travis. There are plenty of other men with similar low-tone voices," he reasoned.

"Grant, please be careful. I know you trust him, but you don't know for sure that I am wrong. I believe I'm right!" she insisted as she stared back at him. She started to pull away, but he held her snugly against him.

Grant leaned in and whispered. "Now we have to convince these men that we are truly sweethearts." He moved his mouth to cover hers in a searing kiss that almost took her breath away.

Ester heard a few low whistles from the men waiting for Grant to join them and some muttered comments she thankfully couldn't understand. She could feel the color rise to her face. Breathing in deep breaths of the cold air seemed to help calm her nerves.

When he released her, he put on his hat and walked briskly to his horse.

"Let's ride!" he said in a commanding voice. Then he turned his horse so he could see Ester. She was still standing in the same spot as though she were rooted to the porch. He tipped his hat and gave her a flirtatious wink. This brought a few chuckles from the cowboys and a few more whistles.

Ester was so astounded she could only just manage to smile and give a slight wave. She knew it wasn't too convincing on her part.

As she turned to enter the house, she was struck by what she had just done. By tomorrow she and Grant would be the gossip of all the ranchers. It amazed her how fast word spread among the ranches, although they lay miles apart. Then an almost devastating thought struck her. What if the rumor reached town and Will heard she and Grant were now sweethearts? What would he think of her? No, please, Lord, don't let that happen, she prayed as she walked into the warm kitchen.

Chapter Eight

An eerie silence seemed to fall over the ranch headquarters after all of the men rode out. Charlie and his group headed west to follow the Comstock Road south toward the Rio Grande. Grant, Travis, and their men headed east to track the Mexicans across several ranches between the McKie Ranch and the border.

As night fell, Corabell, Ester, and the girls sat in the huge living room near the fireplace, each absorbed in their own activity. Corabell continued to work on Molly's new sweater. Ester tried to read as she sat in one of the oversized chairs, with a round wick Aladdin lamp sitting on the side table, giving a brighter light than the other lamp. Molly rocked and hummed softly, and Christine played quietly with the new rag doll Ester had given her for Christmas. Christine pretended she was the teacher and her doll was her pupil.

Her play amused Ester as at times Christine sounded exactly as she did only in her childlike voice.

Although she tried desperately to concentrate on her book, the scene on the porch between herself and Grant kept running through Ester's mind. If only she had had more time to think of another way to tell Grant what she knew, there would be no reason for all the gossip that was bound to follow. She hadn't even mentioned the incident to Corabell. Perhaps she should tell her, but she probably wouldn't believe her either, as Grant certainly thought she was mistaken in identifying Travis as the person she had heard outside the school. Although Corabell didn't seem overly fond of Travis, she might find it hard to think he would double-cross Grant.

As Ester thought about what happened on the porch, it dredged up other memories that she would rather forget. The feel of Grant's strong arms holding her against his unyielding body, the slight smell of whiskey on his breath, the intense kiss they had shared. The strange feelings that had swept through her as he held her close, gently brushing her cheek and neck with his day's growth of whiskers, and the featherlike kisses he had planted on her cheek and neck disturbed her. Suddenly she realized the room seemed to be becoming very warm.

"Mrs. Corabell, Mrs. Corabell," they heard Pete calling from the back door.

"Come on in, Pete, we're in the living room," Corabell answered him, not bothering to get up to meet him at the door.

Pete appeared with his wrist still wrapped and holding his arm level with his waistline.

"How's your wrist?" Corabell inquired.

"Still tender but it doesn't hurt much."

"Sit down," Corabell invited.

Pete took a seat and looked around the room. "I need to speak to you about something, but the little one," he paused as he looked at Christine.

Corabell caught the drift of his statement and turned to Christine. "Take your doll and play in your room while I talk with Pete," she instructed the child.

Christine picked up her doll and did not question her grandma or protest having to leave the room.

When she was out of earshot Corabell turned to Pete.

"What is it, Pete?"

"Me and the fellows have been talkin' over this situation, and we are suspicious of the Mexicans taking cattle from both sides of the ranch at the same time."

Corabell looked at him and nodded her head. "Go on," she told Pete.

"They have about stripped the homestead of men, and out in those two barns are forty well-trained horses ready for the Army to pick up day after tomorrow. We've been wonderin' if stealing the cattle is just a trick to weaken the homestead so they can swoop down and make off with all those horses." Pete paused briefly. "Them horses are likely worth at least twice as much as the cattle they're taking," he stated as a matter of fact. "To our way of thinking, old Pancho Villa needs horses lots more than he needs cattle right now."

Corabell looked horrified. "Good gosh a mighty, you may be right! Why in the world didn't Grant think about that before he took all the men off chasin' cattle rustlers?" she asked, although she didn't expect an answer.

Pete looked down at his boots and back up at Corabell. "I ain't faultin' Grant or nobody. We don't know for sure that's what they're up to, but it sure looks peculiar now that we've had time to think about it," Pete said, in his simple speaking manner.

Corabell let her head fall back against the chair and seemed to be studying the ceiling. She looked up, first at Pete and then at Ester. "What in the world are we gonna do if Pete and the others are right? There's only three men and us two women to defend this place," she said, and Ester could plainly hear the despair in her voice. Ester thought Corabell seemed to have aged ten years right before her eyes. She looked tired, worn out from worry.

It was obvious Corabell was not accustomed to making decisions concerning running the ranch, and now she was at a loss as to what should be done.

"Well, Ma'am, they'd still have to ride past the side of the house where the dining room is and turn the corner and go right past the back porch and kitchen windows to get to the barns. Me and the fellows thought you two ladies and me could hide there and shoot as they ride past us. I'd be in the dining room to get off the first shots and you two would be in the kitchen. Johnny and Sam will be waitin' by the barns. The ones that get past us will meet their fire head-on. That's the best plan we can come up with," Pete finished, first looking at Corabell and then Ester as though he was seeking their approval.

"How good can you shoot with your left hand?" Corabell asked, a serious look of worry evident on her face. Her voice sounded strained.

"Pretty fair, I used to practice with both hands," Pete answered. The memory of his youthful ambition made him grin.

"Why'd you do that?" Corabell asked.

Pete looked a bit sheepish. "I dreamed of bein' another Billy the Kid or somebody like that, but by the time I was old enough to try anything my pa had beat some sense into me."

Corabell's response was, "Hum! Good for your pa."

"I don't think Ester should be involved in this matter. She's just here to teach Christine, not to defend this ranch," Corabell stated in a stubborn tone. Ester recognized that look Corabell got when she was about to be balky as an old mule about something.

"How many do you think they will send to get the horses?" Ester asked Pete.

Pete rubbed his head with his good hand as though giving her question considerable thought. "Well, I reckon at least twelve or maybe more like twenty. Hard to guess what they might do."

Ester looked at Corabell. "I think you are going to need all of the help you can get and that includes me."

"But this ain't your fight," Corabell repeated in her mulish manner. Sometimes it was hard to argue with Corabell once she had her mind set a certain way.

"Corabell, I know this isn't my fight, but in a way, it has become my fight just because I'm here. Five defenders have a better chance to hold them off than just four. What if one of us gets shot and can't help the others? We have to try what Pete said to have half a chance or just let them take the horses. Even if we do that, who's to say they won't try to kill us anyway? After all, we would be witnesses to what they had done," Ester pleaded with Corabell to think reasonably.

Corabell sat with her lips pressed together in a thin line, indicating she wasn't going to give in easily.

"I think Miss Ester is right, Corabell. We need every gun we can manage. Then we might have half a chance of holdin' 'em off," Pete came to Ester's defense.

"Oh, mercy, I wish Grant had thought this thing through better before he took off with most of the men," Corabell fussed, showing she was worried.

Pete sat quietly for a few seconds studying his hands as he slowly turned his hat around and around. "It seems to me and to Johnny and Sam that this was planned out real careful by somebody. Who would expect such a thing to happen, especially on Christmas Day?" he asked, as he looked up at the two women. "The thing is we have to decide pretty pronto what we plan to do just in case we're right," Pete continued in his calm manner.

"I'm helping!" Ester stated, as she looked first at Corabell and then Pete. Her tone left no room for argument.

Corabell looked at the two of them and then nodded. "Go tell Johnny and Sam to get ready. I guess they can take turns watchin' and we can do the same here in the house."

"Yes, Ma'am," Pete said, as he rose and walked toward the back door.

"Ester, put on them ridin' pants and several warm shirts 'cause you'll be crouched beside the window and it's gonna get cold with the window open."

Ester stood to go to her room to get dressed. Then a terrifying thought struck her as she turned back to stare at Corabell. "What will we do with the girls so they'll be safe?"

Corabell never said a word but stood and slowly walked to the corner of the room where a decorative table sat holding a lamp. A rug lay underneath it. She gently scooted the table aside and picked up the rug. There was a small handhold cut in the boards. Corabell lifted a small door, just big enough for an adult to pass through. She picked up the lamp that sat on the table and held it over the hole.

Ester neared and looked down into the semi-darkness. Stairs led down into what she assumed to be some sort of basement.

Ester gave Corabell a questioning look. "Is it a cellar?"

"Of sorts, it's a hiding place. When we first come here there were lots more outlaws and banditos roaming through this country. Allen built this for me and the kids to hide in when they would attack the ranch. There's a bed down there so the girls will sleep there tonight. I'll tell them to not make any noise or try to get out unless one of us comes to open the door. They understand. Even Molly knows if she is put here, it is for her own good."

"No one would ever know this was here unless they moved the table and rug," Ester said, in amazement.

"No, they sure wouldn't. Now help me get the girls ready for bed," Corabell answered, as she turned away from the dark hole.

Ester sat by the open kitchen window wrapped in a wool blanket plus a pair of long johns, riding pants, and three flannel shirts. The loaded guns lay on the floor ready for quick use.

Pete was taking the first watch. Ester heard the mantle clock strike ten thirty. Her official watch would start at eleven, but she could not sleep. She sat wondering if she would see the sun come up in the morning. This could be the end of her short life and for what? She pondered her fate.

At age twenty-two, she had never married, never experienced being intimate with a man, never given birth, never, never. The things she had never done in her short life could go on and on, she thought with regret.

What was she doing here in the middle of nowhere in the late hours of the night waiting for horse thieves that could kill her and the others with just one bullet? Was that the worth of her life or anyone's life? Just the price of one bullet!

Her family would be heartbroken. Would anyone else care much beyond saying what a shame for her life to end so early, she was a nice person?

What about Will? She would never have the chance to tell him how much she loved him. Would he grieve for long? Maybe she didn't mean as much to him as she imagined. Perhaps it was only she that cared so deeply. She wondered about many things, as she sat in the cold, dark night just waiting again for something to happen. A tear trickled down her cheek.

If she survived this ordeal, the first thing she intended to do was declare her love to Will. Tomorrow, she would borrow a horse from Grant, ride to the Cremwelgys', get her buggy, go straight to Del Rio, and find Will. She wouldn't hold back this time. She would speak out boldly of her love for him. Since Will seemed a bit shy about such matters, she would have to be the daring one. She would kiss him full on the mouth, hold his body close to hers, and take pleasure in his warm embrace. Yes, she would take the lead without hesitation this time, since he seemed reluctant to evoke such forward behavior.

She jumped slightly as she heard the clock strike eleven. Had she dozed off?

She called softly to Pete. "I'm coming in to take over the watch."

She crawled into the dining room and took the position where Pete had been sitting beside the window. Pete rolled into his blanket and stretched out on the floor. The rooms were cold, but the wool blankets helped. A short time later she heard Pete's soft snores.

How could he sleep so easily knowing what might lie ahead tonight? she couldn't help but wonder as she listened to his deep breathing.

Ester peered out the window that gave a perfect view of the road leading into the ranch. The pale light of the half-moon illuminated the lighter color of the road enough that she could see anyone coming for quite a distance. The sides of the road changed color where the dry grass took over and spread into the pasture. There were no bushes or trees close enough to the road for anyone to hide behind.

Ester sat for what seemed like an eternity listening to Pete's soft snores and the usual sounds of the night. The night seemed unusually quiet. Eerie!

In the distance near the creek, Ester saw movement. Maybe it was a deer, she speculated. No, it was growing larger and moving toward her.

She gently shook Pete's foot. "Get up, Pete," she whispered, as though she thought her voice might carry into the night.

Pete sat up, scooted across the floor to the window, and peered into the near darkness.

"It's them, go tell Corabell to get ready."

"Are you sure? What if it's Grant and some of the men coming back?"

"It ain't."

"How do you know for sure?"

"They would be making all kinds of noise. These fellows are movin' slow, tryin' to be quiet."

Ester crawled into the kitchen dragging her quilt behind her. "Corabell, they're coming," she said softly, as she tried to spread her quilt on the floor where she would crouch beside the window.

"I'm ready," Corabell spoke in a hushed, unruffled voice.

"Ester," she heard Pete speak her name.

"Yes," she answered.

"Remember, shoot to kill," Pete said in his usual straightforward manner.

A chill ran through Ester that had nothing to do with the cold. She was glad she would be shooting at shadows. Shadows didn't look you in the eyes when they were dying.

Chapter Nine

Charlie, Pablo, and the men they had taken with them from the ranch and the other three they had picked up along the way finally reached the Comstock to Juno Road. Juno lay to the north and Comstock to the south near the Rio Grande. There was an easy crossing about a half a mile west of Comstock, and Charlie felt sure that was where they were headed. Traveling across the rough ranch land at night with the dim light of the pale moon made it slow going until they reached the road. They easily found the cut fences. Once they got on smoother ground, they could make up some time and see how far Rubio had tracked the cattle rustlers.

They rode at a faster pace toward Comstock, but they did not find Rubio. Pablo was obviously beginning to worry.

"Maybe he got too close and they found him and are taking him with them to Mexico," he finally told Charlie. Charlie was all too aware of Pablo's concern and could hear the fear for his son in the man's voice.

"Let's hope not," Charlie answered calmly, but knew in his gut that if they had the boy, they would likely never see him alive again. They wouldn't think twice about killing the kid if they thought he posed any threat to what they were doing. He didn't have to say any of this to Pablo, he knew.

On they rode through the cold night, wishing they were back at the ranch stretched out in their warm bunks.

Suddenly, Charlie spotted movement beside the road ahead. He held up his hand to halt the riders until he could determine what had moved. It could be a deer, stray calf, or man.

The shadow moved out into the road and stood stark still.

"Papa, Papa, it is me, Rubio," the boy called just loud enough for them to hear.

The men rode forward. Pablo smiled at his son.

"I was beginning to worry."

"Why, I am a smart boy, too smart to get caught by the rustlers," Rubio answered. His smug attitude was obvious.

"Ah, youth," Pablo commented. "They know no fear."

"How far ahead are they, son?" Charlie asked. He was anxious to keep moving.

"Several miles by now. It has been quite a while that I have waited for you to catch up."

"I wonder if they're at the Comstock Road by now," Charlie commented, to no one in particular.

One of the cowboys came back with, "If they are we've lost this race."

"Well, let's ride and see if we can catch up before they get to the river."

On they rode through the wintry night, feeling fairly certain their ride was in vain. When they reached the Comstock Road, they could plainly see the tracks of where they had crossed the road. The trampled grass indicated they were headed for the river that wasn't far away at this point.

Charlie sat for a moment studying the signs.

"Me and Pablo will ride on and see if they're already across the river. If we find them still on this side we'll shoot, and you fellers come running."

Charlie almost knew they were too late, and he was right. When he and Pablo reached a low ridge a short time later, they could see the last of the cattle already in the water more than half way across the Rio Grande in Mexico.

"There go about sixty head of prime beef with them thieving Mexicans, and I'd bet my best Sunday hat Pancho Villa will be having steak for his next supper," Charlie said in disgust.

The men rode back to the ranch mostly in silence. Tomorrow they would start mending the fences. About an hour before they reached headquarters a light mist began to fall, chilling them to the bone, making thoughts of their warm bunks even more appealing.

Grant, Travis, and the other men followed the trampled grass path the rustlers had left as they headed south. They would have to cut fences between three ranches to reach the Del Rio to Comstock Road. Once they crossed the road it was still a couple of miles to the river across another ranch.

Grant felt certain they could catch them before they ever reached the road. Thank goodness for the pale moonlight to help show them the way. At one point they had swung east to avoid a deep ravine, so that gave them more time to catch up as they could ride faster than the rustlers, moving about eighty head of cattle at night.

They had already crossed the backside of the Cremwelgy Ranch and were almost across the Hoffman Ranch when Grant caught a glimpse of movement up ahead.

"I think it's about half a mile to the next fence line," one of the cowboys told Grant.

"Yeah, we need to hit them before they cut another fence," Grant answered.

They took little time to plot out a simple plan to approach from the rear and get as close as possible before they started an all-out attack.

"We can round up the cattle tomorrow, just shoot as many of those damned thievin' rustlers as you can," Grant ordered.

When the first shot was fired, the Mexicans tried to stampede the cattle but mostly tried to outwit and outrun the riders descending on them with guns blazing.

Cattle scattered in every direction, bawling in panic. There wasn't anything big enough for the Mexicans to hide behind to take a stand, so they split up, riding in several directions. Grant's men saw their ploy and split up in twos or threes, relentlessly chasing after them at a breakneck speed over the uneven ground. Their guns firing one bullet after another, some hit their mark and a man or horse would go down.

Cotton saw a horse go down. Its rider jumped free and took off running through the brush. Cotton followed but at one point thought he had somehow lost the man. He slowed his pace and soon caught a glimpse of something shiny in the pale moonlight. It was the polished coins that decorated the man's belt glistening in the soft moonlight that gave him away. The man was wrapped around the bottom of a large sagebrush.

"Come out with your hands up, or I'll shoot you where you lay," Cotton ordered in a gruff tone. The man did as he was told and soon found himself tied to a nearby mesquite tree. The ropes were tight, biting into his skin through the material of his threadbare jacket. His captor rode away to rejoin the chase.

One of the outlaws' horses went down in the middle of the milling cattle. The loud gunshots excited the cattle, and they stampeded again. Grant and some of his cowboys heard the man's yells of pain and then nothing. When the cattle cleared away the trampled body was almost unrecognizable, but they could tell by his clothing it was one of the rustlers.

Grant saw one of the riders making a fast getaway toward the next fence line. He spurred his horse, gaining on the man as they rode faster and faster. Instantly the man wheeled his horse and took aim at Grant. In a split-second Grant knew one of them was about to die. Guns blazed! Grant saw the man fall to the hard, cold ground with a thud. Grant rode slowly forward to make certain the man was dead. He was. His coat lay open, and the dark stain of fresh blood soaked the front of his shirt where Grant's bullet had hit him square in the chest.

Both sides suffered losses. In less than a quarter of an hour four men lay dead, three rustlers and one of Grant's men. Grant's men had managed to capture three more of the thieves. One had been shot in the leg and was losing a lot of blood.

Grant stood looking at the dead man who had worked for him for nearly five years. Ian O'Toole had been a man full of life. Grant recalled how much Ian had loved to play the banjo and tap his foot to the beat of the music. Just a few nights ago at the Christmas party, which now seemed like a lifetime ago, Ian had sung and played the banjo. His blue eyes had twinkled as he had sung with gusto in his Irish brogue. What a shame, he thought. A man works hard doing an honest job for a wage, and this is how his life ends. He seemed to remember Ian had family near Waco. He would send a letter telling them what had happened and ask if they wanted Ian's banjo. It would lie silent now, like its owner, unless someone took it and made it play lively music again.

Grant turned and walked back to where the men stood waiting for their orders. He noticed another man had wrapped a bandana around his lower arm but could see dark stains of blood seeping through his coat onto the cloth.

"How bad is it?" Grant asked. He watched the man's face to gauge his pain.

"I think it's just a flesh wound; I'll tend to it when we get back to the ranch," he answered. Grant believed him, as he did not appear to be in much pain.

"Travis, Cotton, and me are taking the prisoners to town and turning them over to the marshal. Take Ian's body back to the homestead," he told the men. A profound feeling of sadness for the loss of a good man washed over him.

He had kept Travis in sight ever since they had left the homestead and had not seen anything to indicate he was in on the rustling. Ester must be mistaken about Travis, Grant mulled over, as they started the long ride toward Del Rio. As he had told her, there were lots of men with deep voices so it must have been someone else.

The lone rider sat perfectly still mounted on his horse as he debated his fate. By the time he and the other raiders had reached the Del Rio to Comstock Road, the men had been talking among themselves about the consequences of returning to Pancho Villa empty handed.

"*El nos matará de seguro.* He will kill us for sure. *El Jefé* no like failure and we failed," one of the men said with apparent fear.

"*Sí,* you are right; he will choot us all for not bringing the horses," another added, just as shaken.

"I think it best to head for the caves further west by the Pecos River. Then we can spread out in different directions on this side of the border. If we step one foot back into Meh-hee-co we are doomed," the first man gloomily insisted with evident fear.

The remaining eight men debated their fate a bit further but finally all agreed they would likely be dead by noon if they returned to their leader without the horses he so desperately needed.

Juan Treviño did not join them. He continued to sit and debate his own fate. He had been a faithful soldier to Pancho Villa for the past four years. He had been with him when he was in command of thousands and scored victory after victory. Now, he remained his faithful servant when his army had dwindled to only a few hundred starving, tired, ragtag men and boys.

Juan had watched Pancho change from being an amigo of the United States to exhibiting hatred for most gringos when President

Wilson's allegiance shifted to Carranza.

The pre-dawn air became colder and the mist increased, making him shiver. He must decide before the sun rose, which was not long off. He could either cross the Rio Grande back to Mexico and face Pancho Villa or take cover in one of the nearby caves.

Did he possess the power to make Pancho Villa understand something had gone dreadfully wrong with the carefully laid plan? Perhaps he could convince him there were more men left at the headquarters to protect the horses than they had expected. When they realized they could not get the horses, the other men ran in fear for their lives, but he, Juan Treviño, knew no such fear and had come to tell his commander why they had not brought the horses. Would Pancho Villa be convinced he was the hero of the raiders, or would he merely pull his pistol, shoot him in the head, and spit on his corpse? He was all too aware of Villa's cruel temper and had seen him shoot his own men for far less offenses.

Juan had survived many battles and was not yet ready to die. He was thirty-seven and envisioned many years of life ahead. He wanted the revolution to end. He was tired of being a Villista. He wanted to return to his beautiful Carmen and ask for her hand in marriage. They could have many *niños* and grow old together.

Juan pulled his worn serape snug around his slim body to ward off the chill. He knew his guns were fully loaded but his bandolier was almost empty. If he stayed, he would likely have to defend himself against other bandits. If he went it wouldn't matter. His fate would be in another's hands. He gently nudged his horse into motion.

Charlie and his men rode back toward the homestead just as the first light of a gray morning dawned. The mist was becoming heavier. Charlie felt like his hands might be frozen in the position he used holding the reins, although he wore gloves. He was beginning to feel old age nipping at his heels. He wondered how many more years he would be able to work on the ranch and pull his own weight. The answer that came on mornings like this did not appeal to him.

"Look, boss," one of the ranch hands broke into his thoughts as he pointed toward the homestead.

"What in damnation happened here last night?" Charlie asked aloud. He stared in disbelief at the carnage they saw strewn about the ranch yard.

"Don't know, but it don't look pretty," the cowboy answered.

They dismounted and led their horses as they walked quietly toward the ranch house. Five dead horses were strewn about the yard. It looked like several bodies were lying near the corral fence. When they were a bit closer, they could see all of the dining room and kitchen windows were gone, apparently shot out. The side and back of the house were splintered from gunshots.

"We better go in easy till we can find out what happened," Charlie told the others.

An unusual stillness seemed to have fallen over the homestead.

Grant, Travis, and Cotton took the three rustlers to Del Rio and turned them over to Marshal Slim Pike, a stern-faced man in his mid-forties. He was not one to put up with any nonsense in his small town. He would escort the prisoners on to Fort Clark and let the Army take care of their fate.

Grant and the two men went to a small, clean café and ordered enough food for six men, but they ate every bite with gusto. They consumed insurmountable amounts of black coffee. As soon as they finished, they began their long trek back to the ranch. The gray over-cast morning was cold, and the drizzle fluctuated between heavy to light and back to heavy again. It even seeped through their slickers and chilled the riders through and through. Oh, how good their warm beds would feel tonight. By the time they got home and helped finish chores, it would be close to dark and quite possibly colder.

They talked intermittently about the attack they had suffered and wondered how Charlie and his hands had come out with the rustlers they had chased after.

As they rode past the Hoffman Ranch, suddenly Cotton pulled his mount to a halt and let loose with a string of curse words. "Damn it, I left one of them Meskins tied to a mesquite tree!"

Grant and Travis looked at him in disbelief. "You did what?" Grant asked, hardly believing what he had just heard.

"I did, I left one of them fellers I chased down tied to a mesquite tree. Reckon he's still there?" he asked, feeling bad for forgetting the bandit, yet dreading the long ride to the backside of the Hoffman Ranch to see if he might have escaped or was still there, dead or alive.

Grant wiped the dampness from his forehead. "Damn, Cotton, I guess you better go see. You took his guns and knives, didn't you?"

"Sure did! I just wouldn't feel right leavin' even him out there to die a slow death," he said, as he turned his horse and headed east.

It was late afternoon before Cotton found the man just where he had left him hours before, still tied to the tree. As he rode closer, he could see the man's head was down; his knees were drawn up with his old worn serape draped over them for as much protection from the cold and dampness as possible. Cotton thought he was dead, probably frozen from being in the cold mist all this time. Cotton felt a twinge of guilt even for the bandit.

Slowly the man raised his head when Cotton was dismounting. He looked at Cotton through weary eyes and then broke into a big grin that revealed about half of his tobacco-stained teeth were missing.

"*Oye, señor, mí amigo,* ju forget me." His expression became somber. "*Me dejaste aqui toda la noche y todo el dia en el frio,* ju leave me here all night and all day in the cold. *Estoy casi muerto y mí vida está en sus manos,* I am near death, and my life is on your hands," he said accusingly. Then he ended his remark with a string of Spanish that Cotton felt sure was a good cussin' out. However, the tenor of his voice did not sound like he was near death.

Cotton had learned to understand a good bit of Spanish although he spoke very little of the language.

Cotton untied the man from the mesquite and even helped him to stand.

The man studied Cotton for several seconds. "Now what ju do, choot me?" the man asked in broken English.

Cotton looked at him and couldn't hold back a grin.

"Now why would I untie you if I was gonna shoot you?"

The man shrugged his shoulders. "*No sé lo que piensan los gringos,* I not know what ju *gringos* think."

Cotton couldn't quite understand it, but he felt sorry for the poor fellow. In daylight, Cotton could tell he was not a young man, likely in his fifties. No doubt he had endured a hard life. Likely he was only doing what it took to survive, he thought.

"Come on, I'll take you home with me, feed you, and you can rest tonight. I guess I'll have to take you all the way back to Del Rio tomorrow and turn you over to the marshal like we did the others," Cotton sounded miserable at the thought of the long ride back to Del Rio. "We can ride double back to the ranch, but you better not try anything, or I'll shoot you and leave you for the buzzards and coyotes."

Cotton suspected the man understood most of what he was saying.

They rode along in silence for quite a while. Finally, the Mexican spoke.

"*Señor,* I know Meh-hee-co *es* behind us," he pointed over his shoulder toward the south. "*Que está adelante?* What's in front?" the man gestured toward the north.

"The rest of Texas," Cotton answered.

"I make ju *un acuerdo,* deal. *Es* long ride back to Del Rio, *no?*"

"Yes," Cotton answered.

"*Mañana me dejas ir, sin arma, sin cuchillo*, tomorrow ju let me go with no gun, no knife, and I will *me voy* to rest of Texas away from Pancho Villa. I cause no trouble; just *me voy* to rest of Texas."

"I'll think about it," Cotton answered, but he knew this fellow had just gotten a free pass for the rest of Texas because there was no way he wanted to make that long ride to Del Rio and back again. Grant may have his hide when he found out he let the man go, but he could take it.

About a quarter of a mile after they entered McKie's property, Travis rode off to the east to the cabin he and Cotton had shared with Ian O'Toole. It would certainly be a quiet place without Ian's jolly chatter and playful nonsense that helped pass the long evenings. He would often take out his banjo and play lively and sometimes melancholy Irish tunes and sing along in that strong Irish brogue. Then he would tell a few Irish jokes and laugh as though it were the first time he had ever told them.

Grant rode on alone pondering the events of the previous night. He had carefully watched Travis as well as the others but found not one hint of betrayal in anything Travis had done. In fact, he had seemed concerned about how Charlie and his hands were faring. That was the only thing the least bit out of character for Travis was to show concern for Charlie. It was no secret; the two men were not overly fond of one another.

Grant felt satisfied it was the work of Pancho Villa's men. He maintained an army of four to six hundred men to feed and any free cattle left more pesos for his pockets. But why him? Grant wondered. Why not hit some of the ranches closer to the border? Of course, they had all suffered losses at times, if not to the Mexicans to the other outlaw rustlers. The only reason he could think of was his cattle were generally of higher quality. It was a puzzle how the Mexicans thought.

As the homestead came into view at near dusk it was a welcome sight. Grant spurred his horse lightly to increase his pace. He was ready to get home, change into dry clothes, sit down to a good supper, and hit the sack. Of course, he would have to discuss the rustling with Charlie, but hopefully that could be taken care of during supper.

The house was coming into plain view now and he could not see any light coming through the dining room windows. It looked strangely like they had boards over them.

Instantly, he slowed his horse and looked closer at the homestead. To the left of the corral, he saw a heap of something piled up that he did not immediately recognize in the dim light. He nudged his horse a bit closer and saw it was dead horses piled up near the corral. "What in the devil happened here?" he mumbled in shocked dismay.

Then he heard the bang, bang, bang of hammers. What in the devil was going on? He rode slowly into the yard and around to the back of the house where the hammering grew louder. He saw two of the men hammering boards over the last of the kitchen windows.

When one of the men saw Grant, he stopped hammering. "Hello, Boss," and with a wide gesture of his free hand said in a derisive tone, "Welcome home!"

Grant just looked at the boarded-up windows and bullet holes in the house, and saw where something heavy had been drug across the yard toward that pile on the other side of the corral.

After looking everything over, he spoke in a hushed tone, "What in Hell happened here?"

Before either man could answer he went on. "Where is my family; are they—safe?" he asked, with a tremble in his voice.

The back door opened, and Pete came out onto the porch. "Yes, they're safe; well, Corabell took a bullet in the shoulder but she's gonna be all right, I reckon," Pete told him in his quiet, calm manner. "She put the girls in their room and told them to stay put."

Grant knew what room Pete was talking about. It wasn't general knowledge that such a room existed. It wouldn't be very safe if too many people knew about it.

It had always amazed Grant how different Pete was when he hadn't been drinking. Give him too much liquor and he became like a different man. Like him and Rowdy trying to rope Smoky and see who could ride him the longest. All of it probably over a dollar wager at that.

Grant slowly dismounted, still surveying the damage done to the house alone. "Go on," he nodded to Pete.

"Well, sir, after you and the other fellows left, me and Johnny and Sam got to thinkin' and things just didn't seem quite right. We put our heads together and kind of decided them Mexicans might be pullin' you all away so they could come get those forty head of horses you've got ready for the Army. We knowed they was likely worth lots more money than them cattle, and we know how the Mexicans like your horses, 'specially old Pancho Villa," Pete paused and rubbed his good hand over his whiskers. "Seein' as how there was just three of us left, when I told Corabell what we was thinking, of course, she was in on the deal. She tried her best to talk Miss Ester out of helpin' but she weren't havin' none of that. She was a real trooper too. Me and the two women took cover in the house, and Johnny and Sam stayed at the barns. Sure enough, a little past eleven, here they come. We surprised the heck out of them when they come sneakin' in here thinkin' it was gonna be easy pickings. I was in the dining room and Miss Ester and Corabell in the kitchen. We waited for about six of them to round the corner of the house, and we let loose." Pete never got overly excited in his telling of the events but just told it straight out.

"We got three of them and several horses that first time. They took off back toward the creek and waited a while. Then here they come at us again with their guns blazin', and we let 'em have it again. Only that time was when Corabell took the bullet, but she wouldn't let us stop shootin' to see about her until they took off toward the creek again. By then they had lost four men and five horses, and we have three prisoners that are pretty shot up," Pete concluded his account of the attack they had endured.

The men all stood in silence for several seconds.

"Oh, yeah," Pete added, "All the horses are still in the barns waitin' for the Army."

Grant cleared his throat. "I sure appreciate what all of you fellers have done. I'll go check on Mama now," he said with a slight catch in his voice, as he removed his hat and looked at each man in turn.

As Grant walked up on the porch, Pete added, "Miss Ester sent Sam to fetch a doctor as soon as it was daylight, and as luck would have it, he found Will Hudson at the Cremwelgys'. Seems half the family and ranch hands are down with the flu. He come on over and tended to Corabell."

Grant glanced around the yard. "He's still here?" Grant asked, when he saw Will's buggy parked near one of the barns.

"No, he was on his way to Juno after he left here. Seems half the town is down with the flu and dying like flies. We told him just to go by horseback, and Rowdy took him up to Big Rock crossing, so he wouldn't have such a long trip back around by the main road. Miss Ester can tell you what he said about Corabell."

Grant nodded his head, put his riding gear in the closet, now shot full of holes, and entered the kitchen that was lit by several kerosene lamps. The delicious smell of some kind of stew simmering on the wood stove met him, and his mouth started watering for something warm inside his belly to soothe the chill.

He walked through the quiet house and knocked gently on the door to his mother's room. Christine opened the door and grabbed him around the legs as she squealed, "Daddy, you're home!"

Grant picked up his daughter, hugged her to him, and thanked God she was safe and waiting for him to come home.

Corabell opened her eyes and looked at Grant standing in the doorway.

"Come on in," she told him in a weak voice.

As he approached her bedside, she could see the exhaustion on his face and that familiar stance that spoke volumes of him carrying all of the blame for what had happened.

"Mama, what did the doctor say?"

"He took the bullet out, dressed the wound, and told Ester how to care for me. He said I might not have much use of my right arm as the bullet did lots of damage to the muscles," she said in an unusually weak voice.

"I'm so sorry, Mama. I feel like a damn fool for falling for their plan to get as many of us away from the homestead as possible so they could steal the horses. It all happened so fast. It just never occurred to me what they were really aiming to do."

Corabell watched Grant and listened to his words. She saw this ordeal had taken a toll on her son. He was beating himself up for making a mistake. It was a clever plan somebody had plotted. Fooled most of them, she thought. Grant shouldn't be so hard on himself —after all, he was just human—but she knew him well enough to know he would shoulder the entire blame for what went wrong.

"Don't be too hard on yourself, son. None of us knowed what they was up to till Pete, Johnny, and Sam got suspicious. Thank the good Lord they figured it out in time for us to get ready for 'em. I got to rest a bit now," Corabell said, as her tired eyes drifted shut. Grant stood still holding Christine, listening to his mother's breathing. It soon became even, and he knew she was just resting.

Ester finally had a chance to go to her room and change out of the clothes she had been wearing since last night. Corabell's blood was on the outer shirt and she needed to put it to soak. As she brushed her hair, she thought about Will's short visit. When she had tried to talk to him about the rumors he might have heard, about her and Grant, he had brushed her off.

After he had finished with Corabell and had stood at the kitchen sink washing up, she had approached him again.

"Will, I need to have a few words with you before you leave for Juno."

"What about?"

She took a deep breath. "You may have heard some gossip about me and Grant being sweethearts but that is all it is, just gossip. There was a situation where I needed to tell him something private and of great importance. The only way to do so was to make it look like we were sweet on each other. I know how fast gossip spreads around here and thought it might have even made it all the way to town. There is nothing to it, so please don't think ill of me," she pleaded.

Will had turned and looked at her as he finished drying his hands. Mercy, he looked so tired already. Dark shadows were under his eyes, he hadn't shaved in a couple of days, and his color looked sallow. It was a shame how little rest doctors got at times of illness like all this flu going around.

Will studied Ester's face and knew she was telling the truth. If only she knew he wished it were true that she and Grant had become sweet on each other. It would make what he was going to have to tell her soon so much easier. Now was not the time to approach such a subject. He needed to be on his way and what needed to be said between them must not be hurried.

"Ester, I have no doubts about you. When I get finished at Juno I am coming back and we need to have a serious talk, but it just can't be today," he said, as he laid the towel on the edge of the sink and walked to the chair where he had left his coat.

Ester was standing beside the chair. He put on his coat and turned to her. He wasn't sure what to do next, so he did what his heart told him he probably should not do. He took her in his arms and held her snugly against his body, relishing the feel of her against him. He breathed in the fresh scent of her hair and felt her soft cheek against his. Oh, how he wanted to kiss her as a man kisses a woman he desires and to tell her of his love for her. Will knew that could never be. Will gathered all of his courage and quickly kissed her on the forehead, released her, and walked out to his horse tied by the corral. He could not bring himself to look back.

Ester watched him leave, once again feeling let down. She so longed for him to declare his love for her and to treat her as a man in love treats a woman. Her resolve of last night to go find him and declare her love for him had faded with the dawn. So much had gone on between the attack last night and the reality daybreak brought.

As she watched him ride away, something in his manner warned her the talk she anticipated might not turn out the way she wanted.

As Grant left Corabell's room, he put Christine down. "Go check on Molly while I have a word with Ester."

He had taken a few steps toward Ester's closed door when she opened it and started out. She flinched with surprise to see Grant standing so nearby. She had no idea what to say to the man standing before her, but to start with, Corabell's wound seemed the most practical place to start.

Ester started toward the kitchen to check on the stew, and Grant walked beside her.

"I hear you called for Will to come take care of Mama," he stated as they reached the living room.

Ester whirled and glared at him. "Yes, I did! I certainly didn't know how to get the bullet out! Even Charlie said it was too deep for him to be messing around with, so what else was I supposed to do?" she asked angrily, as though she thought he was accusing her of taking advantage of the situation. Her eyes flashed with fury. "Don't worry; I'll pay the bill since I was the one who called him!" she continued in her defensive mood just as they reached the dining room doorway.

Grant halted and leaned against the door leading to the dining room, preventing Ester from passing.

"I wasn't accusing you of anything. I'm glad he was nearby and could get here so quick. Why do you always act so defensive when anything is said about Will?" he asked, a bit exasperated. "Don't you worry, I'll pay the bill!" he half shouted in irritation.

Ester saw the frown lines appear between his eyes and knew he was seething with anger.

Ester could not hold her temper any longer. She stomped her foot and yelled back, "No, you won't! I don't want you thinking I used this as an excuse to see Will!"

Grant stared at her as though he could not believe what he had just seen. Then in a calm, quiet voice laced with fury he said, "You stomped your foot at me."

"What?"

Still in that quiet but hostile tone Grant repeated, "You just stomped your foot at me."

Ester stared at him but was not going to let him intimidate her. "So, what if I did!" she shot back.

Grant straightened to his full height, glared at her as though he might like to wring her neck. "Miss Hammon, I run a good size ranch, I am in charge of forty-something men, and not one of them has ever shown me the disrespect you have just displayed by stomping your foot at me. I know you are here to teach my daughter and have just been through a hell of a night, but the rest of us haven't been on any Sunday picnic either!"

Ester knew she had gone too far and should at least apologize for stomping her foot, but somehow, she just could not bring the words out of her mouth. Instead, she made matters worse by stubbornly continuing to challenge Grant's authority.

She narrowed her eyes, trying to carry out her bluff of not being intimidated by him. "So, what do you intend to do about it?" she asked, in an almost arrogant tone.

Grant slowly moved his right hand to the butt of the pistol he still wore strapped around his waist. Without blinking or changing expression he said, "I guess I could shoot it off!"

Ester saw the lethal look in his eyes and was no longer sure how mad she had made him. She wasn't taking any chances that she may have pushed him too far this time. She caught sight of one of the large chairs nearby. Without hesitation, she gave herself a strong push, jumped into the chair, and quickly sat on her feet. She never took her eyes off Grant to see if he was really going to pull his pistol.

It took all of Grant's willpower not to laugh when he saw Ester almost fly into the chair and sit on her feet. It reminded him of something Christine might do and was the most comical thing he had seen in a long time. He watched her as she stared at him with huge, rounded eyes trying to figure out what he would do next.

He probably should shake her or, or, what? It was obvious this spat had gone far amiss. At that moment he knew it was up to him to put an end to their differences. After all, she had just risked her life because of him. It was time to show Miss Ester Hammon his more benevolent side.

Grant steeled himself and walked to the chair where Ester still sat and lifted her by her upper arms and swung her away from the chair. She kept her feet tucked up as though she were afraid for him to even see them.

"Put your feet on the floor, Ester, or I'll drop you and you won't like the landing," he said in a gentle voice.

He felt her take her own weight as her feet touched the floor. Still, he held her by her upper arms and stared into her distrustful face.

"Ester, I apologize for upsetting you. You put your life in danger last night, and I am grateful. I'm truly glad Will was nearby to tend to Mama. I am glad you are here to teach Christine."

Ester started to speak but Grant held up two fingers and gently placed them over her lips as a signal he wasn't finished. He was so near she could smell the fresh scent of the out-of-doors he carried mixed with the faint odor of leather. His nearness and change in mood made Ester tremble, not in fear but in… she wasn't sure what.

"It's true, if one of my men had shown disrespect the way you did, I would have knocked him into the middle of next week, but you aren't one of my men." He took a deep breath. "In fact, you are a lovely woman. A woman any man would be proud to have for his own. I know you care for Will," he paused, and Ester thought he had finished his unexpected apology. "I must admit I am a bit jealous of Will. I hope he knows how lucky he is." With that said, he turned and walked through the quiet living room, down the hall to his own room, and closed the door.

Ester stood stunned as she watched him go.

Grant wondered if he would ever understand women, but right now he was too damn tired to give it much thought. He couldn't remember the last time he had been this tired, and he never remembered being so let down by his own decisions. All he wanted was a hot bath, clean clothes, warm food, a stiff drink, and a good night's sleep.

Chapter Ten

Will followed Rowdy's lead along the Devils River for several miles until they came near a huge rock sitting on a bluff above the river. It reminded Will of a sentinel guarding the crossing.

Rowdy looked back. "The crossing is just the other side of Big Rock," he said, as he pointed toward the landmark ahead. "Once you cross the river, just ride straight west till you come to the Juno Road. Then it's only a few miles north to town."

Will followed Rowdy's instructions and easily found his way to the road and on into the small town of Juno. By the time he had reached the road the coughing had set in, and he knew it wouldn't stop as long as he was out in the cold. He felt weary, drained of most of his strength. But the folks in Juno needed him, so he had to keep going a while longer, he tried to convince himself, hoping it would restore some of his vigor.

Every step of the way, he seemed to think of Ester and pondered on just how to best handle telling her what he had to. Doc Williams had given him some sage advice on the subject, but it didn't seem to make the daunting task any easier now that the time was growing near to take care of the problem.

Only about a hundred or so people lived in the small town of Juno. There was one church, one general store, one saloon, one livery stable, and one school. Most of the houses were within spitting distance of one another so it was no wonder the flu epidemic was spreading so quickly.

As Will rode past the small church that looked as though it had once been painted white, he reined in his horse at the gate to the cemetery. He noticed the freshly turned earth on a number of new graves. He counted nine but there may have been more. The bleak day made the sight even more austere. Who were the people now lying in the cold ground, the place of their eternal rest? Three of the graves were obviously children or perhaps babies. A sad sight indeed, he thought as he continued his ride toward the livery.

The man at the livery stable directed Will to the home of two widowed sisters that had been taking care of most of their neighbors, and thankfully neither of them had come down with the flu.

He left his horse at the livery, took his black doctor's bag, and walked about a block and a half to the home of Dottie Jones and Mary Jasper. Dottie was the oldest by eighteen months, and there was no doubt they were sisters. They had the same round face, rosy cheeks, bright brown eyes, and full lips. In their fifties now, a bit on the plump side, it was evident they had been beauties in their younger years. They welcomed Will as though he was one of their own sons. "You sit right down here by the fire and warm yourself," Mary instructed, as Dottie ladled a bowl of soup and sat it on a small table beside his chair. "Maybe it will help soothe that cough," Mary commented.

It smelled delicious and he needed its warmth to warm his insides.

"Now you eat every bite of that broth. It will put some color back in your face," Dottie told Will, as she inspected him from head to toe. "You look nearly as bad as most of the sick folks," she commented to Will and her sister.

"We got to keep you up and going to help us get folks well 'afore the whole town up and dies," Mary added. "I've seen lots of sickness but I ain't never seen nothing like this 'un."

"I noticed a number of new graves as I rode past the cemetery," Will commented.

Dottie shook her head from side to side and clicked her tongue. The sadness showed on her now wrinkled face. "I believe there have been twelve in all. Nine are buried by the church and three of the McIntire family are buried in the cemetery at their ranch, a mile or so up the road."

"It's losin' the little ones that hurts the most," Mary added. "I know. I lost two children at young ages. My son, Fred, looked the picture of health, but got a fever and died two days later. He was just past a year old. Marylee was always sickly and died when she was three. It nearly broke my heart with each one, but there were seven more to care for, so you just learn to go on," she said. Her sadness still lingered after all these years.

"You finish that soup and take a little nap there by the fire until we're ready to go take soup to all the sick folks, in about an hour," Dottie suggested.

Will did not argue and soon dozed after his coughing subsided. Mary stood a few feet away studying him. She turned and walked quietly to where Dotty was working in the kitchen. Mary shook her head and whispered, "I think he's got the same thing my Zeb died of."

A slight frown crossed Dottie's face. "But he's so young to have such a thing. Do you really suppose that's what it is, or is he just wore down from tendin' all the sick folks?"

They woke Will and started their rounds taking the pot of chicken broth to share with each family. After the first two homes, Will urged them to go ahead as he was taking longer to examine each patient and people were waiting for their evening meal. They told the man of the house where to direct Will when he finished with his family. Will moved from house to house examining and tending to family after family until nearly nine o'clock. He gave each family instructions that if he was needed to come for him at any hour. When he returned to Dottie and Mary's house, nearly exhausted, he found they had left him another bowl of warm soup on the stove. He drank it down and almost fell into the warmth of the feather bed that was usually used by Dottie.

It seemed sleep had just begun when he heard a loud knock on the front door. He quickly pulled on his pants and answered the knock in hopes of not disturbing the two women. John Kirkland stood in the cold night air filled with a light mist.

"Sorry to bother you, Doc, but the twins are worse."

Will remembered six-year-olds Mary and Perry and was not surprised by the late-night summoning. He had known hours ago the unlikelihood of them seeing the light of another day.

"I'll be right with you, John. Let me dress and grab my bag."

Will lit his lantern and followed John's lead through the alley and to the third house on the next street. He was thankful the cold night air did not start him coughing before they reached their destination.

When they entered the stuffy house, Will immediately knew it was just a short time before they would both be gone. He looked at John, who was the only well person in his family of eight. Will slightly shook his head and John nodded, understanding the silent message.

John's wife, Martha, lay in a bed of tangled sheets and covers on the far side of the room. In a weak voice hardly audible she asked, "Will my babies live?"

John walked to his wife's bedside and sat beside her. He took her hand and gently raised it to his mouth and kissed her clammy hand. "I got the doctor. He's doin' all he can."

Will heard the tender love and concern for his wife reflected in the burly man's voice.

At 3:20 a.m., December 27, 1916, Mary Kirkland passed from this life to the next. At 4:12 a.m., December 27, 1916, Perry Kirkland followed his sister to the next life. Will bowed his head and prayed they would truly rest in peace and pass to a new life of health and eternal love.

John tenderly told Martha their two precious children had departed this earth.

"John, bring the twins to me," Martha said in her frail voice. John obeyed her wishes. "Put one in each of my arms," she whispered. She cradled each child in her arms for a long while, gently kissed their cheeks, and whispered words of motherly love.

After a while, Martha looked at John. "Have a casket built to hold both children. They come into this world together, and they will depart in the same way." Then Martha relinquished her children to be prepared for their final resting place together.

Will thought it was the saddest funeral he had ever attended. Martha was so weak a chair was brought to the graveside for her. John stood with his hand resting on Martha's shoulder, gently patting her. Tears rolled down the huge man's ruddy cheeks. The sound of Martha's inconsolable weeping could be heard throughout the small town. Will thought it was the most forlorn sound he had ever heard. It was the sound of a mother's broken heart.

Chapter Eleven

At ten o'clock on the morning of December 27, 1916, the ranch hands gathered in the yard behind the ranch house to prepare for the trek up the hill to the McKie cemetery to bury their friend, Ian O'Toole.

Two of the men had built a plain wooden casket. Two more cowboys carefully cleaned and dressed Ian's body in his best clothes for his burial.

Normally at ranch funerals, of which there had been three besides Grant's father and Zora Mae, Corabell read some scriptures from the family Bible and led the cowboys that knew it in the Lord's Prayer.

Corabell was not able to make the trip up the rough trail to the small cemetery, so Charlie asked to borrow her Bible. Charlie was not particularly a religious man, but he did believe every man deserved as near a Christian burial as they could manage.

Grant led the procession out of the yard, past the barns, up the road, such as it was, and Charlie drove the wagon bearing Ian's body. Ester sat beside him. Christine and Molly sat on the second seat. Everyone was dressed in his or her best clothes as a show of respect. Twenty-two of the cowboys followed riding by twos. The men spoke not one word. The only sound to fill the silence was the creaking of leather, horses snorting occasionally, and the clopping of their hooves on the rocky ground. As they made the climb Grant finally heard Charlie ask Ester to sing. He agreed that would add a nice touch to the simple service, especially since Ian loved music so much.

As they bumped along, Charlie turned to Ester and asked, "Miss Ester, I've heard you sing while cooking; would you sing some church song at the graveside?"

Ester was a bit surprised that anyone would think her singing good enough to hear other than in the kitchen.

"Well, yes, I'll do my best. What should I sing?"

"Ain't *Amazin' Grace* a good church song?"

"Yes, and I do know the words to that one," Ester answered.

"Ian loved his music, so I think that would please him to have a song sung over his grave," Charlie commented.

Once the crude coffin was placed beside the waiting open grave, Charlie opened the Bible and turned to the 23rd Psalm. He read it with more passion than Ester expected. He then nodded to Ester and she began to sing. When she finished *Amazing Grace*, she wasn't sure what inspired her, but she instantly lifted her voice and began to sing—

"Oh, Ian boy, the pipes, the pipes are calling
From glen to glen and down the mountainside."

She saw big, strong men's chins begin to quiver. Several removed handkerchiefs from a pocket and swiped at their eyes.

"The summer's gone and all the roses falling,
It's you, it's you must go and I must ride."

Two of the cowboys, rumored to be the toughest of the tough, turned and walked several paces away from the small group keeping their backs toward the grave. Ester could see their broad shoulders shake; she heard more than one sniffle and clearing of throats. Somehow, she managed to maintain her composure and let her mellow voice drift across the hillside like a bird singing to announce the coming of spring. She was glad she did not have to look at Grant at this moment. For some reason she could not grasp, she was afraid if she saw any of the emotions displayed by the other men on his face, she would indeed lose her composure.

"But come ye back when summer's in the meadow,
Oh, Ian boy, Oh Ian boy, I love you so."

Grant stood holding Christine's hand, listening to Ester's clear, mellow voice. He felt the lump in his throat growing bigger. The haunting words of the Irish tune he had heard Ian sing many times left him with an empty feeling. He had been considering promoting Ian to foreman when Charlie or Travis stepped aside. He was one of the hardest working men on the ranch and a man of trust. Grant knew he had lost more than just a fine cowhand; he had lost a true friend.

Charlie ended the service with the Lord's Prayer. Most of the men joined in but some remained silent just holding their hats in front of their chests.

Chapter Twelve

During the next two days four more people died. The freshly turned earth in the small cemetery was a bleak reminder of the fragility of life. Ten days before, all of those now lying in their graves had been healthy people full of life. Now their lives had been snuffed out like a candle at the end of the day.

On the third day, it was apparent the brunt of the flu epidemic was waning. Will was near exhaustion. Dottie and Mary insisted he stay another night to rest before returning to Del Rio. As anxious as he was to see Ester and make things right between them, he knew that rest was what he needed.

He awoke on the morning of December 31, 1916, feeling more refreshed and ready to ride to the McKie Ranch. After seeing Ester, which filled him with dread just thinking about what he had to do, he would stop to check on the Cremwelgy family and spend the night there. He would check on other families the next day on his way back to Del Rio.

Will bid Dottie and Mary goodbye at mid-morning after consuming a huge breakfast they had prepared especially for him.

When he reached the spot to turn his horse toward the Devils

River and Big Rock Crossing, he knew from the looks of the heavy clouds he was about to get caught in a rainstorm. He dismounted and put on his rain gear. Before long, large drops of rain began to pelt him, and the north wind swooped down in biting gusts. The dry earth soon turned to mud as the continuing downpour become worse. As he neared the stand of trees lining the riverbank, a loud crash of thunder burst overhead. A streak of lightning snaked out of the dark sky, hitting a tall tree not twenty yards ahead of him. Before Will could react, his horse reared, throwing him to the muddy ground. Will felt an agonizing pain shoot through his body when he landed on his back with a thud. He thought he was about to lose consciousness as his head pounded into the earth. He tried in desperation to move his limbs but lacked the strength. He lay there feeling helpless with the rain hammering his face. Within seconds he felt the water seep beneath his rain slicker, soaking his clothing, chilling him to the bone. He told himself he had to move, he had to find some kind of shelter. First, he gingerly moved his head from side to side to see if his horse might still be nearby. He saw nothing but flashes of lightning and rain coming in sheets soaking everything in sight.

Eventually, he spotted a fallen tree about fifteen feet to his left. He half crawled, half drug himself until he reached it. He lay as close to the trunk as he could manage, hoping it would give him some protection from the wind. In reality, he could not feel any difference as an absolute chill had taken over his entire body. The coughing had already begun, and the storm raged on.

Two-and-a-half miles south and an hour or so later, seventeen-year-old Charles Miller spotted a horse with no rider near the corral. He caught the reins and led the soaked animal into their barn. When he began to inspect the animal, to see if there was any sign of identification, he found the doctor's black bag tied to the saddlebag.

"Pa, Pa!" he yelled. He darted through the rain toward the house.

His father heard the panic in his son's voice and met him on the front porch.

"Look, Pa, I found this doctor's bag tied to a horse I found by the corral. I think I better go see if I can find the doctor. He can't be too far away, I'm thinkin'."

Wilber Miller looked at the sodden bag, then turned his gaze to the dark sky and the pouring rain.

"I don't much like you going off in this kind of weather, but I suppose somebody better see about the poor fellow. I heard that young doctor has been at Juno for about a week, tendin' all them sick folks," Wilber Miller said, as he continued to watch the storm. "Get Albert to go with you and get back as soon as you can. Your mama is gonna have a fit when she hears I let you go off in weather like this," he said with a worried expression on his wrinkled face.

Charles and Albert saddled two of their most gentle horses that could be easily managed during a storm and led Will's horse, thinking he could ride him back with them.

"I'd bet he was headed for Big Rock Crossing," Albert told Charles as they gently picked their way north toward the crossing, figuring that was the direction the doctor was headed.

"Yeah, he was likely headed back to the McKie Ranch to check on Mrs. Corabell and on to Del Rio," Charles agreed.

The two young men rode on, scouring the countryside for any sign of life. Charles was seventeen but fully grown in size, standing well over six feet with a husky build. Albert was sixteen and almost as big as his brother. They took after their father in that respect.

They rode on in silence.

Suddenly Charles yelled above the increasing wind, "There!" He pointed to the inert body of a man lying against the trunk of a fallen tree.

They dismounted and approached the still figure. Charles turned the man so he could get a look at his face. "He sure looks pale," Charlie said.

"Yeah, and his lips sure are blue. He's soaking wet and I think he's near about froze," Albert observed.

The movement brought forth a weak cough from the man they felt certain was the young doctor that had been to Juno.

Albert looked at his older brother. "I don't think he's gonna be ridin' that horse back to the house."

"No," Charles agreed. "We've got to get him on my horse, in front so I can hold him on. You bring his horse."

The plan sounded simple but proved to be a battle of pull and tug to finally get the almost lifeless man on Charles' horse and him in position to hold the man in place. The saddle was wet, and they were wet. It wouldn't be an easy task, but Charles knew they had to do it.

The trip back to the Miller ranch house was slow going. By the time they arrived, Charles' arms were numb from holding the unconscious man. Both young men were glad to see the warm glow of lights in the house coming into view.

Charles rode up to the porch and called for help. Immediately the door was flung open and Wilber emerged to help his sons. Maggie was not far behind, giving orders to the men.

"Bring him in the kitchen by the fire and lay him on the blanket I put on the floor. Strip off all of his clothes so we can clean him up and then get him warmed up," she ordered in a tone that left no room for argument.

After Will was clean enough to suit Maggie, a bed was moved into the kitchen and placed near the wood cook stove. He was gently lifted onto the clean sheets and covered with two thick blankets Maggie had warmed by the fire.

By then Will appeared to be in a semi-conscious state. He managed to lift his head slightly, looking around as though trying to figure out where he was, but did not speak. He still emitted a weak cough at times and then lapsed into a deep sleep.

Wilber and Maggie exchanged concerned looks.

"Goodness' sakes, I hate to send anyone out in this weather, but I think somebody better go to Del Rio and fetch Doc Williams," Maggie whispered to her husband.

"It's getting too late to start out today, soon be dark. If he makes it through the night, I'll send one of the boys first thing tomorrow," Wilber whispered back to his wife.

"Do you think anyone can cross the river by tomorrow?"

"Yeah, the rain is lettin' up some, and if it don't get worse tonight they should be able to cross," Wilber assured his wife.

Maggie looked at the man lying in the bed. "We better keep the young'uns out of here; he might have the flu or no tellin' what after being in Juno," she said, with deep concern that was reflected in her worried look.

"Yes, they can eat in the big room by the fireplace tonight and until we get the doctor here to take over," Wilber agreed.

The rain stopped about one in the morning, so at first light, Charles Miller saddled the fastest horse they owned and took another in case he needed to change horses during the fifteen-mile ride to Del Rio. If luck was with him, he could be back with the doctor by nightfall.

Charles set a steady pace. The Devils River was on a rise but not high enough to prevent him from crossing safely. He reached Del Rio about noon. He went straight to Doctor Williams' office to tell him about finding his partner out in the rain near Big Rock Crossing.

Doctor Williams was almost worn out himself after Will being gone for nearly a week. Most mornings, when he looked in the mirror to shave, he hardly recognized the face staring back at him. It was the face of his father, old, with dark circles under his eyes, and lines that belonged to a much older man, not a man in his early sixties.

He had Ethel, his wife, fix him and Charles a hot lunch and gathered his medical bag and the few medicines he had that might help Will.

Charles hitched Doctor Williams' team of horses to his black two-seated buggy. They started the long journey back to the Miller ranch at one o'clock. It was indeed almost nightfall when they pulled into the yard.

"Go on in and tend to your friend," Charles told Doctor Williams, as he led the horses toward the barn.

After a brief greeting by the Miller family, he was ushered into the kitchen. Doctor Williams walked to Will's bedside, and just one look told him all of the medicine in the world would not save this man's life. He took out his stethoscope and listened to the rattling in Will's chest. It only affirmed what he already knew.

Doctor Williams turned to Maggie and said, "Go on about your chores; I'll just sit with him for a while."

Maggie motioned for one of the boys to bring a chair for the doctor, and the family retreated to the other room.

Doc Williams sat and looked at the shell of the man he had met such a short time ago. He remembered the day he had met Doctor Will Hudson at the train depot. When Will stepped down from the train, Doc smiled to himself knowing the female complaints were about to triple. Doctor Will Hudson had indeed been a strikingly handsome man. His manners matched his good looks, and, as Doc Williams predicted, their office was overrun with women of all ages with some of the gall-darn-dest complaints he had ever heard. Will had treated each one with respect, but the two doctors had a few good laughs over some of the more outlandish complaints.

After several hours Will opened his eyes and looked at Doc Williams in disbelief. In a weak voice, he asked, "What are you doing here, Doc?"

Doc looked at him and asked in return, "Do you know where *here* is, Will?"

Will looked around and it was apparent he did not recognize his surroundings.

In a weak voice, Will said, "I was on my way to the McKie Ranch to talk to Ester, but this isn't it." He started to cough, followed by brutal, bone-jarring shaking. Will shook so violently, the bed frame gyrated so hard Doc Williams became concerned it might fall to the floor. After several minutes, he began to calm again and fell into a deep sleep. Occasionally Doc Williams would reach out and check Will's pulse.

Doc dozed in the chair, waking at the slightest sound to see if Will was still breathing. Shortly after midnight Will awoke again.

"Doc," he whispered. "I never got to explain to Ester; I don't think I'll make it back to the McKie Ranch," he managed to say between gasps for air.

"Tell her I never meant to hurt her. I just couldn't prevent myself from giving in to my," he hesitated, "my love for her."

Doc Williams leaned slightly forward and looked his cherished friend and colleague in the eyes. "Don't worry, Will, I'll talk to Ester. She'll understand," he gently assured him.

Will nodded and closed his eyes. He coughed several times and fell into a final sleep. At 1:32 a.m. on January 1, 1917, Doctor Will Hudson succumbed.

Doctor Williams sat looking at the pale remains of a man that had a rare gift for healing. What a damn shame he never had the chance to put all of his knowledge and skill to use, Doc reflected. A new doctor would arrive soon, and if he had half of the skill and knowledge Doctor Will Hudson had possessed, he would be one fine doctor, but no one could take Will's place.

Doc Williams did not pull the sheet over Will's now still, ashen face. He just sat by his beloved friend's bedside until morning. He reflected on the months they had spent practicing medicine together, but, most of all, he thought about what a short time it had taken for them to become true friends. Oh, how he would miss Will Hudson.

When he heard Maggie quietly open the door at around five in the morning, Doc rose and turned in her direction.

"He passed during the night," he simply said. "Thank you for taking him in and caring for him," he told Maggie, fighting to hold back his tears.

Tears filled Maggie's eyes although she did not know Doctor

Hudson. It seemed such a shame to lose such a young doctor they so desperately needed.

They wrapped Will's body in the two quilts that had warmed him and placed his body in the back of the farm wagon before the family awoke for breakfast.

Doc Williams told Maggie and Wilber about what had really killed the young doctor and advised them to burn the mattress and sheets and to scrub the metal bed frame with lye soap.

Charles led the way back to Del Rio with Doc Williams following close behind in his buggy. They reached the only funeral home late in the afternoon. By bedtime that evening, most of the residents of Del Rio had heard about the passing of Doctor Hudson. They attributed it to the flu.

Charles spent the night with Doc and Ethel. He headed back to the ranch at daybreak as the rain had started again.

By noon the rain had turned to a downpour that lasted through the night and until late the next afternoon. By the time the sky began to clear, the streets and yards were flooded. But by the next morning, the water had receded, leaving a muddy mess that would likely last for several days.

They could not delay the burial any longer. Almost the entire town turned out for the funeral of Doctor Will Hudson. Standing room only in the Methodist Church, and some even stood outside in the cold, overcast day, but fortunately, the rain did not return.

A long funeral procession followed the new, shiny, black, auto-mated hearse to Westlawn Cemetery, located on the west side of the small town. The dirt streets were now filled with puddles of muddy water. Before long the automobiles and buggies often became stuck in the mud. Some mourners walked the mile or more, trying to avoid the mud as much as possible by walking across people's yards or some graveled walkways instead of trudging along in the mucky street. Often men and boys would get out of their conveyance to push it out of the mud again and again. By the time the long procession reached the cemetery, many folks were covered with the wet, cold muck, but they stood reverently in the chilly air during the graveside service.

Doctor Williams stood beside the grave after everyone else had departed the sad occasion. Weighing heavy on his mind was the letter he would have to write to Will's parents tonight. He bowed his head and prayed;

"Lord, give me the right words of comfort
to soothe the aching hearts of the parents
of this remarkable and fine man. Amen."

Chapter Thirteen

Two days later, on a bright, cloudless Saturday, Doc and Ethel Williams traveled over the almost dry but scarcely passable roads and made it safely across several low-water crossings to reach the McKie Ranch. They arrived late in the afternoon, so they had come prepared to spend the night.

Christine spotted the black buggy headed their way and ran inside to announce company was on its way. Grant rose and went to the front door. He was surprised to recognize Doc Williams and Ethel pulling into the yard. He had been wondering when Will would make it back from Juno to pick up his buggy. Maybe Doc would have heard something about how things were going in Juno, he thought, as he stepped out onto the front porch to greet their guests.

"Hello," Grant greeted Doc and Ethel as they came up the walkway to the front porch.

Doc tipped his hat toward Grant in greeting. "How are all of the sick folks doing?" Doc asked, as the two men shook hands.

"Everyone is doing much better, including Mama. We've been wondering how things are going at Juno since Will hasn't come back for his buggy. Have you heard from him?"

Doc looked around to see who might be in earshot. They appeared to be alone on the porch. "That's what I've come about," he said in a somber tone. "I'm afraid I have some bad news for Ester."

"Oh?" Grant replied, as one eyebrow lifted in question.

"I think it best I speak to her alone first, if you don't mind."

"Whatever you think is best. She's in her room napping or reading. I'll get her."

"Ethel, would you like to go on in to visit with Mama?"

"I sure would. I've been so worried about Corabell ever since I heard about what all happened out here."

"Have a seat, Doc. Would either of you like something to drink?"

"No, thanks," Ethel answered. "We had a picnic lunch and brought extra coffee with us," Ethel answered.

"Nothing for me, yet," Doc answered, emphasizing the yet.

As Grant led the way to Corabell's room, he was wondering what had happened to Will for Doc and Ethel to come all the way out to the ranch to talk to Ester.

Grant gently tapped on Ester's door.

"Come in," she called.

Grant opened the door slightly. "You have a visitor."

"I'll be right out," she answered, thinking it must be Will come back from Juno.

She quickly ran the brush through her hair and tied it at the nape of her neck with a pretty green bow that matched her housedress. Ester considered changing into something nicer. She inspected herself in the almost full-length mirror on her dresser and decided the dress looked okay. It was one of her older dresses, so she wore it on the weekends to help with the housework. Since Grant had hired Juanita to cook and do housework, Ester had fewer responsibilities. Corabell was recovering well and beginning to take on more of the chores again although she had limited use of her arm and hand. Ester smiled; Corabell was one tough woman.

Ester had dreaded coming to the McKie Ranch, as they seemed so different than the Cremwelgys. Now that she had gotten to know them, she had gained great respect for Corabell, and they had gotten along fine. Her feelings toward Grant were even softening some since she had been around him more and saw the huge responsibility he carried. It was true he could still be trying at times and get on her nerves. Lately, it seemed he was making an effort to be more agreeable. Their quarrel after Corabell got hurt and Ester sent for the doctor seemed to have changed Grant's attitude toward her. She was glad, as she didn't like being at odds with Grant.

Ester left her room expecting to see Will waiting in the large room but was disappointed and surprised when she saw it was Doctor Williams. Now why in the world would he---? Then it came to her that Will must be very sick, and Doc had come to tell her. She wouldn't be too amazed to hear he had the flu or pneumonia after tending to so many sick folks all the way from Del Rio to Juno.

As she approached, Doc stood and extended his hand in a warm greeting.

"Did Ethel come with you?"

"Yes, she's in visiting with Corabell. She'll be out in a bit. Come sit, I have some news to share with you," he said, as he motioned Ester toward one of the large sofas. He sat in the chair placed at a slight angle at the end so he could see her as he talked.

"Is Will sick? I know he was tired when he left here, and he hasn't come back to get his buggy." Nor to have that serious talk either, she was thinking, as she seated herself.

Doc took a deep breath, reached out, and took one of Ester's hands. "Ester, I hardly know where to begin," he said in his kindly manner.

Ester drew in her breath. The sad tone of Doc's voice and the look of compassion on his weary-looking face told her something was terribly wrong.

"Ester, Will started back here and got caught in a bad storm. His horse threw him, and he lay out in the cold rain for several hours. Charles Miller found his horse by their corral. Charles and his brother,

Albert, searched for him and found Will huddled by a fallen tree near Big Rock Crossing. They got him to their house and Maggie nursed him through the night. The next morning Charles came for me, but by the time I got there he was in serious condition."

Ester covered her mouth with her other hand and let out several soft sobs as tears filled her eyes. She did not want to hear what Doc might be about to say, but she knew she must.

"Will woke about midnight and asked me to come tell you that he never meant to hurt you in any way, but he just could not get a grip on his feelings and prevent himself from falling in love with you."

Ester took in several deep breaths to steel herself to speak. "Why would falling in love with me hurt me?"

"Will had consumption." He paused. "Tuberculosis. He knew his days were numbered."

"What do you mean by *had* and *were*?" Ester asked, in a trembling voice as the meaning of Doc's words sunk in.

Doc cleared his throat. "Will passed away around one thirty in the morning on January first. When we got to town the rain started in, and by the time it stopped, we couldn't delay his funeral long enough for the water between here and Del Rio to recede enough for me to get word to you. I am truly sorry, Ester, truly sorry," Doc's voice shook.

Ester let out a shriek as though her body were racked with pain. She could feel her body being pierced with a thousand spears. Unbearable, excruciating pain decimated her body, her heart, and her soul. She gasped for breath as she fell to her knees and bent her head to the floor crying, sobbing, "No, no, no! It can't be! It can't be true!"

Doc looked at the young woman lying at his feet in a heap, shaking with sobs of sorrow and disbelief. It was a hard thing to accept, even when he had witnessed the death of his dear friend, so he could imagine the feelings of denial Ester must be experiencing. He wished there had been some way to spare her this pain, some soothing words to lessen her grief. As a doctor, he had experienced seeing grief by those left behind all too often. He was tired. He needed to see happiness. But for now, he had to deal with what was at hand.

Grant heard the cries of grief and emerged from his office to see what had happened.

His eyes met Doc's as Doc motioned him to come nearer.

In a soft voice, he told Grant, "I just told Ester that Will passed away six days ago, and we couldn't hold his body long enough to get her there for his funeral."

Grant felt a wave of shock at the news, and then looked down at Ester still bent double on the floor, sobbing as though her heart were broken. He suspected it was indeed, as he recalled the almost unbearable pain he had felt when Zora died.

He started to reach down to lift Ester back to her seat, but Doc held out his hand in a motion to stop him. "Let her be a while. I think I'll take a drink of whiskey now and bring one for yourself and one for Ester."

Grant turned and walked back to his office to get the whiskey.

Grant returned with three glasses and a full bottle. He sat the items on the table beside Doc and poured two full glasses and half a glass for Ester, knowing she didn't imbibe.

Doc looked at him questioningly when he saw the half-full glass.

"Ester doesn't normally drink alcohol," he stated.

"If she won't drink it, I have something I can give her to calm her."

Grant reached down and gently helped Ester resume her seat on the sofa.

Her eyes and face were swollen and red from the constant crying. She still cried with sniveling, softer sounds.

"Doc wants you to drink a little whiskey to calm you," Grant suggested, as he extended the glass toward her.

Ester shook her head to indicate no. She did not attempt to reach for the glass. Grant sat it back on the tray and turned to leave.

"Please stay," he barely heard Ester speak.

"If you wish," he answered, and sat on the sofa next to her.

Ester took a deep breath and wiped her eyes with the once clean, white handkerchief Doc had provided.

"Tell me what Will wanted you to tell me," she stated in a quiet voice.

"Will and I had several discussions about his condition and his feelings for you. He said he would vow each time he saw you to tell you the truth about the tuberculosis, but, then, he just couldn't bring himself to do so. He couldn't bear seeing the hurt in your eyes and know it was because of him. Will wanted me to tell you he truly loved you and to ask for your forgiveness for the hurt and pain he has caused you," Doc told her in a tender voice.

Ester sat quietly, still letting the tears run down her swollen face, but she did not speak again for several minutes.

The two men remained silent with her, waiting for her to take the lead in whatever was to come next.

"What about a marker for his grave?" she finally asked, in a quivering voice.

"When you come to town next, we'll decide what to place there, and I plan to pay the cost," Doc told her.

"Not all, I want to help with the cost," Ester answered.

"That will be fine, Ester. Think about the wording you want on the marker and then we'll take care of it."

"Did you write to his parents?"

"Yes, it was probably the hardest letter I have ever had to write through the years, and I have had to write quite a lot. The difference was, I didn't know the others well, but Will Hudson had become not only my colleague but also my friend. It's a damn shame; he was truly a brilliant doctor! During the short time he was here I assisted him with two surgeries that most doctors wouldn't even have attempted.

He did them with such precision; it was truly an experience I'll never forget. Both patients recovered, and both would likely have died on the operating table with anyone else doing that complex of a surgery," Doc stated with a tinge of anger in his voice at the injustice of the situation. "Yes, it's sure a damn shame to lose such a brilliant doctor and fine man," he almost whispered, with deep compassion.

Ester rose, stood for several moments, and then murmured, "I think I'll go lie down for a while."

The two men watched Ester walk across the large room, down the hallway to her room, in such a downcast manner she might have been walking to the gallows.

Grant knew all too well the sorrow she was feeling and also knew there was little he or anyone could do to relieve her pain. Only time was the great healer of such heartache.

Chapter Fourteen

Monday morning Ester woke with a determination she would make every second of this last week with Christine count. She would pour her heart and soul into Christine's lessons. That would not only be to Christine's benefit but to her own. Perhaps she would think of something, anything, except Will.

Her determination worked well for the most part in the daytime, but the long hours of each sleepless night were wearing her down. Her restless sleep was filled with dreams of Will. In one dream, Will was kissing her at the Christmas Eve dance, but when she opened her eyes it was Grant, not Will, kissing her with such feelings of desire. How ironic, it had indeed been Grant who kissed her at the dance, not Will. She would never know the touch of Will's lips on hers. The man she loved had never kissed her the way a man in love kisses his sweetheart. Now she knew why, but it did not ease her pain. Each morning she was glad when the sky brightened, and it was time to get up and start another day. At night she would read, or try to read, until the words became blurry. Yet, sleep eluded her for most of the night.

On Thursday, Christine awoke with a sore throat and by noon just could not go on with her lessons. Corabell directed Ester in mopping her throat with iodine. Ester had never performed such a procedure but managed to get the swab where it would do the most good. Then Molly came, opened her mouth wide, and pointed inside. Corabell told Ester to go ahead and mop Molly's throat too. "I never know for sure if Molly's throat really hurts or if she just wants the same treatment as Christine," Corabell confessed. "It won't hurt her even if it isn't sore," Corabell explained.

Ester glanced up to see Grant standing in the doorway watching Ester wielding the throat-mop stick.

"Is your throat sore too?" Ester asked. "Just step right up, and you can be next," she said, with a slight smile at the expression on his face.

Corabell laughed. "You'd have to hog-tie him first. Even when he was a little boy he would run and hide to keep from getting his throat mopped," she told Ester, as she laughed even harder at the memory.

"Well, since I haven't mastered hog-tying, I suppose you're safe," she too found herself laughing for the first time in days.

"You two girls better go take a good nap, so you'll feel better," Grant told Christine and Molly.

Neither argued but headed straight for their rooms.

Grant started to leave but turned and looked at Ester.

"Since you can't teach this afternoon, come go riding with me. It's really nice out. I need to go check the sheep in the west pasture, just past where there are some really nice Indian pictographs you might like to see," he coaxed.

"That's a good idea," Corabell agreed. "It'll be good for you to get out in the fresh air for a while. You've been cooped up in the house too much."

Ester only hesitated a few seconds before taking Grant up on his offer.

Within half an hour, they were riding along the Devils River. Grant was right: the temperature had risen, and the afternoon was very pleasant. Ester only wore a lightweight jacket. The sunshine on her face felt warm and soothing.

They had ridden a couple of miles when Grant turned and said, "We're going to cross the river just ahead. It's about a quarter of a mile from there to the pictographs."

"This is so pretty here along the river, the water is so clear, and even in the winter, with the greenery of some of the bushes, it's nice," Ester observed, as she gazed at the surrounding area. "Are those big pecan trees up ahead?" she gestured toward a stand of large trees near the river.

"Yes, they have small native pecans that are hard to peel, but they do have a good flavor."

They continued on in silence until Grant reined in his horse, dismounted, and came to help Ester dismount. He tied their horses to a small tree. "Take hold of my arm; the walk is a bit rough." Ester did as he instructed. She clung to his muscular arm several times when she slipped on the loose rocks. She had been walking with her head down trying to watch where she was stepping.

"There," Grant said, pointing to the cliff face just ahead of them.

Ester lifted her head and was shocked to see all of the pale figures that had been painted on the rocks thousands of years ago. She stood studying the scene before her, admiring the faint colors that had lasted through all of these centuries. It was incredible to think of the times the river had flooded and reached these paintings, the wind and sand that had battered the cliff face, and yet they survived. "This is amazing, truly splendid," she said, as she studied the ancient drawings. "Do you know what they mean?"

"Some archeologists came here several years ago to study and document the different sites and sent me a copy of their findings. We have seventeen distinctive sites on this ranch. I believe this one is depicting a buffalo hunt," he said, as he gestured toward the drawings.

Ester studied the crude drawings a bit longer. "I think that's right; I can see the buffalo and the Indians chasing them with bows and arrows."

"Look, there's another one," Ester pointed further along the cliff face. They walked slowly over the loose rocks until they stood near the next drawings.

"It looks like they ran the buffalo off a cliff," Ester suggested, a bit shocked.

Grant looked at her and grinned. "You're pretty good at this. That's right. That was an easy way to slaughter a large number at once, instead of having to chase them down one at a time."

"Are there more nearby?"

"A few miles downriver but too far to ride today. We'll have to turn back soon before it gets dark. I just need to ride a little farther to check the sheep before we head back home."

As they walked along the riverbank back toward the horses, Grant would pick up a small, flat rock and make it skip across the surface of the water.

"That looks like fun; where did you learn that trick?" Ester asked, feeling lighthearted being away from the house and constant reminders of Will.

"I don't remember. One of the foremen, when I was a kid, had two boys about my age, and it was something we used to do. It was a contest to see who could make their rock skip the most times or the farthest," he laughed. "You know how boys are, everything has to be a contest."

Ester looked at him and smiled, intrigued by the story he had just shared. "Not really, I grew up with three sisters but no brothers. I mostly thought all boys were a pain, especially the boy that lived across the street."

"Why was he such a pain?"

"Oh, he used to tease me constantly. His favorite nickname for me was *frog face*, which, of course, I hated and would fly into a rage every time he said it. That only encouraged him to do it more. Then one evening, while I was sitting on my front porch swing, when we were thirteen, he came over and begged me to do him a favor."

"Oh, and what was the favor," Grant asked, watching her expression change as she told the story.

"We were having a major history test the next day, and he hadn't studied the two chapters it was over, so he begged me to fill him in on the chapters so he wouldn't have to stay up half of the night studying. I got up my nerve, and I told him I would help him out if he promised never to call me *frog face,* ever again."

Grant chuckled. "I'd bet my last five dollars he promised."

"Oh yes, so I told him in great detail the major points of the chapters and quizzed him when I finished. He was really rather smart, and I knew he would pass the test. Just before he left, he suddenly leaned over and kissed me on the lips. It wasn't just a quick peck but a real kiss to a thirteen-year-old. He never said another word, got up, and walked across the street. I could hear him start to whistle when he was about halfway home. I just sat there stunned, but he kept his promise and never called me *frog face* again."

"Did he become your boyfriend?"

"No, we actually had very little to do with one another after that until he started to leave for the Navy after we graduated. Again, I was sitting on the front porch swing and he walked across the street to tell me he was going to the Navy. We talked for a while, and he asked me to write to him. I said I would. I got a couple of letters and answered them. Then one afternoon we saw two men in military uniforms ride up to their house. In a few minutes, we heard his mother screaming. He had been accidentally killed. It was so sad," Ester paused. She looked at Grant. "It's funny the memories that just come to mind for no particular reason, isn't it?"

"Yeah, it is strange at times the things we remember."

Ester had a sad, faraway look in her eyes as she softly spoke, "The first boy to kiss me is gone. The first man I truly loved is gone too."

"Grant," she paused and looked up to meet his gaze. "How long does it take before it stops hurting so much?"

Grant didn't have to ask what she was talking about; he knew.

"I suppose it's different for each person."

"Does it still hurt a lot when you think of Zora?"

"No, not like it used to. After a while, the memories become easier. I still miss her. I'm sorry she didn't live to see Christine grow up." He took off his hat and ran his fingers through his blond hair that needed to be cut. "It's hard to explain, Ester. I guess it's just something each person works out as best they can."

Ester looked out over the placid river flowing gently southward and then up at Grant. "Thank you," she whispered, and walked toward their horses.

Grant watched Ester walk away. He took several long strides to catch up with her. She still had her back to him when he reached out gently, surrounding her with his strong arms. They stood for several minutes, bathed in the warm winter sun, not speaking, but communicating feelings neither could have put into words. She could feel Grant's breath gently caress the side of her face.

"Ester," he spoke her name softly. "I have heard it said that time is the great healer, and I believe that to be true. You must give yourself time for the pain to ease. Then your memories will be the good ones."

Grant opened his eyes. Some nondescript noise had awakened him. He sat up in the dark and reached for the pants he kept on a chair near his bed. He slipped into them and then put on his socks to ward off the cold from the floor. All the while he listened intently for the noise to come again. He heard the old mantle clock strike two times. Then the strange sound reached him again. He eased off his bed, picked up the loaded pistol he kept on the small table beside his bed, and crept to the door of his room. He always left it slightly ajar. He could see a pale light coming from his office. The unusual sound came from the same direction.

Grant wondered why anyone would be in his office in the middle of the night. He moved quietly through the door leading to the hallway. He crept slowly and noiselessly down the hall toward the open door. Just outside the door, he halted and cautiously peeped into the room. The sight before him was the last thing he had expected to see.

There stood Ester in her long white nightdress with a bottle of whiskey turned up to her lips. If it hadn't been for the whiskey bottle, he would have thought he was looking at an angel. Her hair hung loose in soft waves around her shoulders and seemed to flow down her back. The white gown made her look as innocent as a lamb.

She took a big slug and swallowed. Instantly, she covered her mouth with her other hand to muffle the sound of her sputtering, wheezing, and coughing as a result of the harsh, burning liquid. She was turned with her profile to him, and he could see her rapidly batting her eyelashes as tears were running from the corner of her eye. Grant could hardly believe his eyes. Poor girl was going to choke herself to death at this rate.

He stepped fully into the doorway. In a commanding voice, he asked, "What in the devil do you think you're doing?"

Eater whirled to face the sound of his intruding voice in the still of the night. She gasped several times and croaked, "I couldn't sleep so I decided to try some whiskey, like you and Doc tried to get me to do the other day. It tastes awful! How can you enjoy it so much?" she asked, in a wheezing gasp filled with doubts.

Grant walked forward and took the bottle from her. He looked at its contents and saw she had downed several good-sized slugs. "You have to develop a taste for it," he answered, as though it would be a pleasant task.

"Let me show you how to drink whiskey without choking yourself. Then you might appreciate its taste a bit more." He poured a full glass for himself and half a glass for Ester. He handed her the glass. "Now take a small sip and swallow it." They both lifted their glasses to their lips and took in the amber liquid. Ester caught her breath and gave a slight cough but did not lapse into the spasms she had previously displayed.

"Now, isn't that better?" Grant asked, with a slight grin.

"It still burns, but not as bad, and I can breathe," Ester admitted.

"Good, you had me worried there for a few minutes when I saw you chugging down that big gulp."

Ester wondered just how long he had been watching her before he intervened. She suddenly felt self-conscious just dressed in her night-gown, but it was thick, and she knew he couldn't see through it.

"Why did you only give me half a glass? I don't feel sleepy yet."

"It takes a little while to take effect. Any more and you might sleep for a week," he said, with a teasing smile.

"That might be a blessing except for moving back to the Cremwel-gys' on Saturday."

"Yes, I expect Christine is going to have a crying fit when you leave, so get set for it."

"I wish the Cremwelgys had more room. I'd take her with me so she could go to school."

Grant didn't say it aloud, but he knew he could never let Christine out of his sight for that long, not even with Ester. "Well, they don't have room, so it's out of the question. Since you have a buggy maybe you could come some Saturday, spend the night, and give Christine some lessons. That would give her something to look forward to."

Ester brightened at the thought. "That's a wonderful idea. Could I bring Lilly with me? They could play together once we've finished with lessons. Lilly won't mind doing extra homework."

"Of course," he said, as he lifted his glass of whiskey to finish it off. "Drink up," he told Ester.

Ester finished the last of the strong drink and was surprised to find she no longer gasped for breath after its burning sensation.

"Come on, I'll tuck you in, and I'll bet in a few minutes you'll be asleep," he told Ester, as he picked up her lamp.

"You don't have to tuck me in, I'm not Christine's age," she stated, a bit defiantly.

Then she started to sway as she took a few steps. Unthinkingly she grabbed Grant's arm to help regain her balance. The situation struck her as being funny. She started to giggle. "Maybe you better walk me to my room after all. I think I'm a bit tipsy," she chuckled even more.

"I'd say that's quite possible," Grant laughed quietly, glad to hear Ester giggling instead of crying.

"Get in bed and I'll put out the lamp," he told her, as he walked to her reading table to replace the lamp. He glanced over his shoulder to see if she was settled. What a picture she made with her hair fanned out over the pillow and a faint smile touching her lips. She had already closed her eyes. If the circumstances were different what a temptation she would present, Grant thought. Instead, he blew out the lamp and walked quietly back to his own room.

Ester finally slept with no dreams, which was a relief. When she opened her eyes to see the bright sunlight, she realized she had over-slept. Ester sat up quickly and then grabbed her head. Wow, what a headache! She had heard about people having hangovers after too much drinking. Maybe this was what they meant by a hangover. She needed some coffee, lots of coffee.

Chapter Fifteen

G rant had been right. When they started to leave, Christine grabbed Ester around the waist crying and begging her to not leave.

"Please don't leave yet," Christine begged between sobs. "Nobody will be here to help me learn my lessons."

Ester fought back her own tears when she saw the sad expression on Christine's face and heard the desperate plea in her voice. Ester wished with all of her heart she could take Christine in her arms and hold her close. She wanted to tell the amiable child how fond she had become of her in such a short time, but she knew that could never happen. Christine could easily get the wrong impression. She might build false hope that her daddy would want to marry Ester after all. No, she could never give Christine false hope. So, instead, she tried to pacify the dear, sweet child.

Ester gently ran her hands over Christine's soft curls and lightly patted her back. "I'm sorry our time together has ended so soon. Remember, I told you I have to go get ready for school to start again. What would all of those other boys and girls do if I didn't come back to teach them?" she tried to reason with Christine.

Christine sniffed several times. "I don't know," she answered in a sorrowful tone.

"I have a surprise for you," Ester said, trying to sound cheerful.

"What is it?" Christine asked with renewed hope.

"Your daddy suggested I come some Saturday and bring Lilly with me. We could do lessons in the morning and then you girls will have lots of time to play," she smiled.

Christine immediately brightened. "Did you really say that, Daddy?" Christine turned her attention to Grant for reassurance.

"Yes, I knew you'd like that idea," he answered and smiled at his daughter.

"Thank you, Daddy. That would be fun. Can you come next Saturday?" she almost squealed.

"I'll try but can't promise," Ester assured her. This plan seemed to appease Christine enough that she finally released Ester.

The scene with Christine clinging to Ester reminded Grant how much Christine not only needed a teacher but a mother. He really did need to start considering remarrying. Not just for Christine's sake but for his sake as well. Ester's presence had reminded him more than once how much he missed the company and companionship of a woman.

Grant and Ester carried on a much easier conversation on the way back to the Cremwelgys' than when he had come for her. About a mile before they reached the road leading to the Cremwelgy house, Grant brought the team of horses to a stop.

Ester looked at him, wondering why they had stopped.

"I've been thinking something over but need to know how you'd feel about it," Grant said.

"Oh, and what would that be?"

"They have started work on this road and should have it finished in a couple of months. I'm thinking about buying an automobile and a farm truck. You could come back to the ranch, and you and Christine could drive to and from school. That way, Christine can go to school with the other children, and you can have your own room again." He looked at her, waiting for her answer.

"I, I don't know if I can learn to drive an automobile. What if I wreck it?" she asked, very unsure of herself.

"You can do it. I'll learn first and then teach you," he said, with confidence. "It can't be all that hard," he mused, with an encouraging smile.

"What about Corabell? Couldn't she learn to drive it and bring Christine to school?"

Grant threw back his head and gave a hearty laugh. "I'm not sure I can even get Mama to ride in it, much less drive it. Besides with her arm the way it is, she probably couldn't drive, even if I could persuade her."

"You're right, I'm sure it would take both hands to manage. Well, I suppose I could give it a try. I must admit it has been nice having my own room. The Cremwelgys are lovely people and make me feel so welcome, but it really is crowded in my little partitioned-off corner. Most of all, Christine needs to be in school with other children."

"I agree. Good, as soon as the road is finished, I'll get the auto and start driving lessons. I'm not going to say anything to Christine yet, as she will pester the devil out of me about it every day," he chuckled.

"Now, won't you be the dandy rancher with an automobile and a farm truck," Ester teased.

Grant laughed. "Yes, my ambition in life, to be a dandy rancher."

Then he looked at her and his face became serious. "I know it wasn't easy, all you went through at the ranch, and I thank you again for all you did to help, way beyond what you should have had to do."

"I admit, it was quite an experience. I'm glad I was there to help when needed," she answered truthfully.

Grant surprised her again by reaching out and giving her a quick hug. "Remember what I told you about giving things time. It will all sort itself out eventually." He kissed her gently on the cheek, and they drove on to the Cremwelgys'.

The Cremwelgys welcomed Ester as though she were a member of the family returning home. The hustle and bustle of the lively household, strangely enough, gave Ester a feeling of calm. Maybe it was because there weren't so many memories here of Will and the frightful night she had spent helping hold off the horse thieves. Whatever the reason, she found a measure of serenity in her little alcove as she sat in bed reading, as there was no room for a chair and table like at the McKies'.

She had been surprised when she had unpacked her boxes earlier to find a full bottle of whiskey and a glass. A note in Grant's bold hand-writing read, *One-half glass at bedtime, sip only. Grant.* It made Ester smile and feel good to know he was concerned about her feelings and willing to show it.

They all attended church service on Sunday morning. Everything seemed to be returning to normal. It lifted Ester's spirits to see all of the other families and especially the children. They were all, for the most part, excited about school starting again the next day.

Everyone was anxious to talk about what had taken place at the McKie Ranch on Christmas night. The men speculated that someone at the ranch was in on the attack, but they couldn't pinpoint or agree on just who it might have been. Ester never said a word about what she had overhead at the school one Saturday since she had no proof to back up who she suspected. She also knew Grant was convinced she was wrong about it being Travis.

Talk also turned to Pershing's inability to catch Pancho Villa and that he would likely be returning to the U.S. before long. Delmer Hoffman said he didn't think Pershing could catch a jackrabbit, much less Pancho Villa. Most of the other men laughed but basically agreed with his statement.

The men also speculated that President Wilson would soon have the U.S. involved in the war in Europe. Ester noticed the Millers exchange a worried look knowing their oldest son, Charles, might be drafted. All in all, the talk was rather depressing.

The most painful part of the conversation was when it turned to the loss of Doctor Will Hudson. Ester wasn't sure how much they knew about their relationship but a few of the women discretely gave her a hug and offered their condolences, along with words of encouragement like, "You're still young; you'll find someone else." Ester graciously accepted their well-meant words but had doubts as to the truth in the old saying.

Monday morning, Daniel had the horse and buggy ready when it was time to travel the three miles to school. All of the students were present. They had many stories to share about Christmas and the rest of their time off. It seemed it was the norm for each child to receive one gift; a small bag of fresh fruit, some hard candy, and a few nuts were a special treat.

Ester thought about all of the gifts her nieces and one nephew received in comparison. They would be considered quite well-off compared to these ranching families. These children knew no difference and were pleased with whatever they received for Christmas.

Ester immersed herself in planning the lessons and grading each child's papers. Most of the students were still making good progress in their studies.

Some things didn't change. Walter still spent a lot of time in the outhouse. Eventually, Ester worked up her nerve and summoned Walter to her one day as she watched the children at morning recess.

"Walter, I am concerned that you spend so much time in the

outhouse. Do you have difficulty with your bowels?" she asked, as delicately as possible for such a personal subject.

Walter looked at her with his crooked little smile that formed at the corners of his mouth and then ducked his head in embarrassment. "I guess you might say that. At home, we only have one outhouse, and there are seventeen of us to use it. Every time I get in there somebody's poundin' on the door tellin' me to hurry up. I just put things off until I get to school where we have two outhouses, and usually, nobody's poundin' on the door."

"Oh, well, I can see where that might cause a problem. Can't your pa build another outhouse, since there are so many of you to share just one?"

"I guess he could, but he just says to get your business done and get busy with the chores," he answered, fidgeting a bit from the embarrassing topic of their conversation.

"I see," Ester answered, thinking about exactly what to say next. "Well, take the time you need but don't dawdle," she advised.

Walter looked relieved their conversation was over. He ran off to play ball with the other boys. Ester was also relieved the conversation was over. Although it was a delicate subject, she was reassured to know there was nothing wrong with the boy's health.

Two weeks had passed since returning to the Cremwelgys'. Ester seemed to be settling into a more normal routine every day. She still filled her days with the students' schoolwork and tried to fill the evenings with things other than thinking about Will and what might have been. Why hadn't she guessed he had a health problem with all the coughing he did during the damp, cold weather? Would it have changed her feelings toward him even if she had known earlier? Would he have ever married her, even if he had lived longer, or would he have thought it too risky for her health? Why did these and many other questions keep running through her mind? There were no clear answers to any of them.

Each night when she crawled into bed to read, she was thankful for the whiskey Grant had sent. She would sip the half-glass of the amber liquid as he had instructed. Then she would try to read. At times she found herself just holding the book, but her thoughts were on Will. Eventually, the whiskey did seem to help relax her, and at last, she would sleep. Some nights were filled with mostly senseless dreams, some dreams about Will, and others involved Grant. Sometimes she would be with Will. Suddenly the dream would change, and she would be with Grant. She was most grateful for the nights when no dreams disturbed her.

She and Lilly were going to the McKie Ranch this coming Saturday as planned earlier to spend the night. She knew Christine would be counting the minutes until they arrived.

Vincent and Daniel said they would be going to Del Rio the next Saturday, so she would go with them to see Doc and select the marker for Will's grave.

Saturday morning dawned bright, without a cloud in the sky, and with the promise of a nice day. Hopefully, by afternoon, it would be warm enough for the girls to play outside. Ester and Lilly left just after breakfast and reached the McKie Ranch about mid-morning. Ester remembered the impressive view the first time she had seen the ranch from a distance as they came over the rise in the road that led to the valley below with the meandering creek, and fields filled with grazing cattle, horses, and sheep. There seemed to be more sheep than before. Grant had said they were moving in that direction as the once-rich grassland couldn't produce enough new grass to support the large herds of cattle anymore. It was as tranquil a scene as it had been before, but Ester knew how fast that tranquility could change to pure mayhem. She said a silent prayer this would be a peaceful weekend.

After greeting the cowboys working the horses in the corral near the house, Corabell, Juanita, Ester and the girls started their lessons.

She was pleased to see Christine had improved her reading and writing skills.

"Has your daddy been helping you with your lessons?" she asked out of curiosity.

Christine bobbed her head up and down to indicate he had. "He likes to hear me read after supper, and then he checks my writing. He says my math needs to be better, so maybe you can tell him how to teach me math."

"I'll talk to him after supper, but let me show you some new problems to work on for now." They stopped for a light lunch and continued working until about three o'clock.

"Lessons over for today," Ester announced. "It's time for you two girls to put on your sweaters and go outside for a while. Play in the front so you won't get in the way of the horses," she reminded them.

Ester smiled when she heard their excited voices and giggles as they scurried off to get their wraps.

Ester put away their materials and went to find Corabell. She and Molly were in the large room sitting near the fireplace that only contained a small fire to take the chill out of the house. Ester and Corabell visited while Molly rocked and hummed softly.

After a while, Ester suggested they move to the porch to take advantage of the warm afternoon. Corabell rose to follow her but Molly continued to rock.

Corabell looked at Molly. "Come on, Molly, it's nice and warm outside," she coaxed.

Molly shook her head from side-to-side and continued to rock.

Ester and Corabell moved their chairs to take advantage of the winter sun. Corabell confided that she used to worry about what would become of Molly once she was gone. "Grant says he will take care of Molly right here at home. She's always listened to him better than me, so I leave it with the Lord," Corabell told Ester with assurance.

Chapter Sixteen

G rant had seen Ester and Lilly arrive but had not taken lunch in the house as he and several of the men were getting more horses ready for the Army. He grabbed a bite to eat at the bunkhouse and got back to work. He had to admit he had missed Ester. At times, he wondered if he waited a while longer if she would be interested in him courting her. After she left, he had visited a widow woman in Comstock a couple of times but did not feel interested enough to continue the visits.

Near quitting time, Grant saw Travis and Cotton riding toward the homestead. That was a bit unusual for the two to come to the homestead together, he thought, as he was putting his gear in the outside closet on the back porch. As they drew closer, he could see Travis was not sitting on his horse as he normally would. Then he saw his hands tied in front and his head was down as though he didn't want to look Grant in the eyes. Cotton rode slightly behind him. As they drew nearer, Grant walked out into the yard to see what was going on.

Before Grant could speak Cotton called out, "Here is your cattle and horse thief! He was in cahoots with Pancho Villa's men!"

Grant felt like someone had hit him in the gut. Of all people to betray him, it was hard to believe it really had turned out to be Travis. Grant had been so sure Ester was wrong, but now her warning about Travis came back to haunt him. She was right after all, but that did not console Grant for what Travis had done. He was a traitor, the lowest of men, and a double-crossing thief. He had been the cause of Ian's death as well as a number of the banditos. Grant's anger boiled over! It outraged him when it sunk in, to think about the misery and unnecessary loss of life Travis had caused.

Grant cleared his throat and looked at Cotton. "I suppose you have proof of those accusations?" he asked, although he knew the answer before Cotton said anything else.

Cotton pitched a leather drawstring pouch and Grant caught it. He could feel its weight as he opened it to find it full of silver coins.

"I happened to get back to the cabin a little early and heard Travis talking to a Mexican on the front porch. I could tell Travis was mad as hell. I slipped along the side of the cabin, careful to stay out of their sight. That's when I heard the Mexican tell Travis he was lucky to get this much money since the plan he hatched up got botched and they couldn't get the horses. It was really the horses they wanted. The cattle's rustling was just a way to draw most of the men away from the homestead. They thought it would be an easy mark to get the horses. Well, I guess they found out different, but it was Travis' idea," Cotton finished in disgust.

"What do you have to say for yourself, Travis?" Grant demanded, barely controlling the anger boiling inside him.

Travis remained silent with his head still downcast.

Most of the ranch hands had come out to see what was going on but kept their distance.

"If you have anything to say you best do it before I beat the living hell out of you," Grant spoke with a fury no one had ever heard before. They could see the fire of rage in his eyes and hear it in every word.

"I wanted a place of my own. Damn! I'm forty years old and don't have half the money I need to get started on a place of my very own! If everything had gone right, I would've left and headed far away and started over. You could handle the loss!" Travis flung out sharply, showing his resentment for all Grant had.

"I've worked hard for everything I have and never stole one thing to get to where I am. I always treated you fair and this is the repayment I get!" Grant bellowed.

"Untie him, Cotton!"

Cotton dismounted and cut the leather strap that bound Travis's wrists.

"Now get down off that horse and get ready for the beating of your life. Don't even think about running unless you're ready to die!" Grant snarled through clenched teeth.

Ester and Corabell had heard the commotion in the yard and stood at the kitchen windows watching the men.

"Should I try to stop them?" Ester asked, afraid of what was about to take place.

"No! Women don't meddle in men's doins'," Corabell answered emphatically. "It might be best you don't watch."

Ester heard Corabell leave her vantage point at the window, but she could not tear herself away from the scene taking place in the yard.

Travis dismounted and the fracas began. Ester wasn't sure who threw the first punch, but she could plainly hear the pounding of fists and curses coming from both men. She saw blood running from Grant's nose and then noticed Travis spitting blood. They fell to the ground in a wild frenzy of blows, kicks, rolls, and moans.

Ester finally realized she had been holding her breath. She wanted to turn away from the ugly scene, but her feet wouldn't move. She continued to watch with her hand clasped firmly over her mouth to hold back the scream she felt building inside. She wanted to yell at them to *STOP! STOP!* But Corabell's warning to not interfere in men's doings kept sounding in her ears.

Grant managed to stand. Stumbling forward, he grabbed Travis and drug him to his feet. Then Grant landed a blow to his face that sent the man reeling backward several steps, and he fell to the ground again. Travis lay there, not moving.

"Get up you dirty, low down, son-of-a-bitch!" Grant yelled. "Get up, I said!" he yelled again and started toward Travis.

Cotton stepped between the two men. "You've whipped him, Grant; that's enough," he said, in a strangely calm manner for the situation.

"Get out of my way, Cotton; I ain't finished with him yet!" Grant threatened and took several steps forward.

Cotton stood his ground. "No, sir, you've whipped him. Tomorrow, we'll take him to Del Rio and let the law do the rest. I don't want you put in jail for murder," Cotton said, unflinching.

Those words seemed to penetrate Grant's blood-boiling rage. He stood looking at Cotton for what seemed like an eternity. "Get him out of my sight. Put guards on him tonight," he ordered.

Cotton and one of the other cowboys picked Travis up by the arms and drug him toward the barn, leaving a trail of his two boot heels in the dust.

Both Grant and Travis were covered in dirt, their clothing ripped, and blood ran from scrapes on various parts of their bodies.

Grant came in the back door and stopped short when he saw Ester standing near the kitchen window staring at him.

"What are you doing here? I thought you were teaching the girls," Grant snarled, as though her presence annoyed him, and his expression matched his tone of voice.

"I, I was just watching to see if one of you would kill the other," she answered defensively, as she looked him in the eyes.

"Well, we didn't!" Grant answered, still glaring at her.

"Go take a bath and get all of that dirt off your wounds. I'll put some of Corabell's salve on them. Be sure to wash good with soap so they don't get infected," she told him, as though she might have been talking to Christine. She was certain that didn't set well either.

Grant just looked at her but did not answer. Then he walked, or rather limped, out of the kitchen.

Ester gathered some bandages and Corabell's concoction that she put on everything from a burn to mosquito bites or a sprained ankle, and headed to Grant's office.

It was quite some time before Grant appeared in the doorway with a towel draped around his neck, blotting his damp hair with one end, wearing only his trousers. The sight of his broad, bare chest, muscular upper arms, and wide shoulders made Ester want to gawk, but at the same time, she felt embarrassed for looking at a man so nearly naked. It would probably be best to look elsewhere, she told herself, but her eyes seemed riveted to the man standing before her. She could see the muscles in his chest and arms ripple as he moved the towel drying his hair. She steeled herself for the task ahead and did neither gawk nor avert her gaze. She tried to act in a professional manner like a nurse would do under the circumstances.

"Sit here." She pointed to one of the extra chairs near his desk that did not have a high back.

Grant sat and laid the towel across his knees so she could see all of the scrapes on his back, chest, and arms. Some were superficial but several were rather deep where rocks had apparently gouged into his skin.

"I had a hard time reaching my back and thought about calling you to come wash it for me," Grant said in a teasing manner, thinking it would fluster her just a bit. Little did he realize how flustered she already felt just seeing him without his shirt. He didn't know why he liked to shock Ester so much except to see her different reactions, the changing expressions on her face, and in her pretty eyes. She was much easier to read than she thought, and that gave Grant the advantage. Something about that intrigued him.

"If you had, I would have used that bar of soap in your mouth as well," Ester shot back, not about to let his rather personal insinuation get her rattled. "I heard all of those curse words coming out of Travis' and your mouths out there," she said, in a bit of a scolding tone.

"That's probably another reason you shouldn't have been watching and listening. Men don't always adhere to polite chit-chat like ladies do."

Ester laughed. "That's for certain."

They remained quiet while Ester applied the salve to Grant's back. Occasionally he would wince slightly when she touched one of the deeper wounds but said nothing.

Ester broke their silence. "That wasn't a pretty sight out there, but I think you gave Travis what he deserved. He caused Ian's death as well as those bandits. They probably had families that cared about them, too. Some may have left a wife and children behind to fend for themselves now. I'm not defending them being thieves, but maybe they were doing all they knew how to do to survive. I hear conditions in most of Mexico are deplorable at best."

Grant could hear the sadness and the fury reflected in her voice. Before he could answer she went on.

"He also cost you a good deal of money in the cattle you lost, plus the danger he put all of the men in and the long hours all of you spent riding out in the cold," she paused briefly.

Grant turned his head slightly and looked at Ester. "Ester, you have a soft heart," was all he said.

Ester did not respond to his comment but went on. "Well, now I hope he rots in jail for the rest of his life!" her words became harsh in her final judgment of what Travis had done.

Ester moved so she could look at the scrapes on Grant's face.

"Did that sound soft-hearted?"

Grant chuckled. "Not exactly, but it sounds like what he deserves, and, believe me, I'll see to it that it happens!"

Ester lowered her eyes to Grant's chest and suddenly it seemed the room was way too warm. To be touching Grant on his chest seemed a bit too intimate. Perhaps she should suggest he do that part himself.

Ester could feel Grant's eyes on her. She knew he was going to taunt her about not wanting to touch his chest if she hesitated. Once again Ester steeled herself for the task and started applying the ointment to the red scrapes that almost covered his chest. She could feel sweat on her forehead and hoped it didn't start to run down into her eyes. She did not want Grant to think it bothered her one bit as she gently ran her hand over the firm, bare warmth of his skin where she had never touched a man before. And, Ester told herself firmly, don't you dare blush!

When she had finished, Grant said in a husky voice, "I think that calls for a drink." He stood and reached for the whiskey bottle.

"I'll wait to have a drink at bedtime, but you go ahead," she said, as she busied herself placing the unused bandages and ointment back on the bookshelf. Then she left the room.

Grant poured himself a full glass of strong drink and was tempted to gulp it down and then have another to calm his nerves. He was amazed at how calm Ester remained while putting the ointment on his chest, but her light touch certainly wasn't calming to him. It made his thoughts wander in directions best left unexplored. He finished off the whiskey and went to his room to find an old white shirt.

Corabell had always insisted on using white cloth for bandages as she said the dye in material wasn't good for open wounds.

Grant sat at his desk, trying to concentrate on the bookwork, but thoughts of what Travis had done kept creeping into his mind. If that wasn't enough of a distraction, the memories of Ester's delicate touch tortured him even more.

Ester appeared in the doorway at about nine o'clock.

"I've come for my bedtime toddy," she said, with a slight grin.

"Help yourself." Grant gestured toward the bottle and watched Ester pour the glass half full as he had instructed.

"I really appreciate you sending the bottle of whiskey when I went back to the Cremwelgys'. It has helped a lot. It is getting low, but we will be going to Del Rio next Saturday. Where would I go to buy another bottle?"

"You won't go anywhere in town to buy a bottle. I'll give you all you need," he said, as he reached over and opened a cabinet door beneath the bookcase. He sat another bottle on the desk. "Now how would it look to folks for the schoolteacher to be buying whiskey? Next thing you know you'll take up smoking cigarettes. Now, what a picture that would make: a cigarette-smoking, whiskey-drinking schoolteacher," he teased with a laugh.

"Oh, you left out part of it," Ester said, laughing with him.

"What's that?"

"A cigarette smoking, whiskey drinking, old maid schoolteacher!" Ester said and laughed even more.

"I don't think of you as an old maid. I know it's not considered polite to ask, but how old are you, if you don't mind me knowing?"

"On March 20th, I'll turn twenty-three. That is considered an old maid by most folks."

"Well, I don't agree," Grant answered. "I think of an old maid as being rather grouchy, disagreeable, a woman that doesn't particularly like men. You don't fit that description in the least."

"Thank you, but I don't think my family would agree. That's part of the reason I came here, to get away from my family's constant match-making. They seemed shocked to think they were going to be stuck with an old maid schoolmarm. My sisters married before they turned twenty. Mother and my sisters introduced me to every eligible bachelor in Dallas. I dated a couple of them several months but knew by then they were not the one for me. After a while, my only defense seemed to be to leave. I saw the advertisement for this teaching position in the *Dallas Morning News* and decided to apply. Apparently, Twelve Mile School is not overrun with applicants. I received a letter right away from Mr. Cremwelgy, offering me the position, and here I am."

Grant studied her for several minutes. Then he asked, "If you had known then what you know now, about the living conditions and other hardships of living on isolated ranches, would you have come?"

Ester was a bit taken aback by his question. Although she had thought about that very subject on several occasions, she had never really decided what she would have done. "Oh, I don't know. I suppose it's good we can't see into the future. It might keep us from having many experiences we would have otherwise missed." Ester gave a short laugh. "I will say this has indeed been quite an experience. I've learned to shoot a pistol and a Winchester, been in a gun battle, helped deliver a baby, fallen in love, and lost that battle," she said, with sadness in her voice that was reflected in her heartbreaking expression. Then she brightened. "I do love teaching the children. Most of them are really making good progress this year, and coming to teach Christine is definitely a pleasure." She lowered her voice, although Christine was likely in bed asleep. "I do hope they finish the road soon so I can come back and drive her to and from school. She so needs to be with other children."

"I agree, and they have started the road work, so it is just a matter of time. I plan to start looking for an automobile and a farm truck, so I'll be ready as soon as the road is complete."

"Good, well, good night," she said, as she left his office.

Grant awoke at about one-thirty with most of his upper body stinging like he was rolling in an ant bed. He made his way to his office and lit the lamp. Grant was not about to put himself through the sweet torment it had caused him when Ester rubbed the salve on his chest earlier. He applied the salve to his arms and chest but could not reach all of his back. He walked quietly to Ester's room. The door was open, so he walked to her bed and looked at the alluring woman as she slept. She could certainly be a temptation, but it was likely best to keep his mind on the business at hand, he warned himself. Gently he shook her by the shoulder. Ester sprang up, looking around wildly.

"It's me, Ester. I need you to come put some more ointment on my back. Sorry to wake you," Grant apologized.

"That's all right," Ester assured him, as she stifled a yawn.

Ester slipped out of bed and followed him to his office. She could see he had already taken care of his chest and arms, much to her relief. She picked up the jar and gently spread the yellowish salve over his back.

"How does that feel? Did I get everything covered?" she asked, still holding the jar.

"That's fine, thanks. I'm really sorry to wake you, but it was stinging like he--- heck," he finished.

Ester reached past him to replace the jar on the shelf just as Grant turned toward her. Suddenly they were standing very close. She glanced up, and Grant was looking down at her. She wasn't sure just how it occurred but without warning his lips were lightly touching hers. Then he drew back, looked at her again, and his lips descended with more pressure, more longing. They both seemed to realize at the same time what was happening between them and drew back. Ester certainly wasn't the most experienced twenty-two-year-old, but she did recognize the fiery look of passion reflected in Grant's eyes. She wondered what he saw reflected in her gaze. Much to her chagrin, Grant may have seen much of the same as was revealed in his own intense look. Quickly she turned and left the office before either felt it necessary to say a word or try to explain anything.

Ester entered her room, closed the door behind her, and leaned against it for support. Why did Grant have such an effect on her, she wondered? His kisses always left her yearning for something she did not quite understand except, she thought, it must have something to do with womanly desires that were not spoken about aloud. She slipped back into bed and lay awake for a long while thinking about those uncanny, yet breathtaking feelings Grant seemed to provoke.

They were so different from one another. Grant was bound to this land. He thrived on hard work and enjoyed the camaraderie with the rough cowhands. He would rather spend a Sunday afternoon competing in roping, or a wild horse-riding contest, than reading a book and just relaxing. About the only thing they had in common, that she could think of, was he did like to dance.

She longed for a life filled with books and attending book reviews. She loved plays, symphonies, and other more cultured entertainment that would never be offered here.

Now that was strange. If Will had asked her to marry him she would have been content to stay in Del Rio with him, where there were scant social activities offered. At least they would have enjoyed discussing books and entertainment they had enjoyed. They might have even taken the train to San Antonio once in a while to attend a play or the symphony. Well, even that would have been an improvement over being stuck twenty-plus miles out in the country. But that part of her life was over. No need to dwell on what might have been, she told herself for the hundredth time.

No, she was quite certain things would never work between her and Grant, no matter how exhilarating his kisses, she decided, as sleep finally claimed her.

Grant treated himself to another glass of whiskey and then another. Sleep evaded him. His thoughts returned to Ester again and again. He was drawn to her. He hated to admit he had been jealous of Will Hudson and wished it were him she had cared for instead of Will, but that wasn't the way things had worked out.

She had certainly shown more spunk than he had ever expected when he first met her. Now that Will was gone, she probably would never be satisfied living out in the middle of nowhere on a ranch. He could tell from some of their conversations that she missed the more civilized life offered in the city, where she could enjoy plays, music, and other more sophisticated entertainment. He could offer her none of those things.

It was going to be pure torment when Ester came back once he bought the automobile. Well, he would just have to deal with his feelings when that happened. Maybe when he had an automobile, he would have more time to go courting. He might go see that woman who lived near Comstock again. What was her name? He tried to remember but couldn't recall it. Oh well, he'd just have to find someone that had an agreeable nature and things would probably work out. People got married for any number of reasons.

For now, the most important thing was to get Christine in school.

Chapter Seventeen

Ester and Lilly had returned to the Cremwelgys' Sunday afternoon. To her relief, she had not seen Grant again before they left. The alluring sight of him without his shirt kept popping into her mind. She could almost feel the hard planes of his chest and---. Now just stop thinking about him, she chastised herself.

The following Saturday, Ester rode to town with Vincent. Daniel rode one of his horses he was ready to trade. Vincent let her off at Doc Williams' house and went on to tend to his business. Doc and Ester walked a few blocks to the funeral home and looked at a variety of grave monuments. They selected a tall two-tone gray stone and gave instructions for the inscription, *Dr. Will M. Hudson, July 10, 1888 – January 1, 1917, In Loving Memory*. There was so much more that could have been written about Will, but his tombstone was not the appropriate place. Ester felt sad to think that in the years to come, most people would not know who Dr. Will M. Hudson had been or that he was an exceptional doctor cut down in his prime by a terrible killer. Not one that could be hung for his crime, but by a vicious disease. Nor would they know how very, very much a young teacher had loved him. The years would likely wipe away the story of Dr. Will M. Hudson.

The excitement increased about the roadwork as it grew nearer and nearer to the school. When it was finally within view, it was hard to maintain the children's attention.

One morning at recess, Ester walked down the road with the children toward the workers for a closer look. The boys were especially excited about the process. The workers welcomed the children and patiently answered their questions while they took a short break from their arduous labor. The girls soon became less interested and wandered about looking for the first signs of spring, but it was still too early for any wildflowers. Ester used their walk back to the school as a time to teach the students about some of the native plants. They talked about how making a road would change the terrain and the possible changes it would bring to the ranchers that lived along the road.

The students apparently had heard from their parents that Grant was planning to buy an automobile and a farm truck as soon as the road was finished. That was a bit of exciting news as no one had dreamed of such a thing a few months ago.

Now all of the children hoped their parents would buy a farm truck or an automobile like they had heard Grant McKie planned to do. Especially the boys dreamed of learning to drive an automobile, instead of having to drive a team of horses pulling a buggy or farm wagon.

Ester smiled as she listened to their chatter. It still made her stomach quiver at the thought of learning to drive. She was determined she would do it when the time arrived so Christine could come to school with the other children.

After another hour of work, Ester announced, "Time for lunch."

The children stood and marched in order to get their coats and sack lunches.

"Miss Hammon, my lunch is missing," six-year-old Susie Hoffman said, as she discovered her missing lunch bag.

"Mine's missing too," eight-year-old Dorothy Miller joined in. Two more students discovered their lunches had also disappeared.

"I'll bet some outlaw was hidin' in one of the caves across the river and snuck in here while we were gone and stole the lunches," Daniel suggested, not hiding his suspicion. The others joined him in his speculation about the missing food.

Ester looked at Susie and saw her chin quivering, and tears were rolling down her dusty face.

The thought of outlaws nearby terrified Ester, but she had to agree with Daniel, as there was no other logical explanation. She knew all of the lunches had been there when they had left for recess. Someone had been watching and seized the opportunity as they had walked away from the school.

Susie started to cry harder but was quickly consoled by the other children. Everyone was willing to share their food with the four students whose lunches had been stolen. Ester suggested they spread everything out and pretend it was a picnic, or dinner on the ground like they did on Sunday. The students thought that was a splendid idea. Ester was proud of them and their willingness to share what little they had with their classmates. The Hoffmans seemed to be the poorest family, so Ester could understand why Susie had become so upset. The lunch she brought to school might well be her best meal of the day. The thought made Ester want to cry, but she could not afford to do that in front of the students.

At the end of the day, Ester cautioned each family group to stay together and go straight home. "Tell your parents what happened, and we won't have school tomorrow, Friday. I'll let Mr. Cremwelgy know and maybe he can get word to the marshal in Del Rio. He can contact Fort Clark for troops to come patrol the area. Now, remember," she reminded them, "stay together and go straight home. I'll see you at church Sunday and we'll decide about school starting again on Monday," she told the children as they departed.

Ester worried all the way to the Cremwelgys' about the children walking or riding for miles to get home without an adult with them. When Vincent heard what had happened the next morning, he sent Hank Day to town to talk to the marshal.

All day Friday and Saturday, as Ester helped Olga with the chores, she asked herself how long she could manage to live in this wild country. She was committed through the summer. Ester did have the option to leave then as her contract was only for one year. She knew she would have to make up her mind soon so they would have time to find a replacement. On the other hand, she loved the children and was so excited to see the progress they had made this year. They had told her the teacher before her had yelled a lot and had scared the younger students half to death. One day the woman had become really angry and had thrown a chalkboard eraser from the back of the room hitting the chalkboard with a loud thud. Even the older students had slid as far down in their seats as possible. At other times she would slam a book so hard on top of her desk that it sounded like a gunshot. What if they wound up with another teacher like that? Ester worried. Well, she had some time yet to make up her mind.

On Sunday, while they were having lunch after church, a small troop out of Fort Clark, led by Lieutenant Noble Young, rode up to assure them they would be patrolling the immediate area in case some outlaw or outlaws were still there.

The lieutenant smiled favorably at Ester as though to remind her they had met once before.

"How good to see you again, Miss Hammon," he greeted her.

"Thank you, Lieutenant, I'm certainly glad to know you and your troops will be patrolling this area. It was a bit startling for the children's lunches to be stolen so quickly while we took a walk. I'm sure we will all feel much safer now that you are here watching out for us," she replied pleasantly.

"Thank you, Ma'am," he answered, and saluted to the crowd in general as they departed.

As Ester watched them ride away, she was reminded again that the

Lieutenant was indeed a handsome and charming man. He likely had a number of girls constantly chasing after him. She did not find him to be the kind of man to attract her attention in that manner. He seemed a bit cocky and too aware of his own good looks.

It was decided school could continue on Monday. Maybe with the road crew getting closer and the troops nearby they would be safe for a while, Ester reasoned.

The road crew came and went on toward the McKie Ranch, and at the end of the first week in March the road was completed.

It seemed marvelous to ride in the buggy without being bounced from side to side and having to steer the horses to miss the deep holes or rocks.

Grant made the long-awaited trip to town and picked up the new Packard automobile and the farm truck he had ordered. Although they were 1916 models, they were new.

As Grant wrote out the bank draft for his purchases, he felt a sense of pride and considered this to be the beginning of a new era in ranching and travel. He wondered who the next rancher would be to invest in an automobile or more likely a farm truck. He'd bet his best Sunday hat it wouldn't be long before another rancher followed his lead. Times were changing fast, and he intended to keep up with the pace. He felt it was a necessity if he intended to remain a successful rancher, and he certainly intended to do that.

Grant drove the sleek black automobile and Cotton drove the shiny farm truck. At first, they looked as though they had had a few drinks too many as they weaved from one side of the road to the other, but after a few miles, they seemed to get the hang of driving. When they reached the Cremwelgys', they drove into the yard honking the horns to announce their arrival.

The entire family, Ester, and all of the ranch hands within hearing distance ran to the front yard to admire the fine-looking automobile and farm truck.

"What kind is it?" Vincent called to Grant, as he came around the corner of the house admiring the gleaming black automobile.

"It's a 1916 Packard Town Car," Grant answered, with evident pride and a wide grin.

Vincent let out a low whistle. "She's a beauty," he said, as he ran his hand over the smooth, shiny paint. "What about the truck?" Vincent asked, pointing toward the bright green farm truck Cotton was still sitting in, grinning like the cat that ate the canary.

"It's a 1916 Mack Truck, made by International Motor Company. It's also a dump truck. That'll make it easy to drop off feed for the live-stock in the winter."

The children were climbing all over the truck and Olga had her head stuck inside the car window taking a closer look.

"Hop in behind the wheel, Ester," Grant suggested. "Go ahead and get in, Olga," he invited as he slid out to make room for the ladies. The two women didn't hesitate and soon the back seat was full of children.

Ester placed her hands on the steering wheel and ran them around the sleek circle. She looked through the slightly dusty windshield and dreamed about what a comfort it would be to drive to and from school on cold days or when it was raining. It was also a bit frightening to think Grant would trust her with such an expensive piece of equipment.

"Do you really think you can learn to drive this thing?" Olga asked Ester, in wonder.

Ester looked at Olga and then gave an answer filled with more confidence than she actually felt. "I'm certainly going to give it my best effort." Then she gave a nervous laugh just thinking about the adventure of learning to drive. Or was she more apprehensive about the prospect of being so close to Grant during her driving lessons? Ester often felt unsure, and even confused, about her feelings toward Grant now that she knew she would never have Will's love.

~

When Grant and Cotton neared the homestead, the honking started again. By the time they reached the yard, everyone had gathered to greet the two men with loud, excited whistles and numerous "yee-haws" and "ya-hoos!"

Corabell stood on the porch watching and listening to all of the men asking questions and making comments. Christine and Molly were already seated in the back seat of the shiny black automobile when Grant motioned to Corabell.

"Come on, Mama, get in, and see how you think you'll like riding around in this fine automobile," Grant encouraged with obvious pride.

Corabell slowly walked to the automobile where Grant stood holding the front passenger door open for her. She gently seated herself and swung her feet inside. She ran her hand over the plush upholstery and breathed in the unfamiliar smell of the fine new automobile.

"It's mighty nice. I might ride in it if it don't go too fast, but don't get no ideas about me learnin' to drive it," Corabell stated, with a solemn expression.

"Don't worry, Mama; after I really get the hang of it, I'm going to teach Ester so she can drive her and Christine to school and back. That's the main reason I bought the auto, so Christine can go to school."

Corabell gave him a questioning look but only murmured, "Hmm! Have you talked that over with Ester?"

"Yes, Ma'am, when I took her back to the Cremwelgys' she said she's willing to give it a try. She really wants Christine to go to school with the other kids and so do I."

"That's good, I've missed her. She was like a breath of fresh air in this house," Corabell said, as she got out of the automobile. She looked it over again and slowly shook her head. "I never dreamed the day would come when we would be ridin' to town in one of these things."

Grant spent every spare minute the following week practicing driving the car. The rest of the time he and several of the men had their heads stuck under the hoods, figuring out how everything on the car and truck worked. Grant quickly realized he needed to assign only two men to be drivers, as the truck was like the latest toy they all wanted to try. He finally designated Cotton and Pete, now that Pete's wrist was healed. Both men had shown a great deal of maturity since the Christmas raid. He knew, without asking, that Charlie, like Cora-bell, might ride in it if it didn't go too fast but he wasn't about to learn to drive.

After a week of practice, Grant felt confident enough to drive to the Cremwelgys' to get Ester. He was ready to start teaching her to drive. He would have to make time to ride with her and Christine to school and come back for them until Ester was ready to make the trip on her own.

Ester had to admit, if only to herself, she was glad when Grant came for her. She loved the Cremwelgys' but was ready to have her own room again and some time for herself. She also had to admit, if only to herself, that she had missed the McKie family more than she had antic-ipated and that included Grant.

Ester started around to the passenger side of the car but didn't get too far before she heard Grant call her name.

"Ester," she looked around and saw him pointing to the driver's side.

"Now?" she asked, with butterflies starting to flutter in her stomach.

"This is as good of a time as any," Grant answered, with a sly smile as if he knew what was happening to her.

Ester took her seat behind the steering wheel and listened intently to Grant's directions.

In a calm voice Grant said, "Now, it's really not hard, Ester. All you have to do is push in the clutch, pull out the choke, put the gear in neutral, and start the engine."

She looked at him as though he had been speaking in Spanish.

"Could you repeat that just a bit slower?" she asked, trying hard to concentrate on every word.

He calmly repeated what he had just said.

They managed to lurch down the lane to the main road where Ester stopped, letting the motor die. Grant patiently explained how to stop and then go without killing the engine.

She took a wide turn onto the main road. They wove along at what might be termed a snail's pace, but Grant maintained his patience. After several miles, Ester managed to hold the car fairly steady in the middle of the road, and they eventually made it to the ranch. Ester breathed a sigh of relief when she stopped behind the house. She was surprised when she heard cheering from several of the cowboys working the horses in the corral.

Sunday afternoon they went for the second lesson. Ester felt more confident, but still unsure about ever driving without Grant sitting beside her giving directions right on cue as though he knew ahead of time what she needed to know. It gave her an eerie feeling to think he seemed to know what she was thinking.

They drove mostly in silence so she wouldn't get too distracted. Finally, Grant suggested she give it a little more gas to up their speed a bit. Ester was leery but did as she was told.

Ester drove all the way to the road that ran between Del Rio and Comstock. She was genuinely stunned at how fast they seemed to travel that distance. On the way back toward the ranch, as they came to a road leading to one of the ranches, Grant would have her turn onto the road, then back up, and continue on until they reached the next road. She would repeat this driving exercise again at each ranch road. Then he told her to pretend she had forgotten something at school and needed to turn around to go back for it. The road was much too narrow to make a circular turn. Ester would turn the wheel while pulling forward and then stop. Then she would put the automobile in reverse and turn the wheel in the opposite direction to complete the maneuver.

Grant was the essence of patience, even when she made a mistake or didn't exactly follow his instructions for the second or even third time. His attitude surprised her, knowing how quickly he could lose his temper when his orders were not promptly carried out.

They finally headed back to the ranch. A couple of miles past the Cremwelgys' road, a huge wild hog suddenly appeared in the road only a few feet in front of the car. The animal looked as startled to see the huge machine bearing down on it as Ester was to see the hog rooted to the spot. Ester jerked the steering wheel to the right, and they seemed to fly off the road. Instead of slowing down, in her excitement, she pressed the accelerator and they picked up momentum as they bounced over the rough ground. Ester could hear the brush scraping along the sides of the car in that high-pitched screeching tone the offending branches made. She was horrified to think of the damage they were doing to Grant's new automobile.

"Ester! Put your foot on the brake!" Grant almost yelled.

Ester heard his words but couldn't seem to remember exactly what to do as they flew past trees and more brush. The car bounced and lurched as Ester tried to regain control over the runaway machine. A huge rock appeared just ahead and once again Ester yanked the steering wheel hard to the right. Then she noticed they were starting to slow down just as they were approaching a huge mesquite tree. Thankfully, they rolled to a stop mere inches from the tree! The motor sputtered to silence.

Ester sat transfixed. The butterflies were raging in her stomach and sweat was streaming into her eyes. Then she realized something was holding her leg up and away from the floor of the car. She looked down and saw Grant's large brown hand holding her leg in a firm grip. As calmly as she could manage, she finally said, "I think you can let go of my leg now."

"Only if you promise your foot remains on the floor," he said, in a husky voice as he slowly slid his fingers across Ester's leg just above the knee. The sensation sent a jolt of awareness through Grant like he had not experienced in a long time.

Ester caught her breath as she felt Grant's fingers loosen their vice-like grip on her leg and slide slowly to the seat. She could still feel the heat from his hand touching her leg through her skirt. Then she leaned her forehead against the steering wheel and burst into tears.

"Oh, Grant, I ruined your new car and almost killed us both!" she sobbed.

Her reaction caught Grant off guard. It took him several seconds to take in what was happening. He spoke in a calm, quiet voice. "Ester, are you hurt?"

"Nooo!" she continued to sob.

"I'm fine too, so I don't suppose you nearly killed us both," he tried to console her.

"But I'm sure I've scratched the pretty new paint and now it will look just awful!" she continued to weep.

Ester was shocked when Grant slid across the seat and pulled a clean handkerchief from his pocket. He gently reached out and turned Ester's face toward him. She was amazed at the tender touch of his big, calloused hands. He carefully blotted the tears running down each cheek. He noticed streaks of blood mingled with the tears on the left side of her face. Grant leaned forward and turned her head slightly so he could get a better look.

"You've scratched your face on some of the branches," he stated, as he dabbed at the small droplets of blood oozing from the red marks.

"I'm so sorry I ruined your new car," Ester sobbed as Grant continued to tend to her face. His touch was soothing and the look in his eyes was sympathetic, as best she could tell through the blur of tears.

Ester was taken aback when she realized he was looking at her red, swollen eyes, quivering lips, and chin. He leaned closer and kissed her gently on the lips. "It's all right, Ester. You haven't ruined my car. It was bound to get a few scratches and dings anyway," he said, and then his lips claimed hers again. This time the kiss was far more seductive with the increasing pressure that comes with passion. His arm encircled her shoulders bringing her snug against his chest. She knew he was very aware of her fully endowed breasts pressed against his firm chest. Vaguely she became aware he had dropped his handkerchief and his free hand was sliding seductively along her left leg and came to rest on her hip. She dreamily wondered if he would take his exploration of her body further.

Ester was shaken by the near accident and now Grant was assaulting her womanly senses. The first kiss had soothed her, but this kiss was evoking feelings she scarcely recognized. Nevertheless, she felt herself responding to him with equal fervor. She scarcely felt the brush of his whiskers against her delicate skin. What if they left red marks on her face? No matter. Her hands eagerly explored his firm back and taut muscular arms. She wanted to feel his bare chest as she had done once before, but this time it would be for an entirely different purpose. She breathed in his fresh scent mixed with leather, so different from Will's spicy aftershave, she mused, realizing she liked Grant's masculine scent better.

Grant knew he had to stop this madness now, but he didn't want to ever stop holding Ester and touching her as a man touches a woman he wants, needs, and cares deeply for. Yes, it was true he cared intensely for Ester. He wanted to be her protector, her lover, and the only man in her life. That was what he wanted. But what did she want? he wondered, as he loosened his hold and released her sweet mouth.

Ester felt his arms loosen their grip and his mouth retreat from hers. She wanted to protest. However, she wasn't sure how far this might go if she let him, and herself, continue their passionate kissing and touching.

They were staring into one another's eyes. Neither seemed to know just what to say or do next. Finally, Grant cleared his throat and put a little distance between them.

"We best be getting back to the ranch; it's almost suppertime," he spoke softly but as though nothing intimate or intense had passed between them.

"Maybe you better drive home."

Grant glanced at her. "No, you better drive home."

"But," she started to protest.

"It's like when the cowboys break the horses. They get bucked off a few times, but each time they dust themselves off and get right back on. If they don't the horse has won, and the cowboy will always have a fear of the next ride."

Before Ester could think of another reason for him to drive, he patiently started his instructions as to what she needed to do to get them back on the road and headed home.

As Ester drove, Grant contemplated what had just happened between them. He considered the way Ester had responded to his kisses. Was it him she was actually responding to, or was she still dreaming of Will Hudson? He started to ask her but knew she would be truthful, and he wasn't quite sure he would like what she might have to say. Perhaps it would be better not to speak of it and just let time take care of anything that might develop between them.

Chapter Eighteen

Ester, still under Grant's directions, arrived at school Tuesday morning surprised to find Lieutenant Noble Young waiting for her on the schoolhouse steps.

As Ester drove slowly up to the school, the lieutenant jumped to his feet to greet her.

"Good morning, Miss Hammon," he called out cheerfully, ignoring Grant.

"Good morning, this is a surprise to find you waiting on the school steps," Ester said, as she opened her door and got out before he could reach her to offer his assistance. She expected Grant to scoot across the seat and head for home as he had done the day before. Instead, he got out and shook hands with the lieutenant.

"I just wanted to come put your mind at ease about what happened last week when some of the children's lunches came up missing," Lieutenant Young said, keeping his gaze fastened on Ester.

"Thank you, Lieutenant, that was certainly thoughtful on your part. Where are your troops?" Ester asked, as he appeared to be the only one there.

"Oh, I sent them on ahead with the prisoners."

Ester's eyes widened when she heard him say "prisoners."

"We located two men hiding out in one of the caves near the Pecos River. We watched and then followed as they headed south. After a while it became apparent they were intending to rob the train, but the pair weren't very smart. The place they picked to pull their heist was on the bluff above the Rio Grande, so they couldn't just hightail it across the border out of our reach," the lieutenant chuckled.

"On the bluff!" Grant exclaimed and chuckled too, a bit puzzled at such an absurd plan.

"Oh my!" Ester interjected, while she listened attentively as he continued his story.

"I suppose they thought it would be easier to stop the train as it came up the long, steep grade. Naturally, it would be going quite slowly. What they apparently didn't stop to consider was they were over half a mile from the border and on top of a fifty-foot bluff," he said with a short laugh, as though he found their amateurish act amusing in the telling of their ill-conceived plan.

Grant and Ester laughed with him at the ridiculousness of such a plot.

"It turned out they were two brothers from a ranch several miles north of Juno. They said they were tired of busting their butts, beg your pardon, Ma'am," the lieutenant apologized when he realized what he had said. "Well, they were tired of working for their pa and not ever having any time off to have a little fun, so they decided to rob a train to get some cash. Then they planned to head for San Antonio to kick up their heels for a while," he chuckled again.

"One of the scouts said they had to be amateurs as they left a trail any schoolboy could follow. I'm afraid they are headed for some time in jail, which won't be much of a place for kicking up their heels. The sad part is those two boys are only seventeen and sixteen years old," the lieutenant said. His concern and a certain amount of sympathy for the boys were evident, as he talked about the trouble they had already gotten themselves into at their ages.

"Maybe the judge will go easy on them since this is the first trouble they've caused," Grant suggested.

"Maybe, but I hear Judge Jordon is pretty tough even on first-time offenders. He seems to think if they get off easy, they'll try something again. I don't necessarily agree with his way of thinking. If they get put in jail or prison for very long, they come out thinking they have learned how to get around the law, but they don't stop to think about who their teachers have been," the lieutenant concluded, with a serious look on his face. "Yes, sir, it's a shame to get off on the wrong foot so young."

"I'm afraid you're right. Sometimes prison can be the worst thing to happen instead of really teaching a person how to stay out of trouble. Could they go into the Army as an alternative so they could learn some discipline? They would also get away from the life they seem set against," Grant suggested, although he didn't know the boys. He remembered some of the foolish stunts he had pulled when he was younger but was lucky none of it led to real trouble.

"That's a good idea, Grant," Ester agreed.

"I'll talk to the two boys and, if they're willing to give the Army a try, then I'll speak to the judge on their behalf," Lieutenant Young volunteered.

"Oh, that would be so kind of you to try to help." Ester smiled at the lieutenant with obvious approval.

"I'm not so sure how much of a favor it might turn out to be if we get involved in the war in Europe," the lieutenant stated, with some apprehension.

"Do you think that's really likely to happen?" Grant asked.

"Yes, it seems almost a certainty. The thing is, they wouldn't likely send anyone under eighteen, so that would give these two some time before they would be facing the enemy."

"Do you expect to be sent if we go to war?" Ester asked as she looked at the handsome young man standing before her.

"Yes, Ma'am, I expect so, but I am ready to fight for my country if it comes to that," the lieutenant proudly stated. He continued to gaze with adoration at Ester.

"I will wish you only the best in that event," Ester smiled sweetly.

Grant felt his gut tighten when he saw the way Ester was smiling at Lieutenant Young. He just wished the man would get on his horse now and head back to Fort Clark. Grant knew he wasn't about to leave as long as this fellow was hanging around vying for Ester's attention. It was obvious he was flirting with Ester, the way he kept looking at her and giving her his charming smile. Something about men in uniform seemed to attract most women, Grant mulled over, as he watched the two.

"Say, have you heard about the big street dance they're having in Del Rio this Saturday night?" Lieutenant Young inquired.

"No, we don't hear much about what goes on in town."

"Well, since you have this fine new automobile, maybe you two could come to town Saturday night. I hear they will be having dances once a month from now until the weather turns too cool in the fall. I'd like to reserve several dances with you, Miss Hammon," Lieutenant Young invited, in an even more flirtatious manner.

Ester was caught off guard by his invitation and glanced at Grant for an answer.

Grant looked at Ester and then at the lieutenant. "Sure, that sounds like fun, don't you think, Ester?"

Ester was surprised Grant had taken the man up on the invitation but nodded her head in agreement. She wasn't particularly anxious to dance the night away with the flirty officer, but a dance did sound like fun. Maybe there would be so many people there she wouldn't see much of him, Ester surmised, as she turned to enter the school.

Saturday night after supper, Grant escorted Ester out to the freshly cleaned automobile, with fewer severe scratches than it had sounded like when Ester drove through the brush. Off they went to the big dance. He had told Cotton about the dance and said he and some of the cowboys could use the truck to go to town. Ester wasn't too surprised to see it piled full front and back.

Grant had taken precautions to be sure an adequate number of men were still at the homestead, just in the event there was any trouble.

Ester wore the polka-dotted dress she had made for Christmas and felt certain Corabell believed she was just asking for trouble. Ester couldn't help being amused when she thought about some of Corabell's superstitions.

Grant looked exceptionally handsome in his form-fitting western shirt and snug trousers. His boots were polished to perfection. He carried his Stetson hat but laid it in the backseat for the drive into town.

It was dark by the time they arrived. Electric streetlights gleamed on every corner. The town was brimming with people. They could hear the lively tune the band was playing from where they had to park, several blocks from the dance.

The main street had been blocked off from cars and buggies for a couple of blocks. The sidewalks were filled with people sitting on blankets, and the street was overflowing with dancers. People of all ages, from young children to their grandparents, were dancing. Grant took Ester by the hand and guided her into the throng as he swung her into his arms for their first dance. Ester could hear people all around greeting one another as they danced. Before long they saw the Hoffmans and then the Cremwelgys. Ester had never attended such an event but found the atmosphere relaxing. She was having a grand time dancing with Grant. Before long, some of the cowboys from the McKie Ranch cut in, and some from other ranches she had never met before were asking her for a dance.

It was over an hour before she heard a familiar voice say, "Ah, I've found you at last and am claiming the next dance."

"Good evening, Lieutenant Young. Indeed, the next dance is yours,"

Ester said pleasantly, as she felt certain she wouldn't be spending too much time with the lieutenant. Not that he particularly bothered her, but she knew he was a flirt that probably tried to make time with any female, and there were plenty to choose from tonight.

Periodically, Grant would appear for another turn and then wander off when someone cut in. The evening seemed to fly by. Ester was enjoying the outing immensely. Maybe they could come to town more often now that they had the automobile. It would be fun to go to the Opera House again, not have to rush so to get all of the shopping done, even enjoy eating at one of the new cafés, she mused, as the pleasure of being in the midst of people and the anticipation of a more social life took hold.

One of the band members announced with gusto, "Fellers, find your favorite lady for the last dance of the evening. Don't forget, we'll be having a street dance every first Saturday of the month through the summer, so come again!"

Ester felt Grant's hand on her elbow and turned to him as the band struck up a slow waltz. He pulled her to him, their bodies pressed snugly against one another, as they danced slowly. Ester knew, if anyone they knew saw how he was holding her, there would be plenty of gossip.

She cleared her throat and softly whispered, "Grant, you shouldn't hold me so close; what if someone sees us? You know there would be talk."

Grant gave a moan deep in his throat but loosened his hold on her. He started to tell her people were going to find something to talk about but knew she didn't want it to be about them. He also knew with Ester living at the ranch, in his house, they had to be discreet for the sake of her reputation. He wouldn't want to put her in a compromising situation. Grant was all too aware that some folks would be so narrow-minded they might not want to renew her teaching contract if they thought anything unsavory was going on between them. Corabell was, so to speak, their ace in the hole. With Corabell's presence at home, there would be no gossip as long as they did not appear too friendly, especially in public.

Knowing all of these things did not prevent his male instincts from wanting to hold Ester close and kiss her when he had the chance. In fact, he wanted much more from Ester but felt she was not yet ready for a new love interest. He had to be patient and give her time to get past Will's death and the feelings she had for him. How well he remembered the seemingly endless pain, the scarce feelings of hope, and the deep anger caused by the loss of someone you loved. Yes, he had to discipline himself to give Ester the time she needed to go through all of the emotions connected to an eternal loss.

Grant still had reservations about Ester being cut out to be a rancher's wife. Even the automobile might not make enough difference to entice her to embrace living twenty miles from the nearest small town. He supposed time would tell.

Ester knew her feelings for Grant were changing. She had gone from not liking much about the man she had first perceived as being arrogant and self-serving to seeing his softer side. As of late, they were getting along much better. She was glad they had not butted heads since her return to his ranch, and he had been extremely patient when giving her driving lessons. His concern for the well-being of his family had touched her. Especially the lengths he was willing to go to so Christine could attend school like the other ranchers' children. He took such special care of his mother and sister. Ester had seen his agony and anger at himself when his mother had been hurt during the raid and Ian was killed. He shouldered all of the blame. She had come to admire his strength in such situations and just the daily running of the ranch. Grant dealt with his employees on an individual basis, praised them for success, and dealt swift but fair punishment for offenses. Even the fight with Travis, as awful as it was, was what Travis deserved and more. His trial would be coming up soon, and she knew Grant wanted to see Travis spend the rest of his life in prison.

On a more personal level, Ester realized she was becoming far more attracted to Grant. Just what the *far more* entailed, she wasn't quite sure. There was something about his forceful persona that intrigued her. He was certainly an attractive man, not handsome like Will, but perhaps it was his iron will and brawny nature that attracted her. He was certainly different in that respect than any of the men she had ever dated, and that included Will.

Ester's feelings frightened her. She had loved Will and lost him all too quickly. What if she gave way to her feelings, fell in love with Grant, and things didn't work out between them? Could she withstand another heartbreak? Should she flee back to the safety of her family? Could she ever find the happiness she envisioned with a man, or would she forever rely on the whiskey to help her sleep and soothe her longing heart? So many scenarios and questions ran through her mind, and they seemed more negative than positive.

Ester realized she needed to start thinking positively again. Just because her love for Will was destroyed by the cruelty of nature didn't mean another would turn out the same way, she tried to convince herself. But it could be destroyed by many other factors, she contemplated.

She didn't want to think about it anymore tonight. The thoughts were spoiling the fantastic time she was having at the street dance. Ester gently rubbed her head to ease the tension these thoughts were provoking.

Corabell surprised Ester on her birthday when she presented her with a birthday cake piled high with white icing sprinkled with coconut. Ester had mentioned that was her favorite cake. The cake was a special treat they all enjoyed.

Ester had received a package from her family with material for a new summer dress. She had opened it earlier in the privacy of her room. She knew birthday gifts were not a tradition among ranching families.

General Pershing and his troops had returned from Mexico, leaving Pancho Villa still on the lam. Uneasy tension prevailed along the borderlands. A number of people, however, were more concerned with the looming possibility of President Wilson dragging the United States into the war in Europe.

Newspaper headlines screamed the foreboding news. Every article seemed full of grim predictions. Anywhere two or more people gathered, the talk quickly turned to the ominous threat of war.

On Monday, April 2, 1917, the bleak predictions were fulfilled. President Wilson declared war on Germany. Rumors abounded that he would call for a draft to build the American forces, which numbered less than 200,000. It only stood to reason, as the United States would have to quickly build an army; many would volunteer, but it might not be enough.

Sunday morning, the McKie family, including Grant, and Ester enjoyed a fresh springtime ride to church. The air was cool, and wildflowers covered the countryside in a profusion of colors. The purple sage had burst into brilliant hues of lavender to vibrant purple after a heavy rain earlier in the week. The craggy old mesquites had put on their lacy green leaves, which was a true sign winter had passed. It was what folks would refer to as *a glorious Sunday morning.*

As each family arrived, the talk immediately turned to the declaration of war.

They were about to enter the building when they saw the Millers' buggy headed toward them.

"I was about to think the Millers weren't comin' this mornin' as they are usually the first ones here so Charles and Albert can put the benches inside," Delmer Hoffman commented, as their buggy pulled to a stop.

Everyone looked at Wilber's and Maggie's somber faces and knew something was terribly wrong. Maggie's eyes were swollen and red from crying. Wilber's downcast expression left no doubt something distressing had occurred.

Vincent Cremwelgy was the first to reach their buggy. "What in the world has happened?" he asked, with deep concern instead of his normal cheerful greeting.

Wilber swallowed hard and dropped his head. He could not seem to bring himself to answer Vincent's question.

Maggie started to cry softly again but managed to answer Vincent's question. "Charles left to go join the Army this mornin'. We thought he was just out gettin' the team ready, but, when we come out, there he sat on his horse and told us he was leavin'. He said he weren't waitin' around for no draft, that he was going now." Her sorrow overwhelmed her as she burst into grief-stricken tears.

"Just turned eighteen yesterday so 'twernt nothin' we could do to stop him. Albert set in for us to let him go with Charles, but we told him no, not at sixteen you ain't goin' off to war!" Wilber said shaking his head, as though he could hardly believe what was happening.

Grant looked at the children piling out of the buggy and asked, "Where is Albert?"

"He's home sulkin'. I told him it won't do him no good to run off and try to join up, but I ain't so sure that's true. He ain't got no birth certificate sayin' how old he is, and he's 'bout as big as his brother, so he could lie about his age and likely they'd take him." Wilber's voice trembled. "Dear Lord, I hope not!"

Fresh tears were rolling down Maggie's round cheeks. "It just seems like yesterday Charles was a little boy chasin' around after his pa. Now he's growed up and goin' off to war," Maggie said, sadness reflecting on her normally pleasant face. "I don't know how we'll stand it if Albert goes too. We sure do need his help at the ranch, but to have two boys off fightin' a war is a terrible thing to think about."

"Come on into services," Vincent encouraged. "We'll have special prayers for Charles and also pray Albert don't follow in his footsteps."

Holding hands, the Millers followed the crowd into church services. Vincent was right, many prayers were offered for Charles' safe return and for Albert to stay put.

Ester watched the Millers as they sat together in church. Wilber kept a protective arm around Maggie's shoulder. If she started to cry, he would gently pat her and pull her head over to rest on his strong shoulder. The love the two shared touched Ester. They clung to one another for support during this difficult time. They had the kind of marriage she hoped to have someday. She had seen couples like her youngest sister and her husband pull apart during adversity. When they lost their first child at birth, they each seemed to grieve alone instead of together. The rest of the family had feared their marriage wouldn't survive. It had, but the two never seemed quite as close or as happy.

After services, as the crowd ate their lunch, the marshal's deputy drove up in a new automobile with the marshal's emblem on the side. He was a friendly-looking fellow and several of the men invited him to get out and join them for lunch. He didn't hesitate. A tall man, about six foot four inches in height, with broad shoulders, and a big smile, emerged from the automobile.

"Come on over, Buster; grab a plate and help yourself to the food," Vincent suggested.

After Buster was seated, he told the group that Travis' trial would be held on Thursday, May 24, but they better come prepared to spend the night in case it ran over to Friday. He pulled a piece of paper from his breast pocket, where he wore his badge, and read the names. "Grant McKie, Herman Ford, better known as Cotton," he said with a smile, and continued, "Pete McCorkle, Corabell McKie, Ester

Hammon, and Charles Stroud. All or some of you folks may be called to testify at the trial."

Buster looked at Ester. "Guess you better dismiss school for Thursday and Friday."

Ester nodded her head. She heard several of the older boys whoop with delight.

Ester also noticed several of the girls exchange looks of disappointment. Apparently, they would miss getting to see their friends more than the boys would. Ester realized boys enjoyed far more freedom at home than the girls. They got to go horseback riding to help with the livestock, and go hunting or fishing, while the girls were kept close to the house. They had to help their mothers with all of the domestic chores and help tend to the younger children. School was not only a place to learn but an escape from household drudgery for the girls.

Chapter Nineteen

Early Thursday morning, the six adults rode into town in the automobile. Juanita said she would spend the night with the girls.

"I sure hope they get this trial wound up no later than tomorrow," Grant commented.

"Yeah, there's too much work to get done when we're already two men short. Then for all of us to be gone for two days, we'll really be working late to catch up," Cotton agreed.

"Maybe I could scout around for some more help when I ain't needed in the courtroom," Charlie suggested.

"We sure could use two more good hands. You know the kind of men I expect to be working for me," Grant reminded him, unnecessarily.

"I reckon I do after all these years," Charlie snorted.

It took Judge Jordon and the two attorneys two hours and forty-five minutes to select a jury. Judge Jordon had warned Grant ahead of the trial, that the prosecutor often tended to be a bit long-winded. Grant had just smiled. After several pre-trial talks with the prosecutor, he felt confident in the man's ability to get the verdict Grant was hoping for, so being a bit long-winded didn't bother him in the least.

The judge gave the court a one-hour lunch break and the trial started again promptly at one o'clock.

Grant was surprised to see the number of reporters that had come to town for this trial. Of course, the draw was its connection to Pancho Villa. Every witness was asked if he or she had seen Pancho Villa present at the scene of the cattle rustling or the attempt to steal the horses. Each person answered it had been dark and they had not been able to identify anyone's features. The men that had been captured had confessed, saying they had been sent by one of Pancho Villa's captains to steal the cattle to draw most of the men away from the homestead so they could move in and easily take the forty horses Pancho Villa needed. The clincher was Cotton's testimony that he had overheard the Mexican paying Travis for his part in planning the thefts, and then Cotton had witnessed the pay-off.

Travis sat beside his attorney, stone-faced, and his expression never changed. He stared at each witness with obvious animosity.

Court was adjourned at 5:00 p.m. to resume promptly at 8:00 a.m. the next morning.

Grant, Corabell, and Ester drove the block and a half to a new hotel, where they checked in for the night. The three men decided a walk would do them good after sitting for so many hours. After securing everyone rooms, Grant told them he would treat them all to dinner in the dining room in about an hour; after dinner, they would be free for the evening. Cotton and Pete exchanged a sly grin and everyone understood they wouldn't be spending their evening reading in the lobby.

Ester and Corabell shared a room. After they freshened up, they went down to the dining room. Grant sat Ester next to him and then Corabell. The others drifted in and took their places at the table laid with a white tablecloth and napkins, stemmed goblets, and gleaming eating utensils. In the center of the table was a fresh bouquet of spring flowers.

The situation brought back memories of when she had first met Will, only they had dined at a table for two. That seemed like a very long time ago, Ester mused, as she looked around the table and at her present companions.

The food was plentiful and delicious, a pleasant change from their own cooking for Corabell and Ester.

As soon as the meal was finished, Cotton and Pete excused themselves and headed down the street toward one of the saloons. Charlie invited Corabell to join him on the front porch where they could enjoy the comfort of one of the rocking chairs and a pleasant late evening breeze.

"Why don't we go for a walk?" Grant suggested to Ester.

"Wouldn't you rather join Cotton and Pete at one of the saloons?" Ester asked, with a teasing grin.

"No, I'd rather enjoy your company on an evening stroll," Grant assured her.

They walked in silence for about half a block before Grant spoke. "Ester, I've been thinking about school being out for the summer soon, and I think it would be good for you to go visit your folks for several weeks."

Ester was taken aback by his suggestion. "That is very thoughtful, but what about continuing Christine's lessons so she'll be ready for second grade?"

"There will be plenty of time for lessons when you get back." He paused. "That is if you decide you want to come back. I realize this teaching position was not at all what you expected, and I think you need time to think things over."

Ester looked at Grant in astonishment.

"Is this a polite way of saying you don't think I am suited for the job and you don't want me back next year?" she asked with apprehension, hoping that wasn't true.

It was Grant's turn to look at her in amazement. "Of course not; I and everyone else are pleased with your teaching. I just wanted to give you a chance to decide if this is really what you want for another year. It should be a little easier now that we have a car and can come to town more often. But, Del Rio certainly doesn't measure up to the type of life you are accustomed to in Dallas."

They walked for another half a block in silence. Then Ester spoke. "Grant, I truly appreciate your offer. Perhaps it would be a good idea for me to go home for a visit and really think things over. It's certainly true," she laughed, "this was not at all what I expected when I accepted the teaching position. I must admit, it has been quite a learning experience. Little did I ever expect to learn to shoot a gun, get mixed up in a gun battle, a trial involving Pancho Villa's men and Travis, and to lose someone I loved. A lot has happened in such a short time."

Grant couldn't stop himself. When he heard the sadness in her voice and saw her eyes filled with tears he reached out and put his arm around her, gave her a gentle hug, and dropped his arm. He knew how concerned she was about risking anyone seeing them acting too friendly in public.

Ester was touched by his simple gesture of understanding.

The trial resumed promptly at 8:00 a.m. on Friday, May 25, 1917. The huge windows in the courthouse were fully open to let in the cool morning breeze. Everyone knew by mid-afternoon it would become uncomfortably warm. Judge Jordon tried to hold the prosecutor to as little oratory as possible that did not pertain directly to the present case, so the trial moved along rather quickly. At 11:37 a.m. closing statements were concluded. The judge gave the jury their final instructions.

Everyone else filed out of the courthouse relieved the trial was now in the hands of the jury. Grant felt fairly certain the jury was going to find Travis guilty on all counts against him, and he would spend the remainder of his life in prison. A reporter from one of the Houston newspapers approached Grant for an interview, but Grant firmly declined. When the reporter turned to the other men they politely walked away. When the reporter saw the stern look on Grant's face, he had the good sense not to approach Corabell or Ester.

They all went to the hotel dining room for lunch. When they finished their lunch, Grant told them he had asked for a runner to come get them when the jury returned; therefore, everyone needed to stay at the hotel.

Ester noticed Cotton's and Pete's expressions of disappointment in not being able to go down the street to the saloon, but neither man said a word. Ester and Corabell went to their room for a rest. Corabell slept, but Ester sat looking out the window at the bustling little town. It was growing steadily, but she doubted it would ever become a large city. What did it have to offer to make her want to come back? She already knew the answer. It wasn't what the city had to offer that would draw her back but Grant McKie and his family. She was afraid she might be falling in love with Grant but couldn't help wondering about his feelings toward her. Beyond a few stolen kisses, which were most pleasant and made her think about him more and more, she admitted, she had no clue as to his true feelings regarding her. Was she just someone to flirt with because she lived in his house, or did his feelings go deeper? she contemplated, but could not begin to answer her own questions. Christine had woven her way into Ester's heart. The child was so happy getting to go to school, and she had become very attached to Ester. How would it affect Christine if she didn't come back? She worried about the sweet, loving child. Ester was happy that

Christine now had more contact with other children. She saw contentment in the child she hadn't seen before.

Would she be happy staying in Dallas and having her family constantly trying to marry her off to any halfway suitable man? She did know the answer to that question. No, she definitely would not. While she loved her family dearly, with or without a man in her life, she had to make her own way in this world. There were plenty of other places she could go teach, maybe even to another state.

Ester's thoughts were interrupted by a knock on the door and Grant's deep voice saying the jury was coming back in ten minutes.

They hurried to the courthouse, along with half of the town and a growing number of reporters.

Judge Jordon called the court to order. The only noise was the swooshing sound of the overhead fans which did little good as the afternoon heat had increased to an almost unbearable degree. Most of the women opened their fans and fanned themselves in a desperate attempt to create a semblance of coolness.

The bailiff took the jury's verdict to the judge who read it in silence. Then he turned to the foreman. "Has the jury reached a verdict?" he asked in his authoritative, judicial manner.

"We have, Your Honor," the foreman answered, without hesitation.

"How say ye?" the judge asked, as he looked toward each juror.

"Guilty on all counts," the man announced loud and clear so all could hear their decision.

The courtroom burst into an uproar of cheers.

The judge banged his gavel and sternly called for *Order!*

The crowd quieted.

The judge pierced Travis with an unwavering, glowering stare as Travis stood before him. "I sentence you, John Lamar Travis, to ninety-nine years in the Texas State Penitentiary in Huntsville, Texas. Court is adjourned!" he announced, with another resounding bang of his gavel.

Travis was led from the courtroom, shackled and in handcuffs, with his head downcast.

Ester couldn't feel sorry for the man. He had done a terrible thing out of greed. Now he would have plenty of time to think about the path he had chosen.

Grant steered Ester and Corabell through the packed crowd. He managed to avoid answering any questions from the reporters that were snapping pictures and shouting one enquiry after another. At length, they reached the safety of the automobile. Cotton, Charlie, and Pete were already waiting beside the car. They were all relieved to leave the commotion behind. Once they were away from town Grant finally spoke.

"I'm sure glad that's over. Now maybe things can get back to normal at the ranch. Cotton, I'm putting you in charge of the east range, and Pete, you will be Charlie's right-hand man on the west range."

Ester could see Pete and Cotton's reflection in the rearview mirror and saw each man smile slightly. She knew they were pleased with their new assignments. She wondered how Charlie felt about the new arrangement but didn't have to wait long for an answer.

"I'm mighty glad to have Pete as my sidekick. You know these old bones and muscles seem to ache more every time I get in the saddle. It ain't long before I'm gonna be ready for my rocking chair. Just haven't decided yet where to put it," he finished, sounding a little sad.

"I know where you're going to put it," Grant said, without hesitation.

"Oh! And where might that be?" Charlie asked, in surprise.

"On the front porch of a cabin overlooking the Devils River, about half a mile downstream from the ranch house."

Charlie was quiet for several minutes as though letting the idea sink in. "That's mighty nice of you, Grant. I've got a little money put aside to help pay fur some of the cost."

"No, Charlie, this one is on me. After all, you were the one that taught me just about everything I know about ranching, and a few other things, and kept me from winding up like Travis."

"I weren't never afraid of you windin' up like Travis; that weren't your nature. I do recall a few incidents, we won't mention in front of the ladies, that might have got your backside shot full of buckshot." He chuckled at some long-ago memories.

Grant muttered in a low tone, "Yes sir, so do I."

Ester could see Grant grin, but no one pursued the conversation about Grant's escapades in his younger, wild years.

After a while, Charlie spoke again. "Well now, Corabell, reckon that cabin will be too far for you to come and sit on the front porch with me from time to time?"

Ester saw Cotton and Pete exchange an amused grin.

"I reckon I can make it that far. Hope it's close enough to the river so we can go fishin' once in a while."

Grant smiled at his mother. "Don't worry, Mama; I'll make sure there is a good path down to the river and a fishing dock, too."

Ester had enjoyed the ride home– back to the ranch was what she meant– and talk of things besides the tragedy at Christmas. Would she always dread Christmas because of what had happened last year? she questioned as they reached the McKie property.

Chapter Twenty

The last day of school finally arrived, Thursday, May 31. Ester knew the students were much too excited about being out of school for the summer to do lessons, so she planned a fun day. It was a surprise and a reward for their hard work. The girls played jacks until a winner was declared. Then the girls organized several kinds of jump rope activities. The boys ran races and played ball. And then all of the students joined in a three-legged tow sack race. Ester had baked cupcakes and cookies for special snacks. The prizes for all winners of events were writing tablets, and every student went home with two new pencils, just for participating in the games.

Ester bid each student a fond farewell for the summer. She told them she was going away for a while to visit her family. They all begged her to come back to be their teacher again. Their pleas tugged at Ester's heart. When she saw the expression on Christine's face, she was even more undecided about not returning. It was going to be a hard decision, perhaps one of the hardest she would ever have to make.

Ester, Christine, and the Cremwelgy children drove home singing to keep up their spirits. After she dropped the children at their road,

Ester knew Christine wanted to ask her more about her leaving. Ester wasn't ready to try to explain to Christine about leaving and that she might not come back, so she kept Christine singing to avoid the topic.

They had driven about a mile and a half when Ester saw the five riders appear out of the brush and block the road. They sat tall on their horses, facing the oncoming car. Ester had a moment of panic, like when the hog had wandered into the road. She started to jerk the steering wheel, which would send them flying through the brush, but remembered how close she had come to wrecking the car once before. Should she floorboard it and try to run them down in hopes of getting past the barricade they made? No, surely she would wreck the car if she tried to do that. Terror gripped her!

"Get down, Christine!" she yelled. Christine did not question Ester's demand and instantly hunkered down on the floor of the car.

Ester finally made a last-minute decision to avoid immediate disaster. She put her foot on the brake and managed to stop the automobile mere inches from the horses. The five men managed to stay sitting astride the frightened animals as they whirled and danced away from the oncoming noise, tossing their heads, and snorting wildly in fear of the unfamiliar object. One rider was almost bucked off as his horse jumped and reared, but he quickly brought the animal under control. Ester could hear the horses' snorts of protest above the constant whir of the engine. She had to admire the men's courage and horsemanship in not giving up their position in the face of the oncoming automobile.

Ester was breathing as though she had just run up a steep hill as she glared at the five mounted riders. Instantly she knew who they were. She had the uncanny feeling the imposing man in the middle was the notorious Pancho Villa.

The five men stared back at her with controlled contempt. They each wore the traditional large sombrero and white shirt, with the single crossed bandolier filled with bullets. Their gun belts held two holsters tied to their legs over their chaps.

Clammy sweat covered her skin in the heat of the scorching afternoon sun. A chill ran through her entire body as she faced the five imposing figures.

They just sat staring at one another. No one moved. The faint sound of several birds in the brush was now the only sound that broke the silence besides the purr of the motor.

The man in the middle politely tipped the edge of his sombrero. He spoke in a bold, daring voice with a heavy Mexican accent.

"I am Pancho Villa! I have a message for jur man, McKie!"

Ester wanted to set him straight that McKie was not her man but thought better of the idea. It was likely better to just listen and hope he would let her and Christine go without harming them. The dread of what could happen made Ester feel sick to her stomach.

"Tell McKie I still have need of his fine horses and cattle," he said with a big grin. "Ju may hear many bad things about me, but do not believe all ju hear. I am a fair man! A man of honor! I will pay McKie a fair price for his horses and cattle." He smiled with pride. "Now, I no longer fight, but will build un rancho muy grande like McKie's! I will send one of my men in a few days to tell him what I need and make arrangements to get the cattle and horses to Meh-hee-co."

Pancho Villa gave her another big grin and spread his arms wide as though to embrace someone. "There is no reason McKie and I cannot be *amigos*, no?"

Ester still sat staring at the man. She didn't know exactly what to do next. Should she say something or just nod her head?

"Do ju understand my wishes?" Pancho Villa asked, in a forceful manner.

Ester nodded her head and simply said, "Yes, I understand."

The five men turned their horses and disappeared into the brush toward the river.

Ester leaned her head on the steering wheel and took several deep breaths.

"Are they gone?" she heard Christine ask hardly above a whisper, with a slight quiver in her voice.

"Yes, they're gone," Ester answered, in a shaky voice of her own.

"Are you scared?" Christine whispered.

Ester looked at the child still hovering in the floorboard.

"Yes, I was scared, but now they're gone."

Christine resumed her seat. She looked at Ester, nervously batting her eyes, showing her anxiety. She continued to watch Ester for several moments; then she spoke. "You're really brave, Ester," she said, and gave Ester a weak smile.

When Ester drove into the ranch yard a bit faster than normal, several of the men turned to look in her direction. Ester sent Christine into the house so she could find Grant.

Ester slammed the car door and walked briskly toward the corral.

"Where's Grant?"

One of the ranch hands pointed toward one of the horse barns. She almost ran until she reached the open door and entered calling his name.

"Down here," she heard Grant answer.

Ester watched as Grant fastened the gate to one of the stalls. Ester almost ran toward him.

Even in the dim light of the barn, Grant could see the color had drained from her face.

He started toward her in long strides. "What's happened? Has something happened to Christine?" he asked, alarmed.

Ester paused to catch her breath. "She's all right," Ester managed to answer. She continued panting for breath.

"He stopped us on the way home!" she gasped.

"He, who?" Grant asked, confused.

Ester's face was almost white, and her eyes were unusually large.

Grant knew something was terribly wrong or Ester wouldn't be in such a state, but what? He searched her face for some clue.

Grant reached out and took Ester by her shoulders as she looked like she might collapse. "What happened, who stopped you?" he asked again, more intensely.

"Pancho Villa!" she managed to answer as she slumped against Grant.

He held her firmly to steady her.

"Pancho Villa!" he repeated, almost in disbelief. "What the devil is he doing over here and stopping you?" he asked eagerly. Grant felt the anger beginning to boil within. The man was relentless. Would Pancho Villa forever be a rock around their necks? He couldn't remember being this mad since the day he found out Travis was behind the Christmas raid. He had shown Travis what happened when he crossed him. Now he would have it out with Pancho Villa as well. Grant would not tolerate any more interference from Villa or his men. Someone had to convince the man that he was not welcome, nor his business, at any price.

Before he could move, Ester told him about the message. "Villa told me to tell you he still needs some of your fine horses and cattle. He also said he is an honest man and will pay you," Ester finished with a slight chuckle.

Grant let his temper fly and cursed like she had not heard since the fight with Travis. She didn't say a word about his language but wanted to calm him before he did something stupid. She soon realized she was too late.

Grant sat Ester on a nearby bale of hay and quickly retrieved his favorite horse, Smoky. He didn't even bother to saddle Smoky but mounted him bareback and shot out of the barn at a gallop.

When Ester realized what he was doing, she ran after him, yelling at the top of her voice.

"No! No! Grant, please don't go alone! Please don't go alone!" she yelled after him, in a panic.

Grant was so angry he rode like the devil was nipping at his heels.

Ranch hands came running from every direction. They were gaping at Grant's retreating figure and asking Ester what had happened to put Grant into such a frenzy.

"There were five men in the road; one was Pancho Villa, but no telling how many more might be waiting by the river! Grant only has one pistol with him," she answered, in a panic at the thought of what could happen to him. Why did he have to be so hot-headed at times?

Pete quickly took charge, gathering ten men to ride with him. "Arm yourselves to the teeth. We have to go catch Grant before they kill him!" he shouted, as men sprang into action.

In a matter of minutes, the yard was almost empty and quiet. Ester did not like the feeling. It reminded her of Christmas night before the raid. There were a few men left behind. They had taken up positions around the homestead, prepared for trouble.

Ester walked slowly to the house. Now she would have to tell Corabell what had happened.

After Ester calmed herself, she went to find Corabell. She explained what had taken place and saw the worried look on Corabell's face.

"I knew somethin' bad had happened. Christine told me some mean men had stopped you on the way home." Corabell gave a deep sigh. "Sometimes I wonder if we will ever have a peaceful life here. It seems one thing after another has happened ever since Allen and I first started this ranch. He kept tellin' me that things would settle down soon, but I guess *soon* hasn't got here yet."

Grant had ridden his horse through the tall sagebrush. When he reached a small clearing, he could plainly see Pancho Villa and about a dozen men. Grant knew Villa was expecting him. Lookouts were posted to avoid any unwanted surprises.

"Villa!" Grant called as he dismounted. "We need to talk!"

Villa slowly walked toward Grant, leaving no more than six feet between them when he stopped. "Señor McKie, it is good to see ju," he said in too friendly of a manner to suit Grant.

Villa was a tall, robust man with a lighter complexion than most Mexicans. His long but neatly trimmed mustache and strong features made him almost handsome. His piercing dark eyes made Grant feel as though Villa could look into his soul. He wore the traditional white shirt, dark trousers, a large Mexican sombrero, and a double bandolier. His gun belt held one pistol.

Grant thought of several responses he would like to make but knew better than to push his luck in this situation. Grant stared at the man for several seconds before speaking. "Villa, I want you to understand that you and I have no business dealings now or ever. After what you pulled at Christmas and today, how could you think I would ever want to do business with you? Leave me and my family in peace!"

Villa's expression grew grim. "I heard about the attack on jur ranch at Christmas and am glad jur dear mother was not killed."

Before Grant could respond he went on.

"Let me ask ju, McKie, do jur men always follow jur orders?"

Grant was somewhat startled by his question. "No, not always; why do you ask?"

"We have something in common. My men do not always follow my orders either. Ah," he sighed. "Just as ju, I am blamed for many things of which I know nothing," he said, as he spread his arms and shrugged.

Grant stared at the notorious man standing before him. "I see," Grant answered, knowing what the man said could be true. Perhaps he should give him the benefit of the doubt, but he still didn't intend to do business with Villa. "But you and I still have no business dealings. I have all of the business I can handle on this side of the border!" Grant stated with such force no one could mistake his meaning.

When Pete and the others reached the spot near the Devils River where they had trailed Grant, they dismounted and made their way quietly through the thick brush. They expected Villa would have lookouts posted, so they had to be watchful. The men fanned out in pairs and took positions where they could hopefully get clear shots if necessary. Pete had crept closer so he could tell what was going on and try to see how many men they were up against. He counted sixteen in plain view but suspected there were more.

Grant and Pancho Villa stood to one side of the group, and Pete could tell by their stance they were not just passing the time of day. He surveyed the men standing nearby. They appeared to be paying little attention to Villa and Grant, but Pete's gut feeling told him that was not the case.

Pete couldn't make out what they were saying but could sense the tension between the two men. Suddenly Grant whirled, mounted his horse, and said something as he pointed toward Mexico. Then he turned his back and rode toward the road. Pete held his breath as he saw Pancho Villa's face and knew he was spitting mad. Pete half expected to see him or one of his men draw and shoot Grant in the back. He lay still, holding his breath, hoping Grant would make it to the road. Then they could all ease on out of here without a confrontation.

Pete had started to ease back when gunshots erupted from the cliffs on the far side of the river. He watched as several of Villa's men fell to the ground. Pete and the others held their fire trying to figure out what was happening. Why would anyone be firing from the cliffs? Pete strained to get a better view of the clash near the river.

The Mexicans ran for their horses and fled toward Mexico. Several more shots rang out from the cliffs. Gunfire was returned from Villa's fleeing men. Then silence!

Pete watched as a hand waving an almost white hat appeared above a boulder. A man called out, "Texas Rangers!" One man stood slowly, and two more men appeared nearby.

"Hold your fire; we're coming across!" the first man to stand called out.

The men held their positions. He heard Grant's voice behind him. "Don't shoot, it's me," he whispered, as he took his place alongside Pete.

"Everybody, stay down," Grant called just loud enough for the others to hear.

"How did you know there was anybody besides me here?" Pete asked.

"I know you men. I knew a bunch of you would be hot on my tail when I heard Ester screaming at me to not go. That's why I didn't take time to saddle my horse. I didn't want to put anyone else in danger."

Pete chuckled. "Well, damnit, Grant, this wasn't one the smarter things you've ever done!"

"I'm afraid you're right. Thanks for coming," he answered, and Pete could tell he really meant it. Grant could be headstrong and occasionally fly off half-cocked, like today, but he appreciated the loyalty of his men.

The three men had forded the river and now their badges were in plain view. Grant, Pete, and the others stood up to greet the three men.

They were a disheveled-looking crew. Their hats and clothes had all seen better days. It was hard to exactly distinguish the colors of their clothing as they were all covered with a thick layer of dirt. Pete soon discovered, if he stood downwind, the smell they carried was a mixture of sour sweat, unwashed bodies, and clothes, mixed with the breath of a buzzard.

Pete casually changed positions in an attempt to avoid as much of the pungent odor as possible. He wondered why they hadn't taken time at some point to take a bath in the river and at least attempt to wash some of the grime out of their clothing. He supposed they were like old Apache, a half-breed cowboy that had been a scout for the Army. At least he claimed to be half-Indian, although it was hard to tell by his looks. He had worked at the ranch for about ten years now and lived on the far northwest corner of the ranch. Apache apparently had gotten so used to his own pungent smell, that it didn't seem to bother him in the least. Good thing he lived alone, Pete thought, as the introductions to the three rangers were completed.

The rangers said they had spotted Pancho Villa a little earlier in the day and witnessed him stopping the woman in the car. They were just waiting to see what he was up to.

Grant told them about the problems they had experienced with Villa and his men. He added in a matter-of-fact tone, "I told him we have no business deals, ever, so he might as well hightail it right back to Mexico and stay there. He didn't look happy, but I told him if I ever caught any of his men on my property again, they would either be killed or arrested, no questions asked. I think he got the message."

One of the rangers spat a wad of tobacco juice and laughed. "Sounds pretty plain to me. We gonna track 'em to be sure that's exactly where they go and don't cause no more trouble on the way."

"I'd like to know why you started shootin' after Grant left?" Pete asked.

"We wanted them to know we were around, and it was time for them to vamoose!" one of the others answered, as he and the other ranger rolled a cigarette.

The first man spoke again. "We was just sittin' up there dividin' 'em up amongst us when we seen this feller ride up," he nodded his head toward Grant.

"Don't you think the odds were a bit in their favor?" Grant asked. He looked the three over again. Each wore two holsters and carried rifles that Grant felt certain were all fully loaded.

The three men laughed.

"I'd say our odds were a bit better than yours," one answered, as he pinned Grant with a stare, and they all laughed again.

"We don't think in terms of the odds, and, besides, we've already left three of them dead over by the river."

"Well, let's get going, don't want to lose track of 'em in the brush," the first ranger said.

"We'll take care of the three over by the river," Pete offered.

The third ranger who had not spoken gave a short snort of laughter. "We do a lot of things but burying dead outlaws ain't one of 'em. Ain't got time."

With that said, the three mounted their horses and soon disappeared through the brush in the direction of Mexico.

Ester could not bear to drag herself off the front porch. She felt compelled to watch for the riders to return. It seemed like they had been gone for an eternity when, eventually, she saw the group coming down the road. She didn't think it was any of Pancho Villa's men as they were riding at a leisurely pace. To her relief, as they grew nearer, she could identify Grant leading the procession. Ester wasn't sure if she wanted to run and hug him and hold him close or bop him over the head with Corabell's rolling pin for being so hot-headed and reckless.

At supper the story of how they had met the three Texas Rangers that were keeping an eye on Pancho Villa and his men and what Grant had told Villa was all the talk. Ester felt relieved to know some Texas Rangers were in the area. They had a big reputation for keeping law and order. Now that they knew about the problems Villa and his men had caused, maybe they would be especially watchful about what he was doing.

Grant finally looked at Ester and gave her that cocky little grin. "I'm sure Villa knew I was coming," he said, still looking at Ester.

"What makes you think that?" Charlie asked.

"He could probably hear Ester screaming at me to not go," Grant answered, with a chuckle.

Ester tried to give him her stern teacher look but failed miserably.

They all laughed with relief, thankful the incident had turned out much better than the Christmas encounter.

After everyone had retired for the evening except Grant and Ester, she decided to go sit on the front porch for a while, in hopes she would soon feel sleepy. She had given up her bedtime nightcap a couple of months earlier. She didn't want to rely on it to help her sleep.

The night air felt cool against Ester's skin. It seemed millions of stars covered the night sky in brilliant profusion. A full moon was peeping over the eastern horizon. Ester swung slowly and listened to the nightly chirping of the katydids. Occasionally, they became so loud the crescendo of their sounds was almost deafening.

In two days, Grant or someone would take her to catch the train to Dallas. She was excited but apprehensive all at the same time. When she left, would she ever see this place or these people again? Once she was away and could think more clearly, what would be her decision about returning to teach another year at Twelve Mile School? It wouldn't just be the school she would return to but this ranch, this family, and Grant.

Chapter Twenty-One

The morning Ester left the ranch, it took an hour to say goodbye to all of the ranch hands she had gotten to know so well and especially to Corabell, Molly, and Christine. It touched her heart when Christine clung to her and tried to get her to promise she would come back. Somehow the child had realized that Ester might not return.

"I promise I will write you a letter as soon as I get to Dallas and tell you all about what I'm doing there. Then you can write to me and tell me all about what's happening here," Ester tried to reassure the little girl that she cared and would at least keep in touch by letters.

Grant picked up her two bags and carried them to the car. As Ester sat in the passenger seat Grant leaned his head in the window.

"Don't you want to drive to town?" he asked, with a teasing grin.

"No, that's all right. You can drive."

"Not me, Pete's going to drive you to the train."

Ester felt a moment of disappointment, but she wasn't quite sure why. Maybe it was because she had planned to talk to him about what had happened with Pancho Villa and try to get a promise out of him to be more careful about the things he did. After all, a lot of people depended on him as the head of the family and this ranch. She knew his temper got the best of him at times, but he really needed to learn to control it better. Why was she even considering such a talk? He hadn't seemed to listen to much of what she had told him in the past.

Or, was she disappointed at not getting to spend any more time alone with Grant? Whatever the reason, she was reluctant to give that possibility much thought.

In a low voice, Grant murmured, "Have a safe trip, Ester. We'll miss you around here."

Their faces were mere inches apart.

"Will you now? I would have thought you would be glad to be rid of me trying to tell you what to do at times."

"I think that's what I will miss. Not that I listen very well, but I will still miss you trying to boss me around," he said with that sly, teasing smile.

Grant leaned closer and brushed her lips lightly with his. Ester felt an intense longing, an ardent desire for a more intimate kiss. She didn't have to wait, as the kiss became more forceful. She instantly felt the heat it created rush through her body. Oh, Grant, she thought, what a temptation you are to me at times. Could it be true that I am falling in love with you in spite of our vast differences? Could we really become compatible over the years? She wished this kiss could last forever.

Grant savored her delicate scent and the tender feel of her lips. He wished they were alone for this kiss, but it was not possible. Even if he had driven her to the train, he felt certain she would not have permitted this kind of kiss in such a public place.

Pete whistled a tune as though to warn them he was near.

Grant ended the kiss but moved his mouth to her ear and whispered, "I hope that wasn't a goodbye kiss but a see you in a few weeks kiss."

Before Ester could think of anything to say, Pete opened the car door and Grant straightened up to remind Pete to pick up the mail and cash the payroll check.

Grant stood watching the car as it became smaller and smaller in the distance and then disappear as it topped the ridge on the other side of the creek. He wondered if he should have said more to Ester about coming back. Perhaps he should have said more about his feelings for her, not just as a teacher and a way for Christine to attend school. He could teach one of the older men to drive, and he could take Christine to school and Mama to town.

He believed Ester was getting over the loss of Will. Perhaps she was ready to look at another man in the same way, a man to love and to love her. Grant was fairly certain that he wanted to be that man.

The train trip was hot and dusty. They arrived two hours late. Ester felt like a wilted rose when she stepped off the train to greet her parents. They didn't seem to notice how exhausted she looked. Ester was certain she must look a mess, but their eager welcome soon lifted her spirits. She was anxious to get home to a warm bath and clean clothes.

Home, she reflected; that sounded strange after being away for nearly a year. Somehow, she had come to think of the McKie Ranch as her home, although she was actually a guest. The idea that now she was home seemed strange, she decided, as they exited the train station.

Ester's entire family awaited her at her parents' home. It was wonderful to see her three sisters, brothers-in-law, and especially her five nieces and the newest addition, a nephew, at last.

The relaxing bath and clean clothes were put on hold.

They besieged her with questions about teaching at Twelve Mile School and living on a ranch. Ester had a strong sense they held a nostalgic, romantic view about living on a ranch and they perceived it to be like life in the Old West. Well, in many ways it still was like the

Old West, but they would not hear about how she spent Christmas night shooting at bandits and being shot at by Pancho Villa's outlaws. They would not hear about being stopped on the road home just last week by the notorious man either.

She did entertain them with stories about living with the Cremwelgys in very cramped conditions, to their apparent satisfaction, after several hours. She made sure they understood what a wonderful family the Cremwelgys were and how they had helped her adjust to such a strange new way of life. Then she described the vast contrast in living conditions when she moved to the McKie Ranch. They all hooted at her story about learning to drive, almost wrecking Grant's new car and scratching the shiny new paint. She did not tell them about the seductive little episode that occurred along with that particular experience. She told them about Dr. Will Hudson, as she had written about him in a number of letters, and what a tragedy for him to die so young. She did not tell them she had fallen in love with Will but led them to believe they had developed a special friendship because they both missed the more cultural life they had left behind.

There were many stories, questions, and more stories. Eventually, they seemed satisfied and pleased to see how well Ester had adjusted to such rural, unfamiliar conditions, and now she was home again, safe, surrounded by her loving family.

Ester fell into bed at about ten o'clock, utterly exhausted. Sleep came immediately. No dreams to disturb her rest. She awoke just as the grandfather clock in the front entry hall struck three. She was hot, sticky with sweat. The air felt stale and oppressive. There seemed to be no breeze at all like out in the country. City noises invaded her senses, distant sirens wailed, the rumble of a train with its forlorn-sounding whistle, and even an occasional automobile purred past her bedroom window at this late hour. Ester sat on the side of the bed for a long time, listening to the nightly noises of the city. It was strange to her now. The sultry air was equally as strange. Even the smell of the city held a mild offensiveness.

She felt a pang of longing to be back at the McKie Ranch where the nights were cool, the smells fresh, and the singing of the katydids were far more pleasant than the rude, intrusive sounds of the city. She longed to be back with her other family, except they weren't really her family. Why did she miss them so much already? Why did she long to walk to Grant's office and pour herself half a glass of whiskey so she could sleep? Why did she still feel the touch of his lips on hers and so strongly imagine she could smell the fresh fragrance of his bath soap while they danced? Tears of longing rolled gently down her warm cheeks and dripped silently onto her white cotton nightgown.

Six days after Ester left, Pete smiled when he picked up the mail in town and saw a letter addressed to Miss Christine McKie, Box 41, Del Rio, Texas. He noticed the return address was Miss Ester Hammon, 621 Peach Street, Dallas, Texas.

Pete was rewarded again when he returned to the ranch and pulled to a stop near the big oak tree in the front yard and waved the letter to get Christine's attention. She came running to the truck wide-eyed and smiling from ear to ear.

She took the letter from Pete as though it were a delicate object that might easily break.

"This is my first letter ever!" she beamed with excitement. "I've got to go find my daddy so we can read it," she said, and started at a full run toward one of the horse barns where she knew her daddy spent a great deal of time.

"Be careful, Christine; remember to stop at the door and call out to see if he's there," Pete reminded her as she ran.

She waved her arm to indicate she had heard him. Grant, and all of the men for that matter, had taught her to not go running into one of the horse barns in the event some of the more skittish horses were out of their stalls. Her high-pitched child's voice might frighten one of the horses.

Christine paused at the barn door and called out as she had been taught.

"Hold on a minute, Christine, let me put this horse in the stall," Grant answered her.

She was bubbling with excitement and called out to him. "Daddy, guess what, I got a letter from Ester! It's my first letter ever! Will you help me read it?"

"Sure, baby," Grant answered his excited daughter, as he walked toward her.

"Let's go sit under that tree and find out what all Ester has to tell you."

Christine carefully opened the letter and pointed out to Grant where Ester's return address was on the envelope. In her shrill little girl voice, she read, "Miss Ester Hammon, 6-2-1 Pe-ach St-r-e-et. What does that word mean, Daddy?"

"In towns and big cities, every street has a special name and a number on the house so people will know how to find you," Grant explained.

"Oh! Dal-las, Texas," she continued. Christine gently removed the pages from the envelope and handed them to Grant.

"You read it this time. You read lots better than me."

Grant took the three pages from Christine and began to read Ester's near-perfect printing.

Christine listened attentively.

Grant came to the last few lines, "Be sure to say hello to everyone for me. I hope your grandma, Molly, and your daddy are all doing well. I do miss all of you very much. My Best Regards, Ester."

Christine gave Grant a quick kiss on the cheek. "Thank you, Daddy. Can I go show it to Grandma and Molly?"

Grant returned her kiss. "Sure, but you'll have to tell them what Ester wrote."

"I know, Daddy." Christine paused and looked at Grant with her childlike inquisitive expression. "Why can't Grandma read?"

"She didn't get to go to school like you do. You can still practice reading to her and Molly and if you don't know all of the words you can ask me later," he suggested, with an affectionate smile.

"Did you get to go to school to learn to read, Daddy?"

"Yes, I went to school through the eighth grade. I hope you get to go all the way and maybe on to college too," Grant said warmly.

Christine eagerly asked, "Then could I be a teacher like Ester?"

"If that's what you want to be, you could. Now go read your letter to Grandma and Molly. I've got to get back to work."

"Okay, Daddy," she answered, as she skipped toward the house waving the precious letter. By suppertime, most of the men at headquarters had heard all about what Ester wrote in Christine's first letter ever.

Immediately after supper, Christine brought a pencil to Grant's office. She sat on his knee so he could help her answer Ester's letter. Then she suggested he write something too. Grant thought about the things he would like to tell Ester. He rather regretted not saying some of those things before she left, but he wasn't at all sure about writing them in a letter. He assured Christine he would write something later but had some other work to attend to first.

Ester felt a surge of excitement when Christine's letter arrived on the Friday of her second week away from the ranch. She opened it and could easily read Christine's neat printing. Her short, choppy sentences were amusing, but Ester got the gist of what Christine was saying. Then, much to her surprise, there was an additional page in Grant's bold cursive handwriting. Ester's heart seemed to jump as she read his message.

Dear Ester,

It was very kind of you to take time to write to Christine. She was so excited about receiving her 'first letter ever,' she pointed out to everyone. She has passed along your greeting to everyone as you requested. Things are going smoothly, at least for now. The Texas Rangers came by last week just to check if there had been any more trouble. There has not. Ester, I want you to know we all truly miss you too and do hope you will come back here to continue teaching. I even miss having you here trying to guide me in the right direction, although I know sometimes I act like a balky old mule. Maybe in time I will improve with your patient supervision.

With Deepest Regards,
Grant

Ester read and reread Christine and Grant's letter, especially the part Grant had written. Was he really trying to say that he actually missed her and wanted her back for more reasons than to continue her teaching career? She was afraid to try to read too much into his statement. She would mull over his words for hours and still never reach a clear conclusion.

Although Grant had made romantic advances toward her, it might have just been a passing fancy for him. Her thoughts would return to their encounter in the car during her driving lesson and she felt there was more to his feelings than just a flirtatious affair.

As the days passed, she was entertained by old friends, introduced to several eligible men, and escorted to a number of trendy functions by one or another of the gentlemen. Not one captured her interest beyond the evening they spent together. One man did call several times for a second date, but she was always busy and truthfully, she was glad. She knew he was not the kind of man she was interested in as a potential husband.

Ester concluded and finally admitted it was only Grant McKie that interested her as a potential husband. With that realization firmly in place, her decision was made to return to the McKie Ranch and teach at Twelve Mile School for another year. That should be sufficient time to see if she and Grant were truly meant for one another. A year would give enough time for their relationship to take on a special meaning, and time for him to fall in love with her.

How strange her life was turning out. When she had first gone to teach at Twelve Mile School, she had marveled that people could live in such rural, rustic conditions and be happy with their lives. Now that was the life she was hoping for.

Ester wrote a letter to Grant and included a page to Christine.

Dear Grant,

I have made my decision to return to teach at Twelve Mile School for at least one more year. Perhaps, during that time, I can work on getting you on the right path more often. Ha, Ha. Please, have someone meet me at the noon train next Sunday. Although it has only been three weeks, it seems I have been away much longer. I need to get Christine started on her lessons so she will be ready for second grade when school starts.

Sincerely,
Ester

Ester contemplated a more familiar ending to her letter but could not decide on what would be appropriate. She didn't want to appear too forward, so she finally settled for the traditional closing.

When Grant read Ester's letter with the news she would be returning in a few days, he couldn't quite suppress a smile. He hoped this was a sign that she had missed him a little more than the others, but he supposed time would tell.

Grant drove to town on Sunday morning to meet the noon train.

It arrived on time, and, when he saw Ester step down from the train, oh, what a picture she made! He looked closely and saw she had a new hairstyle. It was cut much shorter, just above her shoulders, with soft waves ending in large, loose curls. She wore an attractive white, wide-brimmed hat trimmed with a peach-colored ribbon and matching flower. He could see she had bangs that swept in a big wave to one side. He had always liked long hair on women, but he had to admit the new hairstyle looked exceptionally striking on Ester. Her dress matched the peach color on the hat and had lots of lacy stuff on the top. It looked pretty fancy for traveling to him, but then, he certainly was no authority on women's fashions. He just knew Ester looked stunning to him. He also noticed several other men taking a second look too, so he quickly walked forward to greet her.

Ester had spotted Grant in the crowd before the train rolled to a stop, billowing black smoke in the process. Grant stood out not only for his height but his presence as a man. He was one of those men that people noticed even if they didn't know him personally. He embodied the part of being a successful rancher in appearance and demeanor, without swagger or bragging.

Grant stepped forward to accept Ester's two bags as the porter handed them down to him.

He gave Ester an approving smile. "You changed your hair while you were away," he stated wryly.

"Yes, it is much cooler but not quite as easy to manage. It takes a little longer to fix but not that much," Ester answered, not sure if he liked it or not.

"It looks nice," he said, as they walked toward the car. He placed her bags in the back seat and turned to her.

"Come on, let's go have lunch at the new café across the street," he suggested, with a nod of his head in the direction of the eating establishment.

In a gentlemanly manner, Grant took Ester's elbow to escort her across the street.

His firm grip was reassuring to Ester as the street was filled with potholes since the recent rain.

"We had two hard rains last week, and it really messed up the streets," Grant commented, as he guided her in a zigzag pattern to miss the worst potholes.

"That's wonderful; I could tell everything looked much greener, and the purple sage is in full bloom. The sage is a spectacular sight when it blooms. I often wonder how those pale green bushes can burst into such brilliant color after a good rain. It's a shame they don't look like that all of the time," Ester mused.

"Yes, it is quite a sight," Grant agreed.

They enjoyed a leisurely lunch and drive back to the ranch. Ester told him about her visit to Dallas. She described some of the entertainment she enjoyed. She also told him the city seemed strange to her now. Ester described the oppressive heat and no fresh breezes, especially at night. She talked about the noise of the sirens, trains, and automobiles.

When she paused, Grant looked at her with a sly grin. "Did you meet any eligible men?" he asked, in his teasing tone.

"Well, yes, I did. In fact, I met several, but no one that really interested me."

"Are you still looking for another Will Hudson?"

Ester was shocked at his question. "I don't know. I don't think there is another Will Hudson for me to find."

"What kind of man are you looking for then?" Grant boldly asked.

Ester did not like the inquisition of this conversation. She thought quickly and then answered. "Maybe I'm not looking for any kind."

Grant wasn't too pleased to hear her say that, but then he may have been prying too much into her personal feelings.

Their conversation turned to more common matters as they continued toward the McKie Ranch. "Tomorrow, we will be rounding up a large herd of cattle and taking them to the cattle pens in Del Rio, Tuesday, to be shipped east. Wednesday morning, we'll receive a large shipment of sheep and should return to the ranch by late afternoon," Grant said.

"How long does it take to get the cattle to town?"

"We start at sunup and get there just before dark."

"Can't you hurry them along a bit?" Ester asked.

Grant laughed. "Cows have two speeds: slow, and full run. We much prefer slow, even if it does take all day."

"What about the sheep?"

"Same story," Grant chuckled.

"Don't worry about most of us being gone overnight. The Texas Rangers come by about once a week to check on things. They manage to get to the ranch about suppertime and usually bunk down for the night. I'll leave Charlie and five men at headquarters just in case anything happens, but things have been quiet since we last saw Pancho Villa."

"Good," Ester answered, shuddering as she thought about her own, and especially Grant's, encounter with the villainous outlaw.

At the crest of the hill overlooking the homestead, Ester gasped at the beauty of the scene before her.

"Oh, Grant, please stop for a moment and let me look," she exclaimed, with obvious admiration reflected in her voice.

The hillsides and the valley were covered with an array of brilliant hues of light lilac to deep purple. It was as though the sage had put on its Sunday best to impress Ester and welcome her home. The grass was lush and green. Cattle and sheep grazed peacefully along the banks of the meandering stream that glistened in the afternoon sunlight. The panoramic view before her looked like a fine painting.

"It's hard to imagine this country could be so beautiful until you see it," Ester exclaimed, with obvious appreciation for the splendor of the landscape.

Grant chuckled. "Enjoy it while it lasts. It will be gone in a few more days. But, as you know, it will come again after the next good rain."

When they pulled to a stop beside the house, Grant reached over and took Ester's hand. He gave it a gentle squeeze as he smiled at her. "I'm really glad you're back, Ester," was all he said.

The way he said it and the intimate touch of his hand excited Ester. She hoped he really meant it as an expression of his personal interest.

The next morning, Ester started Christine on her lessons. Christine was thrilled to have Ester back and relished doing her homework. At times, Molly would sit and watch them for a while. Then she would lose interest and wander off to swing or occupy one of the rocking chairs in the living room. Ester could hear her singing softly in the distance.

Ester felt a strange restlessness with Grant away. The evenings seemed especially long as Corabell and the girls went to bed by 8:00 p.m. It wasn't quite dark and much too early for Ester to go to sleep. She would read, but she missed the conversations she and Grant had previously shared in the evenings.

Wednesday evening, just before supper, Ester saw the men and a herd of white sheep come over the rise. Soon she realized the three Texas Rangers were riding along with them.

She hurried to the kitchen to warn Corabell.

"Got plenty, made a big pot of stew and two pans of cornbread. That should feed that hungry bunch," Corabell stated, unperturbed.

Ester could see Grant was dead tired and did not try to detain him to visit with her after supper. He was in bed before Corabell and the girls. Ester sat alone again, reading until her eyes began to blur. Tonight, for the first time in months, she walked to Grant's office and poured herself a half glass of whiskey. Soon, she too was sleeping soundly.

The next morning, he had already left the house by the time she woke and went to the kitchen. He often ate breakfast with the men at the bunkhouse so Corabell could rest longer.

Ester made the coffee and took her cup to sit on the front porch swing. The morning air smelled fresh and still remained slightly cool. She thought about the contrast between sitting on the porch here in the country versus sitting on the porch at her parents' home in Dallas. In the city, there were no fresh smells or birds singing like she enjoyed here.

Soon Corabell and the girls were up, and the daily routine began again.

After lunch, Corabell came through the dining room where Ester and Christine sat at one end of the long dining table doing her lessons. "I think I'm going to lie down for a little while. Would you watch the girls while I rest a bit?"

"Of course," Ester answered, as she and Christine continued. Ester had noticed that, when she was at the ranch, a short nap after lunch was a little luxury Corabell afforded herself occasionally.

When Ester heard the mantle clock strike three, she dismissed Christine from her lessons.

"I think I hear Molly on the front porch. Get your doll and go outside in the fresh air for a while. I'll be out in a few minutes."

Christine skipped to her room to get the ragdoll Ester had made for her at Christmas. Ester heard the front door slam in Christine's wake as she finished putting away their books. She went to her room to get paper, ink, and her writing pen, as she needed to write some letters to her family. She knew it would be cooler on the porch than in the house.

As Ester passed Corabell's room, she realized she was still napping. It was unusual for Corabell to sleep this long, she thought, as she walked to the bedside to check on her.

Ester stood stunned when she realized Corabell wasn't sleeping; she wasn't breathing! Ester instantly reached for her wrist but felt no pulse. She checked her neck, but again she could not feel a pulse. A mounting alarm seized her. Ester leaned her cheek almost against Corabell's mouth and felt no warm breath. Dear Lord, she thought in horror, Corabell's dead!

Ester backed to the door, still half expecting to see Corabell open her eyes, but she did not! She gently pulled the door shut and walked quickly to the front door. Molly was still swinging, and Christine was playing under the oak tree.

"Christine," she called.

Christine looked in her direction.

"Watch about Molly for a few minutes, please. I just remembered something I need to tell your daddy."

"Okay," Christine answered, and went on with her pretend tea party.

Ester practically ran to the first horse barn but didn't find Grant.

"He's in the other barn," one of the men called to her, knowing she only came to the barn when there was a problem.

It wasn't far to the other barn. Ester started calling his name before she reached the door.

"Come on in, it's safe," he answered her.

Once again, Grant saw Ester running toward him; her eyes were huge, and her face flushed from running in the heat. The memory of the day she had been stopped by Pancho Villa and his men on her way home flashed through his mind. Ester had that same shocked look. He didn't have to ask. He knew something was terribly wrong.

He started toward Ester, taking long strides. When they met, he took her by the shoulders to steady her.

"What's the matter, what's happened?"

Ester stared at him for a moment. How do you tell someone his mother has died? she pondered, as she took in Grant's worried expression. She also knew this news would turn his world upside down.

Somehow, she managed to speak the words, although they came out almost in a whisper. "It's Corabell, I think…" She paused. "I think she's passed away," she murmured, not holding back the sadness she felt for him and Christine and Molly.

Grant just stared at her as though what she had said couldn't possibly be true. He released her, without saying a word, and ran toward the house, as though he was being chased by the devil.

Ester ran as fast as she could, but he far outdistanced her. She heard the backdoor slam as she rounded the corner of the corral.

The men working the horses were staring at them, wondering what had happened. They exchanged questioning looks. One of the men quickly went to find Charlie and asked him to check to see what was going on.

When Ester reached Corabell's room she stopped in the now open doorway. Grant was standing beside his mother's bed. His broad shoulders were shaking. She could hear his almost choking sob as he wept. Ester stood quietly just watching, not knowing if she should go to him or leave him to grieve alone for a while before the others found out.

Ester heard the backdoor slam again and the heavy tread of boots on the wood floor. She glanced toward the approaching sound and saw Charlie enter the living room. Ester quickly walked toward him and found she could no longer hold back the tears. When she and Charlie met in the middle of the room, she embraced him and whispered in his ear, "I'm so sorry, Charlie; Corabell has passed away while napping." She felt Charlie's arms tighten around her, and his entire body seemed to shake with the sorrow that engulfed him. They stood for several minutes, just holding one another, grieving.

Charlie loosened his hold on Ester and simply said, "Grant?"

"He's in with his mother. I didn't want to intrude on him just yet."

"You're right, let's give him some time. Where are the girls?" he asked, as he pulled a handkerchief from his pocket and dabbed at the tears filling his eyes.

"Molly's swinging and Christine is playing with her doll under the tree. I'll go out and keep them occupied until Grant is ready to tell them what has happened."

Charlie nodded in agreement, and as he sat down, he breathed a deep sigh. "I sure will miss Corabell. I was lookin' forward to us sittin' on the front porch of my little cabin and reminiscing about all the years we've spent here. We both liked to fish but never had much time for it before, and now," he paused and slowly bowed his head, "and now it's too late," he said, in a quivering voice.

Ester stepped out onto the porch and sat beside Molly. As they swung, she listened to Molly half hum and half sing some made-up tune. While Christine played, Ester could hear her childish laughter and constant chatter to her doll.

Oh, dear Lord, what will happen to this family now? She mulled over the possibilities. Ester silently prayed for God's guidance. She asked for comfort for Grant and all of those who loved and depended so much on Corabell.

Word of Corabell's death spread quickly among the neighboring ranches. The next morning people began arriving shortly after breakfast. They brought baskets of food and wildflowers stuck in mason jars.

Corabell lay in a plain hand-made casket built by several of the ranch hands. Ester and Olga Cremwelgy had prepared Corabell's body and dressed her in her favorite navy blue dress with a white collar trimmed in lace. They had put on her Sunday gloves and placed a pretty lace handkerchief in her hands. She looked peaceful, as though she were napping after Sunday services.

Ester had never helped prepare a body for burial and was thankful Olga had come when Cotton went to tell the neighboring ranchers about Corabell's passing.

Christine clung to Ester and cried almost constantly. Ester tried to reassure her that her daddy would take good care of her and Molly. Molly kept walking over to the casket and just looking at her mother. She did not touch her or make any sounds. She would just stand looking at Corabell for several minutes at a time. Ester would go stand beside her and put her arm around Molly's shoulders in an attempt to comfort her. Ester didn't know how to explain to Molly about her mother's passing.

After several minutes, Molly walked over to Grant and took his hand, giving it a gentle tug. He rose and followed his sister to stand beside their mother's casket. Ester watched from a distance as Grant put his arm around Molly and hugged her close to his side. She could hear the low rumble of his voice as he spoke quietly to Molly. The two then stood in silence for a few minutes. Molly looked up at Grant with a faint smile on her face. He leaned down and kissed her gently on the forehead. Molly continued to smile, then turned and walked out to the swing where Ester soon heard her singing.

Grant glanced at Ester and she could see the lines of worry drawn on his normally attractive face. Ester could only imagine the turmoil that must be going through Grant's mind. The sole responsibility he carried for running the ranch and no family he could count on to help with the girls. Ester's heart ached for him. If only she could stay here to help him, but that was out of the question.

Ester stayed busy greeting each new arrival, thanking them for coming, and thanking them for the food and lovely flowers. Olga Cremwelgy, Charlie, and Sarah Day sat up with the body that night, as was the custom.

Ester watched Grant as he talked with his neighbors and friends. The ranch hands came in small groups to offer their condolences to Grant. He seemed still in a state of disbelief, which Ester thought was quite natural considering the suddenness of what had happened. She wanted to go to him, embrace him, and comfort him, but there was no private time for such a show of her personal feelings of understanding.

At three o'clock in the afternoon, when the funeral procession started to the McKie Cemetery, there were well over a hundred and twenty mourners making the trip on horseback and in buggies. The road leading up the rocky hill to the family cemetery was not passable for the automobile.

Grant had asked Ester earlier if she would sing *The Old Rugged Cross* and another song Corabell particularly liked, *In the Sweet By and By*.

The preacher from town came to conduct the services. As they all stood around the open grave, Ester looked out across the countryside and thought this was the perfect place for a person to rest in peace. It possessed a tranquility you did not always feel in other places. You could see for miles across the ranch land that Corabell had called home for nearly forty years. The land was harsh at times, and beautiful at others, just as her life had been here on this ranch.

Christine stood between Grant and Ester, clinging to each of their hands. Molly stood beside Grant and leaned against him, as he encircled her with his other arm.

Ester sang in her clear melodious voice, just as she had done at Ian O'Tool's funeral the day after Christmas. That seemed like a very long time ago, but it actually had only been a little over seven months.

Today the air was warm with a gentle breeze sweeping along the hillside carrying her voice gently into the distance.

Now both of Grant's parents lay here and Zora's grave was only a few feet away. Just above their graves on the hillside were the graves of four of the cowboys that had worked on the ranch through the years. As they had approached the cemetery, Ester noticed a cross at the grave of the banditos that were killed in the Christmas raid. She vaguely wondered who would have put the cross on their grave. It must have been someone with a kind heart, she decided.

When Ester finished singing, she stole a quick glance toward Grant. He stood with his head slightly bowed, and his eyes were closed. Was he praying or was it an attempt to hold back his tears of grief?

The minister ended the service with the mourners joining in saying *The Lord's Prayer.* She noticed most of the ranch hands joined in, but, as at Ian's funeral, a few stood with their heads bowed in respectful silence.

Grant remained beside his mother's open grave after the others had left, except for the three men who would fill the grave. They stood at a distance, allowing him a few moments of privacy to grieve for his mother. He looked into the abyss at the plain wooden coffin and thought to himself, *Now Mother has joined Dad and Zora in the hereafter.* He hoped they all shared a mansion fit for a king. It was for certain their life on earth had been a hard one most of the time. Then he whispered, "Now what, Mama? How in hell am I going to care for the girls and run this ranch without you?" Grant nodded to the men, turned, mounted Smoky, and rode to the house, where most of their neighbors waited to offer their final condolences before departing.

Olga found Ester in the kitchen making coffee for the guests. She approached Ester and spoke in a low voice.

"Ester, you know you can't keep staying here now that Corabell is gone. It just wouldn't do at all."

Ester nodded her head. "Yes, I know, but I have to give Grant a few days to make arrangements for the girls."

"That's true, but then you get right on over to our house again. I know it ain't near as nice as livin' here, but it must be done. You know we love having you with us," Olga said, as she reached out and gave Ester an affectionate hug.

"Thank you, Olga. I know it crowds your family too, but all of you make me feel so welcome. I truly appreciate you making room for me."

"You are always welcome in our home." Olga gave Ester a reassuring smile.

"I will worry about Christine and Molly though. Do you know some older lady from town that might want to care for them?"

"Well, no one comes to mind, but I'll think on it and ask around. There must be someone that wouldn't mind living out here and watching after the girls. Doesn't he have someone to do the housework and cook?"

"Yes, Juanita started helping when Corabell got hurt. She has a daughter who is about fourteen or fifteen who also helps with the cooking and housework, but they go home after supper is cooked. Grant will have to find someone to be here full-time as he often leaves early and gets in late, just like Vincent."

Olga sighed. "Yes, the life of a rancher means long hours away from the house. Sometimes, I wish Vincent wanted a regular job in town so he could be home more, but that ain't for him," Olga said, with a wistful look. "Well, anyway, we'll be expectin' you in just a few days," Olga emphasized.

By late evening everyone had departed. Ester set out some cold meat and sliced cheese, along with sliced cucumbers and tomatoes from the garden. Molly and Christine ate little. Charlie and Grant didn't do much better, but they did finish off the pot of coffee.

It was later than usual when Ester put the girls to bed, listened to Christine's prayers, and quietly closed their doors.

Grant sat on one of the large sofas with a glass of whiskey on the table beside him. It didn't look as though he had touched it.

Ester walked to the front door and stared out into the darkness. The night sky was void of moon or stars as clouds had moved in from the north. She saw distant flashes of lightning and could smell the approaching rain. She felt almost as bleak as the darkness.

She and Grant needed to talk about the situation they were suddenly cast into. Ester wasn't sure how to bring up the subject so soon, but it had to be done.

She turned and saw Grant had leaned forward with his elbows resting on his knees. His large hands were holding his bowed head. She wondered if he was praying for a solution to this dilemma or just thinking. Grant did not seem to be an overly religious man as he rarely attended church, but times like this even brought the backsliders to their knees, she thought, as she watched him.

"Grant," Ester spoke his name softly.

"Yes," came his muffled reply.

"We must talk about what to do about the girls."

"Yes, I know."

Silence prevailed.

"Grant," Ester spoke softly again.

"What, Ester?"

"I think I know what we could do to solve the problem."

"What's that?" he asked, with his head still resting on his hands.

Ester took a deep breath, summoned all of her courage, and blurted out, "I think we should get married!" There, she had said it! She waited for what seemed like an eternity for Grant to respond.

He slowly raised his head and stared at Ester as though she had suddenly gone completely daft. His eyes seemed to turn a deeper shade of blue, and his mouth was agape, indicating his shock at her astonishing suggestion. The only thing she could think was he looked totally thunderstruck.

Grant wondered if he had really understood what Ester had just said. Had she actually proposed marriage to him, or was he mistaken? No, she had distinctly said, "I think we should get married," he realized, as he continued to stare at Ester's expectant face. Before he could answer, she went on.

"You see, I'd be here with the girls until time for school, and then Juanita or her daughter could come stay with Molly until Christine and I get back home. You could tend to the ranch as always without worrying about the girls," she explained, ending with a deep sigh.

Grant stared at her even harder. Then he sat up straight, reached for the glass of whiskey, and took several generous gulps. He had never been caught this much off guard, not even when Cotton told him it really was Travis that had betrayed him. Grant never took his eyes off of Ester's lovely, innocent face. He felt fairly certain that unexpected suggestion had taken a lot of courage. That thought pleased him but brought many questions to mind.

Then he spoke. "Well now, Ester, that sounds just fine and dandy. It seems you have worked everything out very well for Christine and Molly, but what about you, Ester, and what about me? Will this be a marriage in name only?" he asked, without hesitation. "Do you expect to remain in your room at night and me in mine?" he questioned, and his voice was gaining volume.

Ester felt her cheeks turn pink. "No, I would," she hesitated. "I would expect to share your room," she answered, fighting to maintain her composure. She tried desperately to not blush at the thought of what the intimacy of sharing his room would entail.

Grant waited several minutes before he spoke again as though working through what he wanted to say.

"Ester, we need to speak very plainly and truthfully with one another. Would you make love with me because you think that is what a wife is supposed to do, or would you make love with me because you want to, because you feel you can truly learn to love me as a man, and your husband? Think carefully about your answer, Ester," he cautioned, in a straightforward manner.

Ester was a bit shocked at the plainness of Grant's question. She knew she must answer with what she already felt in her heart. She lifted her chin slightly and looked directly into his eyes. "I would make love with you because I have a genuine affection for you, and I believe in time that will grow into love."

Grant sat up straighter, reached for the glass of amber liquid, and took another liberal swallow.

"Let me ask you this, Ester. If I reach for you during the night, will you be dreaming it's Will Hudson wanting you?"

Ester was even more shocked at this question. She narrowed her eyes slightly and mustered the same stern look she gave her students when she felt they needed it. "I know who I just asked to marry me, and it certainly wasn't Will. I have put those feelings to rest and am ready for a new life. A life with you, Grant McKie," she stated emphatically. "Now I ask you. When you reach for me during the night will you be wishing it were Zora and not me in your bed?" Ester was surprised at her own boldness, but she had to know his true feelings as well.

"No, as you said, I have put those feelings to rest. I loved Zora very much, but after she died, I soon learned wishing for her return was useless and only tormented me." He continued to study Ester, as she stood so erect, unflinching, bravely answering his very personal questions. Grant realized he had likely met his match in this woman and somehow that pleased him.

Grant felt a slow smile reach his lips. He stood and walked unhurriedly toward Ester, keeping constant eye contact. When he reached her, they were only separated by mere inches. The faint smell of roses surrounded him, a fragrance that would always remind him of Ester. He took hold of both of her silky, smooth hands, lifted them to his lips, and gently brushed each with a kiss. "Miss Ester Hammon, I feel honored to accept your proposal of marriage on the conditions you have just stated." Then he gently kissed her on the lips, savoring their luscious invitation. He was sorely tempted to deepen the kiss but ended it, not wanting Ester to think he was more interested in a physical relationship than building a solid marriage. "It seems only right that I should confess I have developed deep feelings for you that I too feel certain will grow with time," he said tenderly.

Ester smiled as tears welled up in her eyes. She treasured the warmth of his gentle kiss, as his day's growth of whiskers brushed lightly against her skin, and savored the tart taste of the whiskey he had been drinking.

Suddenly, she looked at Grant, dismayed at what she had done, and burst out, "Oh, Grant, please don't tell anyone it was me who proposed this marriage. I'd be so embarrassed for everyone to know how forward I've been."

Grant looked at her, and his smile broadened. He bent down on one knee and gazed up at her. "Now why on earth would I do such a thing?" he questioned, with his teasing grin. Then he became serious. "Miss Ester Hammon, will you do me the honor of becoming my wife, to have and to hold, in sickness and in health, richer or poorer, and to love and respect one another for the rest of our lives?"

"Oh, yes! I will accept your proposal on the conditions you have stated," Ester answered excitedly.

Ester's heart soared when Grant stood, engulfed her in his strong arms, and kissed her with the fervor of a lover, a protector, and the man ready to become her husband.

Chapter Twenty-Two

The next morning, although it was Saturday, Grant, Ester, and the girls drove to town to get their marriage license. Grant had known the county clerk for many years and knew she would be happy to issue the license, even if it was Saturday.

With the license secured, they dropped by to ask the Methodist preacher to come to Twelve Mile School the next day so he could perform the marriage ceremony. Pastor Warner was delighted at their invitation.

"I always enjoy going out to Twelve Mile School to conduct services. I'm trying to convince the Methodist Bishop to send a permanent minister there," he told them. "I know there are families living on the various ranches that need to receive the gospel, as well as all of the cowboys that work the ranches," he expounded, with great zeal. "Those men need religion, not a Saturday night filled with drinking and carousing in town," he continued, with enthusiasm.

When they left, Grant gave a low chuckle.

"What's so funny?" Ester asked.

"That preacher might get some of those men to church on Sunday morning but that won't stop their Saturday night trips to town."

Ester just smiled, as she knew he was probably right.

Ester shopped for new dresses for the girls. Grant suggested she wear the pretty peach-colored dress she was wearing when he had picked her up at the train. He told her what a stunning picture she had made in that dress, which thrilled Ester to know he had noticed.

As they drove back to the ranch, Christine proclaimed to Grant, beaming, "Now I'll have a mama like all of the other kids and she'll be my teacher too."

Ester spoke up. "You and Molly will wear those pretty new dresses we bought, and you will be my bridesmaids."

"Like at Mr. and Mrs. Adams' wedding we went to in Del Rio before Ester came?" she asked her daddy.

"That's right, honey," Grant answered.

Grant turned to Ester and said in a low voice, "I think us getting married will be more like a shock to most folks." He suspected most folks would think it was a marriage of convenience, but they could think whatever they damn well pleased as far as he was concerned.

Grant told Charlie about their wedding plans and asked him to come stand up as his best man. Charlie was pleased as punch and soon had a group of the ranch workers committed to attending church so they could be present for their boss' wedding.

When the men heard about the upcoming marriage, they all seemed to agree that Grant and Ester were well-suited. In fact, they seemed to fully believe Ester had been good for Grant. He seemed more settled since the encounter with Pancho Villa and now, with Ester here to keep an eye on him, maybe, just maybe, he would stay that way, they speculated.

Sunday morning, Grant sat at the end of the pew, then Christine, Molly, and Ester.

Everyone was pleased but surprised by the unexpected visit of Pastor Warner. They sang several songs and just as Pastor Warner stood to deliver his sermon the door opened and in marched Charlie and fifteen of the McKie Ranch employees dressed in their Sunday best, which happened to also be their Saturday night best.

Waves of whispers spread through the congregation.

"Welcome, gentlemen," Pastor Warner greeted the men. Then he opened his Bible and began his sermon. It was a rather short sermon for Pastor Warner. When he said "Amen" to the final prayer, he motioned for everyone to remain seated.

"Now, I am quite certain the rest of you folks are wondering just why a large number of the McKie ranch hands have honored us with their presence this fine Sunday morning. Well, the answer is quite simple. They have come to witness the marriage of Grant McKie and Miss Ester Hammon," he finished with a flourish.

The whispers turned to gasps and then an outburst of clapping for the couple.

"Grant and Ester, please step forward with your attendants."

Christine and Molly stood beside Ester and Charlie took his place next to Grant.

Pastor Warner lifted his voice as though he were about to deliver the *Sermon on the Mount*.

"Dearly beloved, we are gathered here this fine Sunday morning, July 1, in the year of our Lord 1917, to witness the joining in sacred matrimony of Grant Allen McKie and Ester Adeline Hammon."

As soon as the ceremony was over, Olga came to Ester and Grant, insisting Christine and Molly come spend a few days with them. Grant and Ester were grateful to have some time alone to begin their marriage.

When they arrived back at the ranch and entered the quiet house, there were a few moments of awkward silence. Finally, Grant spoke softly as he took Ester by the hand and led her to one of the large sofas in the living room.

"Ester, I know you are likely a virgin, and, because of that, the first time we make love may not be as pleasing to you as it will be later on." He paused briefly and then went on. "Don't ever be afraid to tell me if I ever do anything you don't like or may be uncomfortable for you. Sometimes, a man doesn't know what is most pleasing to his wife, so you must not be shy with me," he said softly.

Ester was watching his facial expression as he talked to her and knew he meant what he was saying.

"Is there anything you want to ask or tell me, Ester?"

Ester hesitated only briefly. "Yes, how will I know what to tell you pleases me when I've never been with a man before?"

Grant couldn't suppress a smile, but it was a sweet smile. "As we make love you will learn rather quickly what pleases you most, and that is what you will tell me."

Ester felt her cheeks grow pink. "Oh, yes, I suppose that is how it would work," she managed to get out. Then she asked a bit shyly, "Will you tell me what pleases you?"

Grant nodded to answer Ester's question. "Yes, I'll tell you, but you'll soon know. Actually, I'm easy to please," he gave a wicked little chuckle.

"I don't want to rush you, so you tell me when you think you're ready for me to truly become your husband," Grant said, as he put his arm around her and pulled her snugly against him. He kissed her gently on the mouth, then nuzzled her neck, and gently nipped at her earlobe.

Ester felt the heat of desire mounting in her body as she turned to accept the growing passion of Grant's kisses. His hands were touching her, caressing her breasts, and moving seductively over her body. She could feel their heat through the thin material of her dress and layers of clothing underneath. Before long she realized she wanted to feel Grant's hands caress her body with no barriers between them.

Ester remembered the day she had put the ointment on his bare chest. Suddenly, she wanted to feel the heat of his skin beneath her hands again. She reached for the top button on his shirt and gently fumbled to unbutton his shirt. As it gave way the others quickly followed. Grant shed his shirt and quickly removed his undershirt. Ester moaned softly as she felt the warm, hard planes of his bare chest and the tickling sensation of his chest hair. She was amazed to see how tan his skin had become and guessed he must work shirtless when away from the homestead. She could imagine the spectacular sight he would make with a fine sheen of sweat covering his bare chest and the rippling of hard muscles as he worked.

Grant had unfastened the row of tiny buttons on the bodice of her dress to still find the layers of clothing beneath that barred the path he was seeking. "Damn-it! Why do women have to wear so many clothes?" he muttered in frustration.

Ester giggled. "I believe it is expected when we are in public to be fully clothed, but we aren't in public now," she said, suggestively.

They smiled at one another, rose together, and walked arm in arm to Grant's bedroom, now to become their bedroom.

He pulled the shades down to ensure their privacy. The room still glowed from the bright afternoon sunlight. That suited Grant just fine. He wanted to see every inch of his new bride's supple body.

The light gave Ester the opportunity to satisfy her curiosity about the male body, especially the one belonging to the man she had just married.

Now all barriers between them were removed.

Neither had thoughts or desires for any other.

There were no issues of disagreement between them.

Ester and Grant were ready to begin life's journey together. He came to her, gently caressed her at first, and then allowed his enthusiasm to possess her. Ester followed his lead and returned his zealous caresses. Their desires rose to a fevered pitch as their bodies intertwined in passionate lovemaking, transporting them to that ultimate place of euphoric bliss. Yes, they came together as one in the gentle, golden glow of the evening sunlight. Later they became ardent lovers, filled with passion and tenderness, by the soft glow of the moonlight shining through the open windows.

Through the days, weeks, and months that quickly turned into years, as husband and wife the ultimate love they were each seeking came in time and stayed.

Epilogue

It was a pleasant summer night, with a slight breeze out of the southeast that pushed away the heat of the day. The sky was filled with stars, and a full moon had just risen over the eastern horizon.

The longtime family and friends of Grant and Ester McKie had gathered to honor this remarkable couple. They chatted among themselves about one of their favorite topics, the weather, and various other happenings in their area. They reminisced about the earlier years when they had outlaws and the Villistas to contend with. Several remarked about the handsome couple seated at the head table. Grant was still a handsome man with silver hair, only a few pounds heavier than when he was young, and few wrinkles for his years. Ester had grown older gracefully. Her hair was also gray; her body was just as slender as when she was young; a few wrinkles seemed to enhance her pleasant face; her enduring smile never faded.

Ester slowly rose from her seat of honor and gazed around the crowd of nearly two hundred faces she knew quite well. She had known a number of them for a little over fifty years. They were the faces of her beloved family and dear friends.

Ester intended her speech to be short, but then, she also knew at times she could get carried away when talking about the past.

Ester smiled at the faces trained on her. "Thank you, dear family and friends, for coming tonight to celebrate with us this special milestone in our life," she said pleasantly and paused to gather her thoughts. "I was raised in Dallas and at age twenty-two was considered an old maid. Worse yet, I was an old maid schoolmarm."

There were ripples of laughter from her captive audience.

"My family was desperately trying to find me a suitable husband when I saw an advertisement in the newspaper for a teacher at Twelve Mile School, in Val Verde County, Texas. I got my map and finally found Val Verde County. I wrote to Mr. Vincent Cremwelgy to apply for the job. Within a matter of days, I received a reply telling me that I was hired and would be living with the Cremwelgys. Oh, what a shock when I got off the train in the tiny town of Del Rio and was greeted by Olga and Vincent Cremwelgy and a wagonload of children!"

The audience laughed.

"I was told that during the month-long Christmas break I would move to the McKie Ranch, eight miles farther up Devils River, to teach the daughter of a widower. When I first met Grant McKie, I didn't much care for him."

The audience laughed even harder and someone yelled, "Imagine that!" in a teasing manner.

She put her hand on Grant's strong shoulder and he gently caressed her hand as they smiled at one another.

"I thought he was arrogant and hot-tempered! But, after a while, I learned to respect the way he ran the ranch and dealt with his employees. I came to admire him for his devotion to his daughter, Christine, and for the loving care he gave his mother and handicapped sister. Somewhere along the way, I began to have feelings for Grant that went beyond respect for his better qualities and concern for his unpredictable behavior, at times."

The crowd burst into laughter. Ester knew a large number of them could relate some very interesting stories about Grant's outrageous behavior at times when he was younger.

"I had just begun to fall in love with him when Corabell suddenly passed, and we were thrust into a real dilemma. I could not remain at the ranch being a single woman and he a single man, with no chaperone. This situation led to a secret I asked Grant to keep, and he has kept it all these many years."

Ester could tell she had captured her audience's complete attention with that statement.

"I am going to share that secret with you tonight," she paused. "You see, I proposed marriage and tried to make Grant believe it was so I could remain at the ranch to help with the girls. He quickly saw through that ploy and wrangled it out of me that I really wanted to remain at the ranch because of my growing feelings for him. He accepted my proposal, but I made him promise he would never tell anyone it was me who proposed marriage. Back then, I was afraid people would think me to be a brazen hussy."

There were more ripples of laughter. The older generation knew what Ester said was true.

"Grant promised he would never tell my little secret." She paused. "Then he in turn got down on one knee and proposed to me and, of course, I accepted!"

The crowd of family and friends burst into applause.

"Now you know our secret," Ester smiled down at Grant, her husband of fifty years.

"Eleven months later we were blessed with our oldest son, Ian; two years after that came our Julie; two more years came Charlie; and three years later the twins, Timothy and Teresa.

"I taught at Twelve Mile School for fourteen years. By then

everyone had automobiles, the roads were better, and we drove to town, where I taught school for thirty more years.

"Now our children have blessed us with fourteen grandchildren and three great-grandchildren." She paused and looked around the audience. "You know, I'm glad I proposed to this man and that he accepted."

The crowd rose and clapped with overwhelming enthusiasm.

Grant, still a fine-looking man, rose and smiled at the group. "I count myself a damn lucky man to have shared fifty years with this lovely, remarkable woman. You know, when Ester proposed to me, I was just sitting there trying to figure out how to approach her about the prospect of us getting married. Not just for the sake of Christine and Molly but because I already knew she was the woman I wanted to spend the rest of my life with."

Friends and family gave heartfelt shouts of joy and resounding applause!

"Now, ladies and gentlemen, if you will excuse me, I am going to steal a kiss from my lovely bride of fifty years." Grant took Ester in his strong arms, their eyes met, and when their lips touched, the kiss was tender yet laced with the passion newlyweds would share.

Acknowledgments

My sincere appreciation to my son, Brian, for his technological support and unwavering encouragement.

Thank you to Beatriz Lopez McGonagill for your assistance in editing the Spanish in this book and ensuring its authenticity for this area of the Texas/Mexico border.

Honor Versus Lies

THE HEART OF TEXAS, BOOK FOUR

Helen sat beside the fireplace, watching the fading light outside. The sunset was picturesque with streaks of orange, yellow, and purple painting the western horizon. She suddenly leaned forward in her wheelchair and squinted to see what she thought she was seeing.

"Trent, Trent!" she called to him in his office. "Sassy's back early and came riding by, toward the back, like a bat out of Hades."

Trent walked into the room and gave Helen a questioning look. "Wonder why she would be back a day early?"

"I can't imagine, but I'm sure we are about to find out," she answered as they heard the back door slam. Within seconds Sassy came almost running into the living room. She stopped short, seeing Trent standing beside the fireplace and Helen seated in her wheelchair. Both were staring at her as though her presence was a total surprise, and it was.

Trent thought Sassy looked wild-eyed, like a frightened colt, one that has felt a saddle for the first time and wants more than anything to rid itself of its burden. He had witnessed this phenomenon over and over during his years of ranching. He could sense her fear and wondered what could have possibly happened to cause her almost hysterical appearance.

Helen had seen that same look that day at the creek when Jack realized something was terribly wrong. His handsome face revealed it all, fear, confusion, and uncertainty. The difference was, she didn't think Sassy would run away from this problem, whatever the cause, as Jack had done. She had what the old timers called *grit*.

"They're gone!" she blurted out in a voice much too loud for the distance between them.

"Who's gone?" Helen and Trent asked almost in unison.

"She, that Miss Martin, put Timothy and Nathan on the orphans' train and gave Martha to some rich woman." She sounded almost breathless as the tears started streaming down her cheeks.

Trent stood rooted to the floor, but he managed to ask. "Where is Daniel?"

"Thank God he's safe with the Smyths."

Helen put her hands over her face and let out a moan that would have been heard at the funeral of a loved one.

Sassy advanced toward Trent, balled her small hands into fists, and brought them up in a fighting position.

Trent saw her movement but was not prepared for what she did next.

"You did this!" she screamed through the tears as she delivered the first fierce blow to his chest, knocking him off balance. He quickly recovered his firm stance and readied himself for what was to follow.

"You said they would be safe!" She landed another blow to his chest.

"You said they would get a good education!" she blurted out as more tears fell. Wham! Her fist hit his broad chest again!

"This is your fault!" she continued to shout in rage. Wham!

"Do you hear me? It's your fault!" she gasped as she delivered another violent blow to his chest.

Trent was truly surprised at her strength and thought he might wind up with a few broken ribs, but he was not about to stop her from venting her anger toward him. The sad truth was she was right. Right now, he felt it was his fault. His intentions had been good, but they had certainly gone awry.

Available in Paperback and eBook from Your Favorite Bookstore or Online Retailer

About the Author

Judy McGonagill is a native Texan and loves the rich history of the Lone Star State. Judy grew up in a small town where church and school were the focus of the community. She has been married to her beloved husband for many years and has two adult sons. She is a retired teacher with an interest in history and enjoys writing historical novels.

www.ingramcontent.com/pod-product-compliance
Lightning Source LLC
Chambersburg PA
CBHW020547020726
47494CB00006B/1954